DEAD LIGHT DISTRICT

Praise for Jill Edmondson's Debut Novel, *Blood and Groom*:

"*Blood and Groom* is a sprightly read – a promising start to a new series and a fresh writing career."

–The London Free Press

"*Blood and Groom*'s main character, newly licensed downtown Toronto P.I. (and former rock singer) Sasha Jackson, has enough sass and quirk to hold a reader's interest (particularly entertaining is Sasha's occasional moonlighting as a phone sex operator to stave off mounting credit card bills.)"

–Quill & Quire

"The style is fresh, well-paced and for the most part uses dialogue that feels real. Toronto is nicely portrayed as a place fit for dispatching grooms. Edmondson shows the storytelling skill to turn this debut into a Toronto-focused series with room to grow."

–The Hamilton Spectator

"Parts are very funny – especially the sex chat and Sasha's nerdy pal Victor, and her gambler dad… Bizarre! Not as bizarre as the ending, with romance and finance combined to deadly effect."

–Ireland Evening Herald

"A fast-paced, soft-boiled novel with a strong, distinctive voice and a sassy protagonist."

–The Sherbrooke Record

"Recommended for the mystery fan who likes those touches of reality that bring true life into their world. Talented author Jill Edmondson has crafted a set of intriguing characters."

–Newmysteryreader.com

"Edmondson's protagonist clearly recalls aspects of other female private eyes such as V.I. Warshawski."

–Reviewing the Evidence

DEAD LIGHT DISTRICT

A Sasha Jackson Mystery

Jill Edmondson

IGUANA

Editors: Greg Ioannou, Lisa Hamid, Colborne Communications
Front Cover Design and Illustration: Jennifer Stellings
Back Cover and Interior Design: Rick Blechta, Castlefield Media
Author Photo: Iden Ford
Printer: Webcom

Library and Archives Canada Cataloguing in Publication

Edmondson, Jill
Dead light district / Jill Edmondson.
(A Sasha Jackson mystery)
Issued also in an electronic format. Forthcoming.

ISBN 978-0-986683-80-0

I. Title. II. Series: Edmondson, Jill. Sasha Jackson mystery.
PS8609.D67D43 2011 C813'.6 C2010-902412-5

1 2 3 4 5 15 14 13 12 11

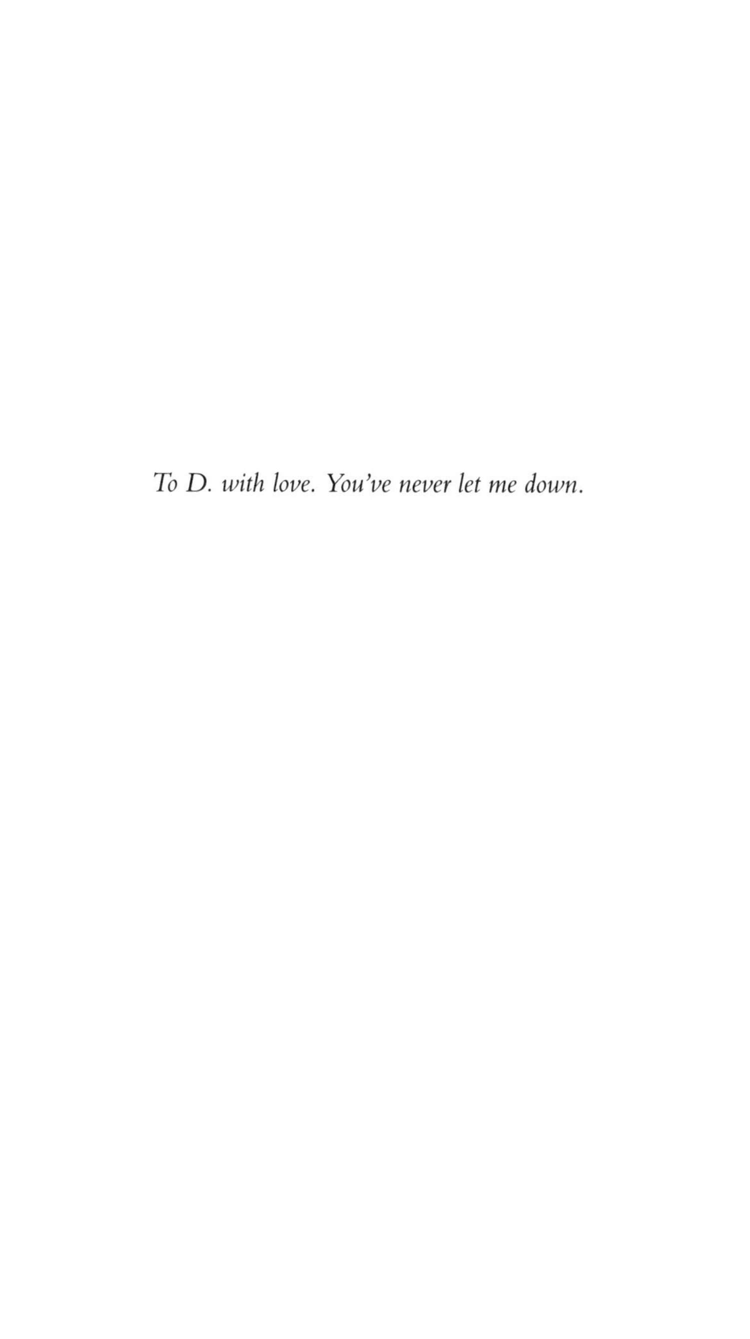

To D. with love. You've never let me down.

Acknowledgements

Warm fuzzy appreciation to dear, dear friends Amaya Chandler, Coco Bernal, and Lesley Walker: Thanks for getting me through those frustrating, surreal, insane days in Borreón. This one's for you!

Heartfelt thanks also to Derek for keeping me sane and making me laugh… sometimes at you, but usually with you.

As well, I'd like to thank Paul Arvisais and John Proano for being such unfailingly loyal cheerleaders and worthy Scrabble opponents.

Many thanks to the magicians and miracle workers who pulled this all together: Greg Ioannou, Lisa Daisy Hamid, Rick Blechta, Jennifer Stellings, Bobbi Olsen, Iden Ford, Drew Arnold, and Alexandra MacLennan. I couldn't have done it without you!

Finally, I'd like to thank my wonderful friend and neighbour Patti Côté: You've been there for all the ups and downs, walks and talks, and experimental bartending. My God, you're patient!

Friday, July 17,
8:57 pm

"So these women get paid to have sex with men?" I couldn't believe I was having this conversation.

"Sasha, I know it sounds bad, but it's not what you think," said Candace, the expertly coiffed, perfectly groomed madam of the first bordello I've ever been inside. I hoped it would also be the last. She seemed matter-of-factly businesslike, almost imperious, sitting there with her legs gracefully crossed at the ankles, absently fingering a thin gold chain as she spoke. Her confident body language was not at all surprising, given that she used her body to make a living. The well-appointed room told me that her confidence was not without merit.

"Sounds to me like it's degrading, exploitative, unsafe, and a whole bunch of other things," I said. "Sorry, I don't want to be judgemental, but I can't get my head around this."

"Maybe if you talk to some of my girls, you'll get a better sense of things. They're in control. It's the men who are being used. The girls have a lifestyle here with me that they could never have on the street. For many of them, working here is the only thing that saved their self-respect."

Never say never, but it was unlikely I would ever get

around to seeing things from Candace's point of view.

"Perhaps for now we should just agree to disagree," I said. "You might as well tell me why you called me today, since I'm here, anyway. By the way, how did you get my name?"

"Let's just say we have a client in common. For obvious reasons, I can't tell you his name. I mentioned to him the other day that Mary Carmen, one of my girls, is missing. We haven't seen her in just over a week, and no one has heard from her. Our mutual acquaintance suggested I contact you, since, clearly, I can't go to the police."

I understood why she wanted to handle things unofficially, but the fact that we shared a client got my curiosity engine going. I'm really stubborn and insatiably curious, two important characteristics for a successful private investigator. I would find out sooner than later which of my clients enjoyed time with Candace's 'employees', but for now I let it go.

"What are the details of the last time you or one of the other girls here saw the missing person?" I asked.

"Last Thursday night. Mary Carmen was here for her regular shift. She usually works Wednesdays, Thursdays, and Fridays. She's slated for the peak hours, from 6:00 pm to 2:00 am." Candace was so nonchalant about this that she could have been discussing the cashiers' schedules at Walmart. "We had a request for an outcall. Terra was on the phones. She said the caller was quite specific about what he wanted. Latina, at least five foot eight, green eyes, long black hair. Mary Carmen came to mind before I even looked at my database."

"You have a database of hookers?"

A stunning, petite brunette in a black satin bustier

and fishnet stockings strutted into the room, grabbed a bottle of single malt scotch and two Baccarat glasses, smiled at us, and sashayed away without saying a word.

Candace paid no mind and kept talking. "Please, don't call them hookers. Most of the girls use the term *intimacy consultant*, though some call themselves *relaxation therapists*. I know they're euphemisms, but they're important to the girls' self esteem."

"Consultants. Right. Got it."

I felt as if I were on the set of a Peter Bogdanovich meets Ron Jeremy film and half expected someone to click one of those black things and shout, "Hot, Wet Con*slut*ants, take two! Lights, camera, action!"

"Yes, I have everything in my database. Before I tell you more about it, I should offer you a drink. Do you care for ice wine?"

Does a bear shit in the woods? I absolutely love ice wine and don't get to love it nearly often enough. At fifty-plus dollars for a 375-millilitre bottle, it's way out of my budget. Of course, since she was offering, I cheerfully said yes and hoped she'd pour it into a giant tankard.

While Candace was getting our drinks, I took a better look around the room. It was understatedly elegant. The drawing room – since in my mind that's what it should have been called – was bigger than the whole first floor of the house I share with my dad, Jack, and my brother, Shane.

Candace had clearly spared no expense on even the most minor details. The coasters were marble, the ashtray was granite, and there was a sterling silver Dunhill lighter beside it. The sofas were the softest leather any cow had ever produced. The sculptures and artwork were all authentic Canadiana originals – something I had learned a lot about on my last case. There was an ebony grand piano in the corner, polished to within an inch of its life (if such could be said about an inanimate object), and there were fresh flowers in every brightly-hued Murano glass vase. The walls were painted in the warmest and richest shade of claret Benjamin Moore had to offer, and the carpet was so plush I thought it would swallow me. Oh yeah, classy joint.

I felt out of place in my faded Levis, amethyst tank top and pewter-toned gladiator sandals. At least I'd recently had a pedicure, so all ten little piggies – painted as they were in *Mauve Magic* – looked really cute.

Candace returned bearing a tray of goodies. She set the platter of flatbreads and artisan cheeses on the coffee table. She then handed me a flute of chilled ice wine and sat down next to me.

"You simply must try this St. Antoine Brie. It's made in Northern Quebec and tastes fantastic with this wine."

I spread a healthy gooey blob on a cream cracker. *Delish.*

"Cheers," she said as she clinked my glass. "To doing business with Sasha Jackson Investigations."

I took a sip of the liquid gold nectar before replying. "I haven't agreed to anything yet. Give me some more details before I decide. What's in the database?"

"Hmmm. Well… prostitution is a business, and maybe even a science. It's certainly a service-oriented industry where knowing clients' preferences and catering to their whims results in loyalty and excellent word of mouth."

"Kind of like the baristas at Starbucks knowing how you like your non-fat, decaf, extra foam cappuccino with cinnamon, right?" I think this is the first time anyone has ever made an analogy between prostitution and take-out coffee. *Venti, VD, Visa.*

"In a way, yes. I have things grouped by the physical characteristics of the girls, and by the educations, the professions, and the hobbies of the men. I have clients sorted by fetish, by lingerie preferences—"

I had to ask, "Lingerie for him or her?"

"Both. They're also sorted by role-playing, and by musical tastes. It's all about finding a match, and combining the right ingredients in order to produce a spectacular session."

I hoped my face remained expressionless, but more likely I was blushing with embarrassment. As if right on cue, we heard some ecstatic moans, and the snapping sounds of a whip coming from the bedroom above us. I visualized the fishnet-clad brunette standing behind an espresso machine with a cup of steamed milk in one hand, a cat-o'-nine tails in the other. *Purr... snap... who's your daddy?*

Candace continued, "Believe it or not, this is as much for the girls as it is for the men. When my employees are paired with someone they actually *like* and enjoy being with, and they get paid for it... well, that's hardly considered work."

"Again, I don't want to seem judgemental, but would you suggest this as a career choice for your daughter if you had one?"

"Probably not. But these girls fell into the life one way or another, and since they're hooking anyway, they may as well do it here. I hire only the very best and I treat them very, very well. I pay top dollar, I give them regular shifts, and I have a high-calibre client roster, not a bunch of dirtbags from the street."

"Uh huh."

"Some of the guys take them out for dinner first. Occasionally, they bring the girls gifts. My workers get paid a flat hourly rate no matter what they do during their shift, and they get to use nice, clean, safe rooms here."

"How many bedrooms do you have?"

"Six. This building is zoned for commercial purposes, and I have it registered as a bed and breakfast, with common rooms on the first floor. The third floor has been converted to an office and a small apartment where I live."

I suppose, in some weird way, the bed and breakfast claim was loosely true. Sort of. Kind of. More or less.

"Do any of the girls live here too?"

"No. They use the rooms during their shifts. It gets cleaned and changed when they're done, and at the end of their shifts they go home."

"You have a housekeeping staff?"

"No. I have a contract with a cleaning company."

"Would they be able to give me any insights?"

"I don't think so. They keep pretty much to themselves. They just get the job done and get on their way."

"How well do you know them?"

"Not well. They have four or five women who sort of rotate. They come twice a day, do the basic cleaning, take the dirty laundry out, and bring in clean linens."

"I see. You mentioned that the missing girl went on an outcall?"

"Yes. About one-third of the clients prefer to take the girl to a hotel. Clients seem to think it's more anonymous that way. Whatever, it's their money, and to me it's just another transaction, another service we provide."

"Uh huh."

"Many of the girls enjoy the hotel bookings. They say it's like a mini working vacation, although others prefer to stay here on site. They say they're more comfortable here," she said.

"That's a fine bit of spin-doctoring, Candace, but in the end, a strange man sticks his penis into her and fucks her."

"That's true. But if you think about it, who's really getting fucked, Sasha? The guys who pay hundreds of dollars to buy a few hours of intimacy? The guys who naively believe the girls who tell them they're virile, and sexy, and dynamite in the sack? The smitten puppy dogs who come back every week, bringing flowers and jewellery? Or the guys who really believe the girls find them attractive and fascinating? Give me a break. The guys are getting fucked, but they're just too dumb to know it."

Ouch! I didn't have an answer for that.

I still had an almost full glass of ambrosia, so I decided to string the conversation along as long as I had vino.

"Okay, well, why don't you tell me more about the missing girl?"

"Mary Carmen is a sweetheart, and I've been worried sick about her since last week. Let's see; she's twenty-two, she's from Mexico – somewhere in the North. She's gorgeous – an unparalleled combination of ethnicity and good genes. Her background is indigenous, think of an Aztec goddess. She has these amazing green eyes, high cheekbones, caramel skin. She's got a body to die for: tall and slim, quite graceful, really. I can easily picture her on a runway. Her English isn't the best, but despite that, you immediately get a sense of how warm and kind she is, and she seems to have a good sense of humour. What else do you want to know?"

"Where does she live? What's her social insurance number? Her date of birth? Where did she go when you sent her out on that call? Who was her client?"

"I have to protect my clients."

"Then I won't be able to help you." Yummy noble rot or not, I set down my drink and made like I was about to leave. My job is hard enough as it is without having to play by someone else's rules.

I've only been an investigator for about a year and a bit, and it's a more challenging and dangerous job than I ever imagined. I got into sleuthing when I gave up on singing. There are days when the music biz in Toronto seems a more solid and stable profession than private investigating. And, there are times I really miss performing, although some would say that's exactly what my current job entails.

Despite what it says in the private-eye textbooks, real life sleuthing is neither scientific nor predictable. I've been shot at accidentally on purpose; I've sat atop rotting food scraps in a dumpster in the pouring rain; I've chased and been chased by angry, errant spouses; I've uncovered an art fraud ring; and I've done a number of boring, routine background corporate checks that almost turned me into a battery-operated robot. Or a zombie.

I never know what's on the horizon.

As unpredictable as my job is, though, I can't say I ever expected to be employed by a madam in a bordello, and I've never gone looking for a disappeared hooker.

Missing persons is probably my least favourite gig among the myriad cases that fall into my lap. Okay, maybe not exactly myriad. How do you start looking for someone who doesn't want to be found? Or worse, what if the missing person doesn't think of herself as missing, but just decided to walk away? There's no law that says an adult has to stick around. There's no law that says you can't leave without saying goodbye.

On one hand, looking for someone is a challenge; on the other hand, missing person cases could make me prematurely grey, and could frustrate me into indulging in any number of irresistibly tempting coping strategies, such as martinis, wine, single malts, or any sweet concoction with a paper umbrella stuck in it.

Candace said, "I'll tell you whatever you need to know, but only as you need to know it."

To which I replied, "And how will you know what I need to know when half the time I myself don't even know what I need to know until after I know it?"

Good thing I'd only had one glass of ice wine because that sentence would have made a lot less sense if I'd been a bit further into my cups.

"I can tell you where she went and when. If you need to know with whom, I'll eventually tell you that too, but only if it's germane. I just want to be sure Mary Carmen's okay. She may have called it quits, and I'd be okay with that. I feel a sense of responsibility for my girls. If anything happened to them because of a job I arranged, I'd feel terrible."

"I can see your point," I said.

I wondered how culpable she'd feel if any of her girls got a sexually transmitted disease.

"Mary Carmen might have just decided she's had enough. That's happened before. Girls have just walked away from working here, from the life. Others have decided to do exotic dancing instead, some go back to their old pimps, some get messed up on drugs.... Longevity is not one of the hallmarks of this industry. Neither is loyalty. There may be perfectly innocent reasons for why she's gone, but I want to be sure."

It struck me as odd to say 'innocent' in any sentence discussing a prostitute, much less one who was missing.

Mary Carmen

¡Puta madre! *I think to myself. How in the name of* Dios *did this monster find me? Where is Dave? What the hell is going on? This cannot be happening to me.*

The bastardo *stretched his arm way back and then swung his fist forward* muy rápido *and it slammed into my face and made my ears ring. I could taste the blood of where my teeth cut into my cheeks.*

"Did you think I wouldn't be able to find you? Are you fucking stupid? You dumb fucking Spic whore," he said.

"I'm sorry," I say. "Lo siento. *I was scared, please, don't hurt me again," I pleaded with him.*

I knew it was no good. He used to hitted me and harmed me and hurted me before, and the more I cried, the more I winced in pain, the more I tried to shrink myself into a little ball, the more turned on the bastardo *got and the harder his fists on my face was.*

"You had no right to run away, bitch. I paid a shitload for you, you useless fucking slut. Your ass is mine, got it? Nobody

bails on me. You hear that? Nobody."

What could I say?

I whimpered and said I was sorry. I made promises to return to him. I asked him to forgive me. All these things, while the pendejo *was smacking me around.*

¡Dios mío! ¡Jesus Cristo!

He slapped me across the face again, harder. The posts on the back of my earrings digged into my skin. I didn't taste any new blood because it mixed with the salty taste of the tears running down my face.

"Take your fucking clothes off now, bitch," he said.

He pulled me by the hair over to the bed and shoved me down. I wasn't close enough to the bed and slipped down the edge of it onto the floor. The hard corner of the box spring digged into my back.

"Let me help you get undressed, you fucking whore."

He pulled out his knife, and cut all of my clothes right off of me.

Friday, 10:52 pm

Candace had given me a recent photo of Mary Carmen. It was just a head and shoulders shot, but it was a clear, eight-by-ten colour picture of her facing the camera. She was a true head-turner, breathtakingly beautiful: her thickly lashed, deeply set, dusky emerald eyes were absolutely hypnotic.

"She's a looker, all right, but I ain't seen her," said a man in a faded brown maintenance worker's uniform.

I was traipsing around The Grand Hotel on Jarvis Street, showing Mary Carmen's photo to every hotel employee I came across. The Grand Hotel reminded me of a quotation from that oh-so-pithy porcine puppet: Miss Piggy. She once said that you never want to stay in a hotel called *The Uptowne Royal Olde King George the 5th Regal Châteaux and Suites*, or something like that. Her theory was that the longer the hotel name, the greater the disappointment. A good hotel, Miss Piggy claimed, had one name. The Grand Hotel lived up to its mono-moniker: it was classy, bordering on ostentatious, and yet its location was incongruent with its personality. The much hoped for gentrification of this 'hood was still in the embryonic stage.

Jarvis Street is one of Toronto's seedier areas, home to pawn shops, porn shops, and sketchy diners where one could more easily get a cap of meth than a cup of joe. The street was a favourite of the city's destitute, drug-addicted, and downtrodden people. It wasn't altogether surprising to see an abandoned syringe or a soiled condom lying in a saliva and graffiti covered boarded-up doorway. There were panhandlers on any corner that didn't have a hooker or two trolling whatever cars slowed down in passing. There were dealers and transvestites on the alert to purvey whatever other vices were in demand.

Then, of course, peppered between vacant store fronts and boarded up buildings, there were the charities, religious institutions, and government-funded social services all hoping to rid Toronto of one social blemish at a time.

If you build it, they will come.

The Lighthouse offered hope and rehab to drug addicts; St. Paul's Mission offered beds for the homeless; The Salvation Army doled out warm meals to those who usually foraged through garbage bins for their three daily squares. Yet, two blocks up from Jarvis Street's worst stretch stood one of Toronto's finest hotels, with in-room Jacuzzis, room service delivered on sterling silver trays, and complimentary Egyptian cotton robes and slippers.

The contrasts weren't lost on me. Obviously nobody had yet told the area's winos that urban renewal was on the menu.

Knockout that she was, if anyone had seen Mary Carmen, they would certainly have remembered her. But the doormen showed no signs of recognition – ditto the bartenders, waitresses and parking lot employees. Either the staff of The Grand were all involved in an elaborate conspiracy of silence, or they were all very forgetful and possibly visually impaired, or Mary Carmen had never actually been here.

At the front desk, a pimply girl with a bosom that surely must have caused backaches was very helpful and forthcoming, especially after I dropped a fifty-dollar bill in her hand.

"No one checked in. The room was held with a credit card—"

"Name on the card was Candace Curtis, right?" I broke in. "American Express?"

Candace had told me that all hotel room bookings were made under her own name, and guaranteed with her corporate credit card. She later billed the clients for the room, and the, um, extras.

"Yes, that's right. If people cancel before 6:00 pm then there's no charge. But if they don't call to cancel, we hold the room for them, assuming it'll be a late check in. As far as we're concerned, the room is sold for that night, whether they show up or not."

"And you're sure no one checked in?"

"Yeah. They never came. The file note says 'no show' but on the credit card it just goes through like a normal check in."

"Well, thanks for your help."

Another fifty dollars got the housekeeping staff to confirm what the desk clerk had said. They were convinced the room had not been occupied at all, and the day shift workers were glad the next day to have one less suite to vacuum and one less bed to change.

Well, I was only a few hours into this case and was already fronting cash that I could hardly spare. I had discussed money with Candace before agreeing to take on her case. She hadn't even batted an eye when I told her my rates, and that all expenses would have to be covered by her. I immediately wished I had padded my hourly fees. Clients with generous budgets were rare, second only in rarity to clients who paid their bills in full and on time, and didn't pay me with a bum cheque.

I took a walk along Jarvis, then crossed over to Church Street, and then doubled back to Sherbourne Street. Toronto's sex trade was contained almost entirely on these three streets, especially Jarvis. I approached hookers on every corner, but few would even look at me, much less talk to me. I suspected I'd have to refine my approach if I was going to pursue this angle.

After batting zero, I decided to call it a night. It was now well past midnight, and I was tired. I had no desire to hang around the neighbourhood once the bars closed for the night and the nocturnal vices and the flesh trade were out in full force.

Saturday, July 18, 10:33 am

"I'll have scrambled eggs, home fries, and white toast, please," I said. I was famished, and a greasy, starchy breakfast would surely hit the spot.

"I'll have steak and eggs, medium rare steak and eggs over-easy, please, a side order of bacon, home-fries, and an order of rye toast without butter," said Lindsey.

Oh yeah, like it's the butter that made the meal fattening.

"I see you're feeling very Hindu this morning," I said.

Lindsey's real name is Lakshmi. Although she was born in Sri Lanka and raised by devout Hindu parents, she is about as Canuck as they come – bring on the beef and bacon.

"I need protein," she said. "I've been working out. Pilates. You should try it."

"Exercise? What, are you trying to kill me?" I said.

"Would you two please whisper?" Jessica mumbled. "I'm hungover and you're giving me a headache. Just bring me a coffee please." Jessica's normally bright blue eyes were today a mottled shade of watery red, rimmed by dark circles.

A bitter old waitress in a navy polyester uniform and crooked hairnet silently took our orders and shuffled away without giving any indication that she'd heard our requests at all.

I was sitting in the Danforth Café, which really should be renamed 'Hardened Arteries Eatery'. 'Café' just has too much of a positive connotation for a place that hadn't had a facelift since its grand opening, back in the days when fire was discovered. I was with Jessica and Lindsey, my two best friends, and in Lindsey's case, my future sister-in-law. Jessica, Lakshmi/Lindsey and I had all known each other since we were teenyboppers. Our friendship is solid, which is why we can get away with saying anything at all to one another.

Lindsey is my brother's girlfriend. She and Shane finally became a serious couple around two years ago – about a decade later than they should have. They had flirted and teased each other as teens but were both too young, too shy, and too stupid to do anything about it. Then, in early adulthood, the timing had just never been right – one was travelling, the other was in school, one was single, the other wasn't, et cetera, et cetera.

Finally, a couple of years ago, at a party involving the lethal combination of a bit too much alcohol plus the sledgehammer subtlety of yours truly, Shane and Lindsey had gotten together at last. Now we were all placing bets on when the wedding would be. Any time I mentioned the nuptials, Lindsey magically shut me up by describing in minute detail the horrific tulle and taffeta, puffed-sleeved, pastel-coloured abomination she wanted the bridesmaids to wear.

Well, okay, then, why don't you just elope? You'd have my blessing.

Lindsey, Jessica and I try to do brunch at least two or three weekends a month. It's the ritual and conversation that matters, not the food. Good thing too, because it looked like today's special was Culinary Armageddon.

"So, you're looking for a Hispanic goddess who was lured into a life of selling her body, and who has now disappeared?" said Lindsey, handing Mary Carmen's photo back to me.

I nodded. "Yup. What should I call this one? The Case of the Missing Hooker seems too obvious," I said.

"The Hooker in Hiding?" suggested Jessica. "The Vanishing Vixen? The Wayward Streetwalker? No, wait, The Streetwalker Who Walked Away?"

"No, no, Jessica, you gotta have the Mexican angle in there," Lindsey said. "Latino something."

"It's *Latina*, not *Latino*. O endings are for boys and A endings are for girls. Don't you know anything?" I said.

Not surprisingly, they both ignored me.

Lindsey shrugged. "Whatever. She truly is gorgeous. I wonder why she didn't go into modelling or something?"

Jessica picked up the photo. "Yeah, she could almost make me switch teams… and after last night's date, that's becoming a more distinct possibility."

"Honey, you'd strike out with the chicks too," I said.

"Why are we still friends?"

"What a shame she ended up hooking," Lindsey said. "What a waste."

"How the hell do you plan to start looking for her?"

Jessica asked. "I wouldn't even know where to begin."

"What makes you think I know? Missing persons cases are tough. I'll chase down every lead Candace gave me and then I'll pray or consult a Ouija board or buy a lucky rabbit's foot," I said.

"Yeah, the furry little paw was certainly lucky for the rabbit it came from," Jessica said.

"Is that woman going to bring our food anytime soon? I'm going to die of starvation." Lindsey was craning her neck around to see if she could spot our unfriendly server.

Jessica sighed. "Who cares about food? I need a lot more caffeine. My head feels like it's wrapped in barbed wire."

For the next hour we did a fair imitation of *Sex and the City*. Jessica filled us in on her night out and the reason for this morning's hangover.

"So, he was a dud?" Lindsey asked Jessica.

"I had to get drunk to keep myself amused. He kept telling the same stories over and over. I couldn't stop yawning. I dug my fingernails into my palms to keep from falling asleep."

"Safe to assume then that you didn't get laid," I said.

"There's no way in hell I would have slept with him. Not even with someone else's pussy."

"What a charming image," Lindsey said.

"Well, Sasha, it'll be interesting to see who gets out of the desert first – you or me," Jessica said.

"Don't remind me. It's been so long since I've had my muffin buttered that I think I've forgotten how to have sex."

The unsmiling 'waitron' eventually showed up with

our food, all of which was either cold and gelatinous or burned to a crisp. I'm sure it takes a special talent to serve food with both ends of the temperature continuum on one plate. Lindsey and I picked at our meals while the three of us talked about men and dating and sex and fashions, then we discussed men and dating and food, after which we chatted about men and sex and shopping. At one point someone mentioned diets and working out, but those veins of conversation were mercifully short lived. Robo Waitress came by with coffee refills, and I dumped four sugars into my cup to make it almost drinkable.

Jessica asked if she could have her coffee served intravenously. The acid-faced server didn't even pretend to smile.

After a while, I tuned out the girl talk. My mind had started racing. I'd been trying to come up with a plan, and a few – probably not very good – ideas had come to me. I was anxious to finish brunch and get cracking on the Case of the... what? We still hadn't come up with a good handle for this one.

Saturday, 1:30 pm

It occurred to me that I had kind of botched up the beginning of this investigation. Last night I had focused exclusively on the girl, not on her client, and not on the bordello business. So now I was back to square one, starting from scratch, back to the drawing board… you get the idea.

"I need to ask you some more things. Can I drop by in a little while?" I asked Candace when I got her on the phone.

"Sure. Have you got any news? Any leads?" Her voice was as well modulated as before, but I could sense eager anticipation beneath it.

"Sorry. All I have for now are questions and more questions. It's too soon for me to even speculate."

Now that I was committed to the case, I was more businesslike than before. Yesterday, I could have gone either way with this client, at least from the point of view of how interested I was in the case, and in terms of my own moral judgments about hooking and the sex trade and feminism and capitalism. However, moral rectitude or ethical certitude pale in comparison with my bank account, which could only be described as fiscal hebetude or economic lassitude, if alliteration, consonance, assonance – or whatever the hell literary term applies – matters at all.

The bordello receptionist – a perky, sexy blonde with a mischievous smile – was seated at an antique desk beyond the foyer, in front of what could only be described as a Scarlett O'Hara staircase. The old, edge-of-Rosedale mansion, off Sherbourne, on the wrong side of Bloor Street, had a centre hall plan, and I took a better look at the surroundings on this second visit.

The banister of the staircase leading to the second

and third floors was a darkly stained carved wood. The front room had Persian rugs that I'm sure were worth more than I could earn from the sale of both of my kidneys. On my right was the sitting room I'd been in before. To the left was what used to be a dining room but now housed a billiard table and a walk-in cigar humidor. Next to the humidor was a glass-fronted case displaying a gun collection. The gun case made me nervous, even though some of the weapons were clearly valuable antiques. Despite my field of work, I hate guns. I have come into contact with them too often, whether directly or peripherally, since becoming an investigator. Even in a locked cabinet, they scare the crap out of me. Beside the gun cabinet was an expensive looking, glass-fronted wine fridge stocked with row upon row of dark green bottles. No Tetra Pak vino for this joint. There was probably a kitchen behind the erstwhile dining room, but I doubted anyone ever used it to bake Tollhouse cookies.

The house had the feeling of an exclusive old boys' club, which I guess was fitting, since that was essentially what it was. Blondie got up and showed me into the same sepia sitting room I'd sat in last night.

Candace and I sipped freshly brewed Ethiopian coffee and exchanged a few minutes of pleasantries before we got down to business. I was struck once again by her style and presence. Even though it was a summer Saturday afternoon, Candace was dressed in business casual. Her pearly grey skirt and blouse looked expensive, her shoulder-length blond hair was perfectly combed and slightly curled under at the ends, and she wore subtle make-up. Classy and traditional, she would have blended in at any of the office buildings downtown, but…

"I need to know more about your business in general, and about Mary Carmen's last client in particular," I said once I'd finished my second finger of almond biscotti.

She replied, "I told you, I have to protect my clients. They pay very heavily for confidentiality. If they can't trust me or my girls to be discreet, I'd be out of business in a heartbeat." She forced a pause by taking a sip of her coffee.

Speaking of confidentiality, I caught a glimpse of a client who had just arrived and was being escorted upstairs. I didn't get a good look, but I could have sworn the man was a city councillor from the west end. Hmm. Hadn't his whole campaign been about law and order?

I took the cue to fill the pregnant pause. "I promise I'll be diplomatic, circumspect, respectful, my lips are sealed, I'll take it to the grave. Whatever. But I need to talk to her last john. Or I can't work for you."

Candace looked about as thrilled as a cat being tossed into the dog pound, but I've had more than enough clients figuratively tie my hands behind my back. I've learned the hard way that playing by someone else's rules screws things up exponentially. If this was going to work, I needed to set the tone right here and now.

"Okay," she said, setting down her coffee. "But please let me make the arrangements. It would be bad for business if I simply handed out his contact info without giving him a heads-up. I'll call him when we're done."

"That's fine. Pave the way and feel free to give him all my contact details." I pulled out one of my generic business cards, which listed my office, cell and email info. Just for good measure, I wrote my home number and home address on the back of the card as well. "Okay. Next, you have to tell me a bit more, actually a lot more, about this operation."

"Where to start? I established this business about four years ago. I'd worked the streets for years and got beat up way too often, sometimes by johns, but mostly by my pimp. He was eventually and thankfully locked up for an unrelated matter, which is how I got away from him."

"I see…"

"I earned lots of money and hardly saw any of it. I had no control over my life and was getting deeper into drugs. I saw the downward spiral and knew I had to make a change. Once my pimp was out of the picture, I finally had some freedom and had no idea what to do."

Her story so far was every cliché of a heartstring-tugging, Monday night made for TV movie. Not to be reductive about it, but I automatically assumed that her childhood had probably included incest or molestation, maybe an alcoholic parent or two, welfare, drugs, dropping out of high school, physical abuse, juvenile records and the whole sorry list goes on. However, that sort of trashy tragic biography did not mesh with the well-bred, articulate, poised woman before me, unless she had gone to one hell of a finishing school. The question was begging to be asked, so I put it to her.

"What about your family? I guess your upbringing was pretty rough?"

"You'd think so, wouldn't you? But not really, not outwardly. I came from a good family. My grandparents on both sides were well-off. It was an inheritance from my grandmother that gave me the capital to buy this place. My folks had money, respect in the community. I grew up in Rockcliffe Park in Ottawa."

"I know the area. Beautiful homes along the Ottawa River, right?"

"That's it. Dad was in property development. Mom was an interior designer. We lived in a sterile but colour co-ordinated five bedroom showplace with an in-ground pool. The perfect home for successful Baby Boomers with both money and taste. They met when my mom decorated some model suites for one of my dad's cookie cutter bedroom communities in the suburbs. A match made in heaven; a marriage made in hell."

"Why so?"

"Appearances mattered to them, so did booze. They kept it together in public, did all the right things, sent me to an expensive private school. They did a bit of community work, climbed the right social ladders, attended the right public events, hosted classy dinner parties with catered meals served on the good china. But, once the guests were gone and we were behind closed doors, the masks came off. Dad would get drunk and hit Mom. She'd get sloppy and would start smacking me. They'd both scream at me, and tell me I was worthless, that they were stuck in a lousy marriage because of me. They'd throw stuff at each other, at the walls, and then they'd pass out on the floor. The next morning they'd be hungover, so they'd scream at me some more before pulling themselves together for the next client meeting.

"I'm so sorry. How are things with them now?"

"We haven't spoken since I was about fifteen."

"God, that sucks. All right, fast forward. What happened after you got away from the pimp? Did you try to find a job? Go back to school?" I asked. The questions seemed dumb even as I asked them.

"Yes and no. I had no official work experience, no references. I had run away from home when I was a teen, and I didn't quite finish tenth grade. So, once my pimp was out of the picture, I tried to get my act together. I applied for a lot of jobs. Evergreen Youth Centre helped me do a résumé and set up some interviews for me. I got a job at McDonald's."

"I saw that one coming."

"*Ba-da-bap-bop-ba*, I didn't love my $6.25 an hour wage. I quit after three weeks. I knew I wanted to get out of the hooking life, but my weekly cheque from Mickey D's was less than I made in one night on the street."

"So, you went back to the life." If I'm not around to state the obvious, then who would?

"Not quite. I became a stripper. It was a slightly better option, but only slightly. If it had just been prancing around naked on a stage and giving the occasional lap dance, it probably wouldn't have been so bad. But it was still prostitution and sex was expected. It was just more covert and usually only oral."

"My God…"

"But really, what's the difference? It was warmer and safer working indoors at a peeler bar than standing outside, shaking my tush in a miniskirt on Jarvis Street in the middle of January."

"I guess so. How did you get from there to here? From what I understand, the strip bars are either run by bikers or controlled by the mob. Either one would be hard to pull away from, probably as hard to divorce as a pimp," I said.

"Well, there are two fairly certain ways out of the sex trade. One is to get a disease. The other is to get pregnant. I got both."

"Oh my…"

"I'm HIV positive and have been for years now. And my son was born HIV positive as well. I named him Adam. He was born on Friday the 13th, which seems fitting. I only held him for about an hour. He was so tiny. So beautiful. His little blue eyes had such pretty little wisps of blond lashes. Then they took him away. Well, I gave him away. What the hell did I have to offer as a mother? He's been in a foster home since then, at least I think so. I don't know if he's alive or dead or healthy or what. He'd be about five and a half now."

"My God. I'm so sorry. I can't imagine how hard that was…is. I don't know what to say…"

"Don't worry about it. It's heavy stuff to deal with. I haven't mentioned it to many people, but everyone I have told has the same reaction as yours. There is no 'right thing' to say."

"I guess not, but still…"

We were silent for a few minutes. The awkwardness of the moment was made even more so by atavistic grunts and groans, and the urgent, rhythmic creaking of some busy box springs in the bedroom above us. Candace took another sip of her coffee and I crunched away on another piece of biscotti. Eventually, Candace broke the weighty silence. I listened to her while I discreetly tried to use my tongue to un-wedge the almond slivers stuck between my teeth.

"So, you want to know about this place? Well, I was on welfare, I was depressed as hell after giving up my baby, and I was, or am, sentenced to a deadly virus. I looked ahead at ways I could make my remaining years comfortable and maybe even meaningful. I doubt you'll get that, but it was one of my motivations."

"Keep going." I was hooked on this conversation, in much the same way people can't take their eyes off a horrible, multi-vehicle highway accident involving a rolled-over eighteen-wheeler and a collection of compact, gas-efficient hatchbacks.

"As you can guess, my only marketable skill was sex. The welfare people and some other youth and women's services found various training programs for me. I got my GED and took a bunch of computer courses. Even with that, I still couldn't get a decent job. So I decided to create my own. As luck would have it, this is about the same time that I received an inheritance."

"And here we are," I said.

We were interrupted by the perky blond receptionist.

"Sorry to bother you Candace, but there's an urgent call for you."

"Excuse me," Candace said as she left the room.

"May I have a glass of water?" I asked Blondie before she left.

"Sure, one sec."

Blondie returned a moment later with ice water in a crystal tumbler. I wasn't exactly parched, but had used thirst as an excuse to get her to come back to the drawing room alone. *Aw, shucks, aren't I a clever girl?*

"So, how do you like working for Candace?" I asked.

Blondie answered with an enthusiasm rivalled only by the home team's cheerleaders at the Superbowl. "It's great. Candace treats us very well. Why? Are you looking for a job?"

Moi? Not in this lifetime...

"Uh, no, I'm doing my dissertation on the sex trade, and Candace is helping me with my research." There might come a day when my natural and almost instant ability to lie will shame me and make me penitent, but for now I considered it one of my greatest assets. "My name's Sasha, by the way." I stuck out my hand.

"Nice to meet you. I'm Jackie, but everyone calls me Jake. So what kind of research are you doing?"

"Mostly about the johns. How they treat the working girls. Any experiences you'd like to share? I guess maybe not, if you work the reception."

"Actually, I work the trade too. We each take one shift a week at the reception desk. It's part of the gig, and believe it or not, being the greeter is one of the funnest things about the job. Best thing is we get paid the same for the desk shift as we do for the sex shifts."

"I guess that's, uh, very...egalitarian. So, what are the clients like?" I asked.

"Well, I can't really talk about the guys from here. We sign a confidentiality agreement. But when I was working the street before coming here, I met some real wing nuts and some real assholes. Which would you rather know about?"

"How about both? I guess that would be wingholes and assnuts."

Jackie or Jake laughed at that. I think it was out of politeness rather than as an acknowledgement of my razor-sharp wit.

"Well, I've had requests for just about every fetish."

"Like what?" I asked. I've been single so long that regular sex wasn't even on my radar, much less anything kinky.

"Well, there's a bizarre trend these days for nursery rhyme characters. I've dressed like Little Bo Peep at least three or four times in as many weeks. It's getting tired. And then there's the routine requests: blindfolds, anal, spanking, and golden showers. You know, the usual."

"Yes, of course..."

What the heck? That's the *usual*?

I was glad Jake-Jackie continued talking because I had less than no idea what to say next.

"The guys who ask for me are mostly into oral, giving and receiving. That's fine with me. It's less physically draining."

Draining? Ugh!

"Have you ever had a bad experience? A rough client?" I asked.

"Not since I came here. Look at my smile. Perfect, isn't it?"

Her teeth were as white and straight as a picket fence in 1950s suburbia. "You could be in a toothpaste advertisement," I said.

"That's now. They're fake. Caps and crowns and bridges and implants. I had just about every tooth knocked out by a vicious john on crack. He didn't touch me below the neck. Just my face. I had a broken nose and two black eyes and a mouth that looked like

I was from the Ozarks. Never accept a "date" with a guy who drives a fully loaded black Ford F-250 pickup truck. They're always dirtbags, but this guy was the worst one ever."

I pictured a Confederate flag in the rear window of the truck, and a rifle standing upright, at the ready. Nothing of the image I had of this man was appealing in the least, but money talks. How sad.

"I came to work for Candace after that experience. After the bruises had faded, and I'd had my teeth fixed. Working here is safe. She screens all the johns and I feel so much better here than working the stroll."

"That's the goal," said Candace as she returned to the room. "Anyhow, Jake, if you could excuse us…?"

"Sure. Nice chatting with you Sasha," Jake said as she bounced out of the room.

"Before I forget to ask, there's one thing in general that you could help me with, Candace."

"Name it."

"For now, you don't need to give me any names, but have there been any changes among your clientele over the last while? Anything in general?" Jackie had me wondering what role a john might have had in Mary Carmen's disappearance.

"What do you mean?"

"Like in clients' patterns. Have any regular clients dropped off the horizon? Do any clients come in significantly more or less frequently than usual? Or has anyone developed a…new taste for the types of services required? That kind of thing?"

"Possibly, although nothing really leaps to mind at the moment. I'll check my records, okay?"

Candace and I talked for a short while longer about her business and how she got started, where she found her clients, how she recruited her staff. I had to admit, it was a pretty slick operation, although it still rubbed me the wrong way.

"While I wait for you to get hold of Mary Carmen's last client, do you mind if I talk to some of the other girls? Maybe one of them can shed some light on things. She must have been close to someone."

"No problem," Candace said. "I'll see who's free."

"Before you do, how do you want me to handle this? I told Jackie that I'm doing research on the sex trade. Do you want me to stick with that?" I couldn't get used to calling a girl 'Jake'.

"I'd prefer you didn't. I don't see any point in coming up with some flimsy cover story. I don't want to freak out any of the girls, but this could be something of a reality check."

"Harsh reality."

"I know, but the truth is that any one of them could disappear… by choice or by chance."

"Sad, but true."

"Did you want to talk a bit more with Jake first? There are three other girls on the premises right now, but they're all…indisposed for the next hour or so," Candace said.

"Might as well pick up where I left off with Jackie."

"So, do you know Mary Carmen very well, Jackie?"

"Please, call me Jake. Yeah, I guess I kind of know her. What do you want me to tell you?"

"Anything. Biographical details. Habits, hobbies, hangouts."

"Well, she's in her early twenties and gorgeous. She's from Mexico, and has the sexiest Mexican accent. She's just a really, really, really nice girl."

"What do you mean? 'Nice' is so vague, even though you put three *reallys* in front of it."

"Well, she always seems interested in what people have to say. She's a good listener. Every time she comes to work she greets everyone with a big smile and that kiss on each cheek thing that Mexicans do."

"Okay, what else?"

"She's always cheerful and really, really generous too. She's always bringing in treats, like candy or chocolates. She brings in a stack of magazines every couple of weeks. *People*, *Cosmo*, *Vanity Fair.* I don't even know if she can read them. Maybe she just looks at the pictures and the fashions."

So far, everything that Jackie had told me was warm and fuzzy and sounded like a typical twenty-something girl next door. Great info if you're assessing demographics for MTV or Fashion Television, but utterly useless for my purposes.

"Uh huh," I said. "What else can you tell me? What does she do on her days off? Who are her friends? How did she end up here?"

"Well, she lives in a rooming house on Carlton Street, a couple blocks before Parliament. I know she's friendly with one of the other tenants there, a girl from the Maritimes, but I can't remember her name. And Mary Carmen does a lot of Spanish things. I guess I should say Mexican."

"Like what?"

"She goes salsa dancing; she loves dancing. I know she goes to the clubs pretty often. And I've heard her mention a few times about going out for burritos or enchiladas. Funny thing, I never heard her mention eating nachos, and I thought those were Mexican too, same with Taco Bell. I don't think she ever goes there, which seems odd to me. Wouldn't it be the place to go for comfort food?"

"Maybe she prefers regional dishes." Yeah, if Taco Bell is authentic Mexican food, then I'm an iguana's uncle. Or a monkey's aunt.

Jake pursed her lips. "I guess so. Other than that, what can I tell you?"

"Know where she goes to eat burritos or to dance salsa?"

"Nah, but I'd recognize the names if I heard them."

I didn't get much more out of Jake-Jackie, and I was getting bored now waiting for a chat with any one of the three other on-site girls. I flipped through some back issues of *The New Yorker*, and sipped on my third cup of Ethiopian fair trade java until someone had time for me.

Next up was a severe-looking woman named Tonya Bartlett, whose name made me think of the compendium of quotations. Martin Luther King's line, "Never succumb to the temptation of bitterness" immediately sprang to mind.

Tonya was clearly unfamiliar with those words of wisdom. Everything about her seemed icy and angry. I wondered how she got clients because if I were a guy, I'd have to be pretty drunk to see anything redeeming beneath her frosty, stern exterior. I guessed she was probably a hit with the guys who hated their mothers, but felt guilty about it, and were ready to be punished.

"Mary Carmen was a nice girl, I suppose, but we were rarely here at the same time," said the Ice Queen Tonya.

I wondered why she was using the past tense.

She continued, "I mostly work afternoons, not nights, so I don't think I can help you."

"Does she ever talk about what she does on her days off?"

"I know she took some English language classes. Other than that, who knows?"

"Does she ever talk about her hometown, how she came to be here, her family?"

"She didn't have anyone here as far as I know. She came to Canada by herself. Her family's very poor and I think she sent most of her money back home to them."

"Any idea how long she's been in Canada?"

"No idea, sorry."

"Can you think of anything else?"

"Not really. As I said, we didn't work a lot of the same shifts. I'd politely chat with her when she was around, but I mainly had the feeling she only wanted to talk to me so she could practice her English. We really had nothing in common," Tonya said.

Nothing in common except taking off all your clothes and being physically intimate with a strange guy who paid for it. Nothing in common except being exploited and degraded. Nothing in common except STDs or pregnancy as an occupational hazard. Nothing in common except… you get the picture.

"Well, if you can think of anything else, please give me a call," I told her.

Candace returned to the drawing room (maybe I could start referring to it as a *salon*, which seems equally pretentious, but somewhat sexier) and told me she had left messages for Mr. X – Mary Carmen's last date – to get in touch with me.

"Thanks, I guess, but I have to tell you how annoying all this secrecy is. It might also be creating a big waste of time. For all we know, maybe Mary Carmen said something to him about her plans, and if we knew that, we could have this all wrapped up in a heartbeat."

"I understand your frustration," Candace said. "But I can't do it differently. Sorry."

I hung around a while longer and talked with the two other girls who had been "in session" when I arrived. Again, neither was much help. *Nice girl, really sweet, but I actually don't know her very well. Mary Carmen hasn't been working here all that long. We aren't usually on the same shift. Blah, blah, blah.*

I touched base with Candace before taking my leave. She pulled up the employee profile for Mary Carmen and I got what I could out of that, which wasn't much. I chastised myself for not having performed this obvious and routine task yesterday. Mary Carmen Ruiz Santamaria's date of birth and the address for her rooming house were listed. I decided to make the rooming house on Carlton Street my next stop.

The rooming house looked like a dump. I had next to no desire to go inside, but I had a case and a real live client, and the hand written sign out front said ROOMS FOUR RENT. I figured anyone stupid enough to spell 'for' wrong would be interesting to talk to. I pressed the doorbell and didn't hear any muted chimes from inside. No liveried butler magically appeared to usher me in. I waited a moment, then pushed the doorbell again. Nothing. A dog barked, and I wondered about their policy on pets. I banged on the door a few times and was eventually rewarded by the arrival of a miserable-looking woman in dingy lime green track pants with spongy pink curlers in her hair. The track pants were tautly stretched across a rolling expanse that could only be referred to as thunder thighs. What a contrast to the beautiful house full of beautiful women that I had just left.

"Yeah?" Her voice was phlegmy and rusty. The only thing missing was a filterless hand-rolled cigarette dangling from her lips.

I gave her my brightest smile. "I was so glad when I saw the sign out front about a room for rent. A friend of a friend told me to look into renting here. Is the room still available?"

"Yeah. C'mon."

We walked up the old, creaking stairway to the third floor. I thought I heard rats scurrying up and down the musty firetrap – or was it just my imagination?

"This one has a shared bathroom. No cooking facilities. Furnished, but you gotta supply your own bedding."

"That's not a problem," I said. If I were actually planning to live here, I'd buy a set of plastic sheets and put them on over a rubber mattress pad, and I'd still try to levitate while getting my beauty sleep. “I’m new to Toronto. I just moved here from Calgary and don’t really know anyone in the city. A friend back home knows a girl who lives here named Mary Carmen. Said I should look her up.”

“Yeah, she’s the Spic who lives on the second floor. Her English ain’t so good. Can you speak Mexican?”

For Christ’s sake… doesn’t anyone know that Mexicans speak Spanish?

“I’m learning. What are the other tenants like? I’m really hoping to meet some people, you know. It might make it easier being new in town. Anyone around my age?” I hope she took me as being in my early twenties. Most people do, and I love them dearly for it, but in truth they’re off by about a decade.

“Yeah, there’s a coupla girls probably about as old as you is. One’s hardly ever here. Name’s Daria, lives on the second floor, hasn’t been here long. The other young girl, Carrie Jo, is on the second also, two doors from Mary Carmen. She seems to have more on the ball than the Spic, but ain’t nearly so friendly. The rest of the tenants ain’t much worth your time. An artist, a coupla no-goodniks, and a few guys I’d never let my daughter date, if I had a daughter.”

“What about pets?”

“Nah. No pets. Only one allowed is my German shepherd, Fritz, and he’s a guard dog, not a pet.”

“I think I heard him barking when I was at the door.”

“That means he’s doing his job.”

Fritz had sounded wheezy and not particularly threatening, and kind of like he was on the fritz.

“How much is the rent, anyway?” I asked.

"Hundred bucks a week, and you gotta give me an extra week's rent as the last week's rent deposit. Everything's payable in cash only, due every Monday by nine in the morning. No rent, and your stuff is on the street by noon. I run a tight ship here."

"Well, I have a couple other places to check out. Can I think it over for a day or two?"

"Suit yourself. Whatever."

Mary Carmen

He raped me twice.

The first like normal sex, like they call misionario. *The second time like a dog from the behind. It feel like he tore the skin of my asshole.*

Son of a bitch! ¡Hijo de puto!

"You know you like it, bitch," he said to me. "It's all you're good for – a piece of fucking tail. Admit it, it's what you want."

"Si, señor, *I do want you, yes," I said, but I sounded* insincero.

God help me.

I think I hated him more at this minute than I could ever hate anyone in my life. ¡Jesus Cristo! *What I am going to do? I cannot cry one more tear for this* pinche *animal.*

"Go get me a glass of water, bitch."

It was almost like God speaked to me in that moment. My purse was still on the floor, in the entrance, right by the door of the bathroom. I started to pray to God immediatamente *for forgiveness for what I am going to do.*

Dios, perdóname…

Saturday, 6:35 pm

I should have felt guilty about showing up at Shane's restaurant Pastiche and expecting free food. I should especially have felt guilty about it given that it was dinnertime on a Saturday, his busiest period. However, I have no shame and very little pride, and at that moment I had an empty stomach and an empty wallet. I walked down the side alley and strode through the delivery entrance that opened onto the kitchen.

"Shane's not in the kitchen tonight, Sasha," said Rolf, the sous-chef and also Shane's partner. "He's out front pretending to be a maître d' or something."

"Oh, this is going to be good."

I love my brother, and far be it for me to say an unkind word about him, but people skills are not his thing. Shane can effortlessly whip up a five-course culinary masterpiece, he's great at fixing any and everything, he has a wicked sense of humour, he's a walking encyclopaedia of music history… and he's anything but extroverted. He seems to be okay with family, or any group of fewer than five or six people, but working on the front line with John Q. Public would have to be a nightmare come true for him.

I headed back to the street and entered the restaurant via the front door. I tried not to laugh at the sight of my darling brother all gussied up in a suit and tie. I've never seen him wearing a cravat before, and I doubt he even knows how to do a Windsor knot. I was tempted to tug on it to see if the tie was a clip-on.

"Well, you're sure out of your element tonight, brother dearest," I said, taking a seat at the bar opposite the entrance.

"Don't remind me. Rolf's been after me for a while now to get more involved in the front-end part of the business. Cross-training or something. I understand his point, but I'll be glad to see the end of this night. Excuse me."

A party of four had arrived, and Shane checked their names in the reservation book. He picked up four menus and a wine list and led them to a table.

Drew, the bartender, asked me what I wanted to drink.

"Surprise me."

Drew got busy with a silver martini shaker and three or four different bottles.

"Here you go. It's called the PB&J."

That couldn't mean what I thought it did, could it? I took a sip and, sure enough, it tasted like I was drinking an adults-only, high-octane version of a liquefied peanut butter and jelly sandwich. "This is good, dangerously good. What's in it?"

"Chambord, vodka, white crème de cacao, and Frangelico. It's one of our new specialty cocktails. We'll be offering it during the Summerlicious Festival."

"It's about as perfect a summer cocktail as you can get."

Drew offered me a menu and I ordered a couple of

appetizers. I knew Shane wouldn't have much time to chat, but who needed conversation when I could amuse myself by watching his level of discomfort increase exponentially as the dining room filled up with hungry patrons? Drew delivered the first of my small dishes: maple-cured salmon gravlax served with beets and dilled fennel. I had just shoved a wad of deliciousness into my mouth when my cellphone twittered to life. Shane shot me an evil look from across the room. I had just broken one of Pastiche's cardinal rules: no cellphones. I told Drew to keep an eye on my place, and took the call in the open air sauna outside.

Call display said *unknown number.* I picked up, "Sasha speaking."

"This is Dave. Candace suggested I get in touch with you."

Ah. Mr. X was finally making contact.

"Thanks for calling me Dave. I don't know what Candace told you…?"

"One of her employees is missing. However, I don't think I can help you."

"Apparently, you were the last client to see her."

"And this was a couple of Thursdays ago?"

"Yes, July 9 at The Grand Hotel," I said.

"Well, that's the problem. I didn't see her then, or anyone else in Toronto for that matter. I was in Montréal giving the opening address to a group of environmentalists, geologists, lawyers, and politicians attending the 'Sustainable Mineral Excavation Conference' at the Queen Elizabeth Hotel. So, you see, there must be some mistake," said Dave No Last Name.

"According to Candace, you called in with a request

for an exotic girl. They pulled up your file and matched you with Mary Carmen, who happened to be free and happened to be just what you were looking for – "

"I am acquainted with the young lady." He was terse, and I could picture Dave No Last Name impatiently glancing at his watch, probably a Tag Heuer or a Rolex, as we spoke.

"You asked for a hotel room rather than seeing her at, uh, corporate HQ," I said.

"It sounds plausible, but it wasn't me. It's been a couple of months since I've used the services of that establishment. I met someone special and have been dating her exclusively. In fact, we got engaged a couple of weeks ago. So, sorry, but I don't think I can help you."

We spoke for a moment or two longer, but I got nothing more out of him. He could be lying about booking an appointment with Mary Carmen on July 9, but if he were lying about that, then why talk to me at all? Why bother to call me? Why admit to using Candace's whorehouse in the past? Why 'fess up to knowing Mary Carmen? Why not just go into denial about the whole thing?

Inconsistencies both perturb and intrigue me. More than that, though, they confuse the hell out of me and make my brain hurt.

I re-entered Pastiche and parked my ass back down at the bar. A glass of wine appeared out of thin air as I was inhaling the rest of my salmon. Drew cleared the plate and then presented me with a chèvre salad topped with cognac-drenched blueberries, followed by a bowl of tarragon-scented, chilled yellow pepper and leek purée. I considered asking Drew to marry me.

While I was outside on the phone, I had picked up a copy of *NOW* magazine from one of the newspaper boxes on the sidewalk in front of Pastiche. *NOW* is a weekly publication listing events, happenings around town, live music, and just about anything else related to the city's nightlife, culture, and entertainment. I flipped through the magazine while I was finishing my dinner and circled the names of a few Spanish clubs and salsa bars. I figured it couldn't hurt to check them out, even though I was definitely not dressed in club wear. Oh well, maybe I could start a new trend. *Dressed down in Clubland. Understated elegance. Less is more.* At least none of my clothes came from Walmart.

After I left Pastiche, I stopped at an ATM on the corner and put myself a bit further into overdraft. I knew I'd need cash on hand if I wanted to get inside any of the clubs to talk to the staff. Looking at the negative balance, it might not be long before my wardrobe actually does come from Sam W's bastion of bargain hunting.

Saturday, 9:45 pm

Momentos is one of those bars that thinks ear-splitting loud music equals a hip and happening club. The room vibrated with the thump of full-throttle bass and I wondered if there was a cure for tinnitus. I think some evil marketing genius with far-reaching powers has convinced club owners around the world that the rhythmic throbbing of bass is subliminally linked to the pulsing sounds of hot and horny sex. There was no other way to justify the über-stentorian *pump, pump, pump.*

I paid a ten-dollar cover charge for the privilege of entering.

Even though the night was just getting underway, there was a decent crowd around the bar and on the dance floor. Most of the people there were young (twenty-something) although I'd bet more than a few were younger than that – but not according to the fake IDs, which they'd probably bought at any one of the tacky head shops near Yonge and Bloor.

I was invited onto the dance floor by a smiling, plump guy who looked about seventeen, or maybe that was just the effect of his peach-fuzz moustache. I half expected Mr. Happy Go Porky to ask me to buy a beer for him. I graciously declined to cha-cha-cha with Chunky and sidled up to the bar.

"A Corona please, no lime." I slid ten dollars across the bar. "Keep the change."

"Thank you!" shouted a very hot bartender with broad shoulders. "I'm Luis."

"Nice to meet you. I'm Sasha!" I had to yell to be heard, and even so I figured he was reading my lips more than listening to me. I handed him one of my business cards. "I'm actually here tonight on business. I'm trying to find this girl. Recognize her?" I passed him the photo.

"Definitely. It's Mary Carmen, right?"

"Yes. Has she been around lately?"

"Not in the last couple of weeks. What do you want with her?"

"She seems to have disappeared. Does she usually come in with a regular group of friends? Any of the people she hung out with here tonight?"

"Nah. She'll talk to whoever's around, dance with just about anyone, but she always comes alone and leaves alone."

"Well, if she happens to come in, please give me a call."

I showed Mary Carmen's picture to the bouncers and some of the regulars. A couple of them recognized her but said they hadn't seen her recently. I gave them my card and loudly recited my usual lines about getting in touch.

The electronic *thump-thump-thump* of the music was giving me a headache and there was clearly nothing more to be gleaned from Momentos. I left my half-finished Corona on the bar and split.

Babalu's, a bit farther down the road in Yorkville, is another Latin-themed club, and I had to admit I preferred the vibe here to that at Momentos. The crowd was a bit older, the place had much nicer décor, and the music was less of an aural assault.

Once again, a couple of people recognized Mary Carmen's picture, but no one had seen her lately.

"Yeah, a few weeks ago," said a tall man with a unibrow, a tattered beige and rust Hawaiian shirt, and thick brown corduroys. "I danced with her all bloody night and then didn't score."

Doesn't everyone know that corduroys must be kept hidden away from Easter till Thanksgiving? And no clothier worth his salt would make a Hawaiian shirt in sombre, muted earth tones.

"Did you have any reason to think you'd score?" I asked. "Was she looking to be picked up? Did you just meet her that night?"

"Yeah, I mean, what the fuck, a hot chick like that, why wouldn't she want to be picked up?"

"Why not indeed?"

"I don't even like dancing, but I danced with her all bloody night 'cause she was into it. I even bought her a coupla drinks. Then, at the end of the night when I was about to ask her back to my place, she said she was going to the can, and she fucked off. Never saw her again, but I'd still like to do her."

What a putz. "Maybe she was just playing hard to get."

I handed out my business card to a few other people, and asked them to call me if Mary Carmen came by. I was clearly batting zero here, too, so once again, I left a half-finished Corona on the bar and split.

After walking a few blocks south on Bay Street, I hailed a taxi. I could have walked, but it was too damn muggy. I could have taken the subway and the streetcar, but I was just too damn lazy. This salsa bar line of inquiry – taxis and cover charges and the tabs for half-drunk Coronas – was going to get expensive. My next stops were El Convento Rico and Mana, both on College Street. Each had another ten-dollar cover charge and my results there were a carbon copy of the first two places, right down to the wasted Latino lagers. A few people recognized Mary Carmen, but no one had seen her recently.

I was tired, frustrated, and ready to call it a night. I only had about seven dollars left in my wallet, so I had to take the streetcar home, since a cab would have been about twenty bucks. Damn it, I'd have to plan tomorrow a bit more carefully, unless I wanted the next day's expenses to be paid for with rolls of coins from my piggy bank.

I had a long, sticky wait for the streetcar. The night was only slightly cooler than the day, which wasn't saying much.

The streetcar stop was at a good corner from which to people watch. A group of teens were staggering along arm in arm. Couples dressed up for date night ambled down the street holding hands. Clusters of hot chicks in slinky club wear tottered along in heels they'd never be able to dance in. It struck me that there were only shades of difference between the nightclub attire of chicks on the prowl versus the wardrobes of the hookers on the stroll. Context is everything, no doubt.

After pacing back and forth for about twenty minutes, not one but three streetcars lurched into view.

Sunday, July 19, 1:15 am

Lucky for me, Dad was away fishing this week, so I had the house to myself until Shane came home sometime around two or three in the morning.

Unlucky for me, I had a rather unpleasant surprise awaiting me upon my return home. Some asshole with a can of black paint had sprayed BACK OFF BITCH on the front and garage doors. Fuck. I should have been scared, but I was pissed off. Dad and Shane didn't deserve to come home to this. They hadn't signed up to play cops and robbers with me.

I lightly touched the paint to see if it was dry. The night's humidity probably slowed the drying process, but my finger came away clean. That meant the asshole who did it had probably been here a while ago, maybe two or three hours. I doubted anyone was lurking in the bushes, so I went inside.

After entering the alarm code, I flipped on the main floor lights. A quick dash through the living room, kitchen, dining room, and den reassured me. Nothing was out of place. Doors and windows were closed and didn't appear to have been tampered with. Okey dokey. Then I breezed through upstairs. Nothing seemed amiss.

Well, someone was trying to scare me off, but it was obviously an amateur who was too much of a candy-ass to do more than pose graffiti threats. A professional would have done more.

I didn't want Shane to be greeted by BACK OFF BITCH when he tumbled home from work, so I dug around the garage for something I could use to obfuscate the message. There were a couple cans of red and green spray paint left over from some Christmas project. Within a few minutes, the garage and front doors looked like rejects from a Jackson Pollock yard sale.

To relax and clear their heads, some people meditate, others exercise, and still others just quietly contemplate their navels. My Zen moments come from beating the shit out of a set of Mapex drums in the basement. After the hell I'd been through on my last case, I'd decided to treat myself to this new set and I love every minute of playing them.

Dad had done his best to try to soundproof the basement, and during the day I could get away with making as much noise as I wanted, but at night the shortcomings of the acoustic padding became obvious, especially when I woke the whole house, or worse, the neighbours.

I didn't have to worry about anyone's beauty sleep in my own house tonight, though, so I let loose. I was wearing a stretched and shapeless old AC/DC concert T-shirt and a pair of pink cotton bikini undies, and I was in a punchy, edgy mood.

I warmed up with "Pleasure" by 2G, Toronto's own rapper on the rise. Rap and Hip Hop aren't usually my thing, but this tune was just right for my mood. Then I started playing along with some golden oldies, familiar faves like The Temptations and Led Zeppelin, followed by some slightly newer stuff like Sublime, The White Stripes, and Franz Ferdinand. From there I segued into improvisation. I really started laying down a groove and created a few beats I quite liked. I whacked and tapped and smacked and smashed away at the drums off and on for about an hour and a half. I loved my new Sabian cymbals. The hi-hat sound was crisp and clear until I pounded it a bit too hard and knocked loose the wing nut thingy that holds a bracket in place, allowing the top cymbal to rise and lower. I got up to fix it and noticed immediately how sore my ass was.

When I had bought the new drum set, I hadn't bothered to get a new throne – you never call the thing a drummer sits on a *seat* or a *stool.* People seldom realize how physical drumming is, although sore arms and shoulders are the obvious occupational hazards. However, most drummers will tell you it's their asses that get sore if they play too long. When you're pounding away on the bass and hi-hat pedals, and your upper body is reaching for the tom-toms and stretching towards the cymbals, all your weight goes on your ass. As you rock it out, the bones in your butt begin to ache. A decent throne with thick padding was only about a hundred and fifty dollars, but considering I couldn't afford cab fare home, a throne would have to wait until someone paid me.

After I fixed the hi-hat, I stuck a pillow on top of my old throne and played a while longer. I even recorded some of my playing, but knew as I did so that I'd be the only person who'd ever hear tonight's improvised session. Too bad, because I'd pulled a couple of rabbits out of a musical hat, and no one would ever have the pleasure of hearing the rhythmic magic I'd conjured up.

When my forearms felt like they were about ready to fall off, and my forehead was beaded with sweat, I called a night to drumming and went upstairs to the kitchen. I made a great big mug of hot chocolate and, as I took the first sip, it occurred to me that hot chocolate was an inappropriate beverage on a close and sultry July night. So I threw in a shot of peppermint schnapps, and that made everything okay. I sat at the kitchen table and started writing notes about this case, a case for which I still hadn't come up with a clever title.

As for the notes, they consisted almost entirely of

questions rather than answers. In my profession, the inverse is preferred.

Where is Mary Carmen? How did she end up working for Candace? What did she do before that? Who saw her last? Did her roomies know anything about her? Where was she taking English classes? Why was she a hooker? Why or how did Dave No Last Name get peripherally involved in this? Was someone using his name? Where did Mary Carmen go if not to The Grand? Whom had she met? Why did her last john pretend to be someone else, if that was indeed what was happening? Is Mary Carmen alive and well? Should I check out more salsa bars? Could she have gone back to Mexico? And why doesn't she eat at Taco Bell?

The writing exercise never seemed to accomplish anything while I was doing it, but it always clarified a few things for me after a good night's sleep. Or maybe it was just the slumber that unlocked the deductive section of my brain.

I rinsed out my mug and went to bed.

Sunday, 8:54 am

My plan of action, which had crystallized while I was off in Never Never Land, was to find out more about Dave No Last Name. It occurred to me that if he was on the up and up, then someone was using him to get to Mary Carmen. But who and why? I also figured that with this case – as well as in politics, international relations, history, and Freudian psychology – the past is the decoder for the present. I should send that startling revelation into "Deep Thoughts by Jack Handey."

Whatever. I needed a clearer picture of the present before I began digging backwards through time.

Shane hadn't come home last night, so I had the house to myself. I went out front and checked out the artwork in my front yard. The word BITCH was still faintly visible, so I sprayed another coat of red paint over it.

Then I went into the den and logged onto the Internet. I searched mining plus conferences, and then minerals plus conventions, and a few other combinations of similar terms. Eventually, I found a website for the conference at which Dave said he had spoken. Yes, indeed, Dave J. Bowring, L.L.B., of the Toronto law firm Gopnik, Guralnick, Purdy, and Roth, had given the opening address that Thursday night at a posh hotel in downtown Montreal. It was kind of amusing that Dave had been so secretive and private, yet he gave me enough details during our brief call to track him down in no time at all. Dumbass. I now knew where he worked and I had his full name. I filed away this new information until I could decide what to do with it.

As I frittered away the morning, it dawned on me, as it had last night while I was waiting for the streetcar, that this case could and would suddenly run up a big expense tab, and I had concerns about that. The obvious concern was my desire to be reimbursed. However, the greater concern – and this is woefully embarrassing to admit – is that my cash flow these days is anything but flowing. Try torpid, frozen, clogged, inert, moribund.

In my last big case, not that long ago, my office had been trashed. Completely ransacked, and everything in it was affected by unsurpassed levels of gratuitous destruction. So, I had rented new office space near the St. Lawrence Market. Since the start of the summer, I'd slowly replaced, redecorated, and redone the workplace of Sasha Jackson, Private Investigator.

Insurance had covered a lot of the damage and would cover the replacement for most of what had been ransacked. But, of course, things always cost more than expected. There was the insurance deductible plus moving costs, the latter not covered since it was my choice to relocate. And there were the myriad little expenses that emerged long after I'd sent in my insurance claim. Naturally, the insurance company was taking its sweet time settling my claim.

I was flat broke these days.

Of course, I shouldn't have recently spent three grand on a new set of drums and cymbals, but I'd needed a boost after having been shot in the boobs.

A friend of mine once listed all the ways he could think of to get money. I believe his list had eleven methods on it: earn, find, win, inherit, steal, borrow… I can't recall the others. I was currently trying to earn money; I did not have any real expectation of finding or winning any; for obvious reasons I truly hoped I didn't stand to inherit any cash anytime soon; and I wasn't desperate enough yet to steal it. That left borrowing and that conclusion made me feel like a loser. Then there was the question of which lucky friend or relative I would choose to use as my short-term banker.

I called Lindsey.

Dad and Shane were ruled out almost immediately. Dad because, as loving and supportive as he is, he's not quite convinced that this private-eye gig is a good career choice for his one and only favourite daughter. Admitting to money troubles could easily tailspin into an "I told you so."

Shane was a no-go because of my pride, even though I knew Lindsey would probably tell him. But, he'd pretend not to know, and wouldn't mention it, and I'd pretend I didn't know that he knew. Kind of like when there are two people in an elevator and one of them silently farts; they both know who did it, but neither one says anything about it.

Sunday, 11:30 am

"Here you go," I said, handing Dingy Track Pants, whose name was Agnes Lynch, the first week's rent plus the deposit for my new fleabag abode.

Lindsey had come through with some cash, and I was renting this room for hopefully no longer than a week in order to find out whatever I could from Mary Carmen's erstwhile cellmates.

"The week begins Monday morning. If you wanna move in today, you gotta pay twenty dollars for the extra night," said my charming new landlord, whose hair was still in the awful pink rollers, but who had swapped yesterday's lime-green track pants for an equally awful pair of peach-coloured ones.

"Here you go," I said, giving her another twenty.

"Here's your key and I'll make up a receipt for you later. No overnight guests, okay?"

"No problem." This was hardly a place in which I'd be entertaining gentlemen callers or hosting a slumber party.

"Ya gotta lotta stuff to move in?"

"Not really. Just one suitcase, and I left it in a locker at the train station."

She gave me my key and disappeared into her bunker.

I killed a few minutes in my new abode by checking the voice mail on my cell and returning a few very unimportant calls. Then I decided to be my own welcome wagon and get out and meet my flatmates.

On my floor I met an effervescent drag queen named Todd. I assumed he was one of the no-goodniks to which my landlord had referred. I immediately took a shine to him.

"Sweetie, you look too normal to be living here," Todd said.

"It's just temporary. I'm new in town."

"Well, get your shit together and go find a place that has running water 24/7. You're too pure for this dump."

"It doesn't seem so bad."

"You must have grown up in a shantytown outside Calcutta if this place is even borderline acceptable to you, sweetie."

I chuckled. "It's a good location. Central."

"Uh huh… and?"

"Actually, a friend of a friend lives here, which is how I heard of this building. Her name's Mary Carmen."

"Oh, sweetie, if I played for the other team, I'd be all over her. As it is, we just do each other's hair and makeup."

"So you're a friend of hers?" The ability to ask deductive, clever, loaded, and insightful questions like this comes almost naturally to me. It's one of the many talents that makes me an investigator without equals. The other talents are chutzpah up the yin-yang, a knack for breaking into places where I don't belong, ad libbing convincing lies on the spot, and being an amazing – but underappreciated – singer. Okay, maybe singing has nothing to do with sleuthing…

"We hit it off as soon as she moved in here," Todd said. "She's a doll and a darling, and what wouldn't I do to have eyes like hers."

"Yes, she's quite the beauty. So when did she move in here?"

"About five or six months ago."

"How could anybody stay here that long?" I asked.

"I've been here over a year."

"Oops. Sorry. I didn't mean it like that. Please don't take offense."

"None taken. It *is* a dump, after all."

"Anyhow, about Mary Carmen?" I asked, trying to steer the conversation back on track.

"You know Mary Carmen's a hooker, right?" I nodded, and Todd continued. "I work a different kind of sex trade. Tricks are what pays the bills, but I'd so much rather be doing a show. You can see me onstage at Woody's every Tuesday night from ten to eleven o'clock."

"Oh, really?"

"Yes. I'm part of the *Divas in Drag* ensemble. I do a wicked Cher imitation. People think I sound just like her. And I really am singing, not just lip syncing."

"I'll definitely check out your show sometime." Not even at gunpoint would I go to any show or event where Cher or any derivative of her or her music was the feature. Never. I'd rather listen to nails on a chalk-board than suffer though songs done in a billy-goat vibrato.

"Anyhow, sweetie, in our kinds of work, we don't get pay stubs and employment records and references. Try to rent a place when you can't prove your income."

"I see…"

"A lot of sex workers live in flophouses like this one. Sucks, but what's a poor drag queen to do?"

"I see…"

"Best thing is to find good, steady, rich clients and stay the night with them whenever possible. Use this dump as nothing more than a pit stop."

"Is Mary Carmen around today?"

"Her room's the last one on the second floor, but I don't think she's home. I haven't seen her for a few days. Mind you, I spent most of the past week at the Four Seasons with an unnamed Hollywood hunk in town filming his latest action flick. I can't tell you his name, sweetie, but let's say that folks in Tinseltown would be shocked to learn he likes to play with the pretty boys. The tabloid stories about him and Nicola Simone are just a cover."

I smiled. "Well, if his secret comes out, you'll make the front page of *The National Enquirer* as the 'other woman.' Any ideas where I can find Mary Carmen if she's not home?"

It seemed odd to refer to this shithole as home, no matter how transient the tenants.

"It's Sunday, so she might have gone to Mass. You know how Catholic those Mexicans are."

No sex before marriage, no birth control. Yup, Catholicism was written all over this case.

Actually, I was well familiar with Mexico and its culture and customs. During my rudderless slacker year after high school, I had spent six months volunteering at an orphanage in Zacatecas, a hilly, bucolic, colonial silver mining town high in the Sierra Madre mountains. During that time, I had grown very fond of Mexico and its people. I had boarded with a Mexican family, and they fed me quite well, corrected my rudimentary Spanish, and dragged me to church every weekend. To this day, we still send each other Christmas cards. And to this day, I swear I get an allergic reaction whenever I enter a house of worship.

"Yeah, but the whole church thing seems so incongruous with Mary Carmen's chosen profession," I said.

"Maybe the profession chose her. Or maybe it wasn't a choice."

"*Touché.* Any idea which church?" I asked.

"It's Saint Something or Other in the west end. They give the Mass in Spanish."

"*Si…*"

"She usually goes for Mexican food after church," Todd said. "You know that place on Augusta Street, just south of College Street? El Toto or Toro, something like that?"

"I think I've walked past it."

"She says they have the best corn tortillas in the city. Who knew there were varying degrees of corn tortillas? All I need is a bag of Doritos and I'm happy."

"I'm with you on that, but I suppose I'll have to check it out."

I tried a few more doors on my floor and the fourth, then wandered down to the second floor to try my luck there. Daria and Carrie Jo were both out, but I did meet the artist, or more appropriately, the starving artist. Think of a younger, anorexic Iggy Pop and you'd have Laramie. I didn't know whether that was a first or last name and didn't much care.

He answered the door with a short, fine paintbrush clenched between his teeth, and a longer, broader brush clutched in both hands like a Samurai sword. He didn't invite me into his shoebox, but from the doorway I could see several small canvases, and I could smell a noxious bouquet of paint and solvents and other stuff that could get me high as a kite if I were to continue breathing. The paintings were all angular abstracts, covered with hasty, violent brushstrokes done in shades of black, blacker, and blackest, with a little battleship grey splashed in to brighten things up. Obviously not a student of the Impressionists.

"Sorry, but I can't tell you much," Laramie said, still gnawing on the paintbrush.

"It's not important. It's just that I lost her cellphone

number, and we have some mutual friends, and I said I'd hook up with her when I got to Toronto."

"She comes and goes. Doesn't seem to really have a schedule."

"I knocked on her door, but there was no answer."

"Then she's probably not home."

"Right. Any ideas where I can find her?"

"Maybe at Burrito Boys. She usually gives me her doggy bags from there. They make motherfucking big-assed burritos. I can't even finish the half she brings home for me."

Judging by his poster-child-for-Oxfam physique, he should have eaten the whole damn thing and asked for seconds.

I wasn't about to go on a wild goose chase looking for a church that delivered its Sunday sermon in Spanish, so I hightailed it to El Toto or Toro or whatever in Kensington Market off College Street. Actually, truth be told, I hightailed it to the streetcar stop, got on the trolley car and let the Red Rocket do the hightailing for me while I zoned out to Muddy Waters on my MP3 player. It was far too hot to walk.

"*Si*, I know this girl, she come for *gorditas de requéson* and chorizo all the Sundays," said a matchbox-shaped Latina gnome in a colourfully-embroidered cotton dress typical of Oaxaca. The Mexican place was actually called El Topo.

"Mmm. I haven't had *gorditas* in ages. Give me a couple." The Gnome took my money and threw a couple tortillas on the grill. "So, did Mary Carmen come in today? What time does she usually get here?"

"No, I no see her today. I no see her the last Sunday, too."

"Is that unusual?"

"*Si*. She normally come this time, after the mass. She have the lunch here, and we talk a while. Maybe she sick. Why you ask questions for her?"

"Apparently she's missing. No one has seen or heard from her in over a week."

"You like the *gorditas* with cilantro?"

"Yeah, please, lots." She handed me a paper plate, and I took a big bite and burned my tongue. The chorizo was zingy, and the cheese had the velvety, gooey texture I remembered from my days in Mexico.

"Maybe she with the old lady, the rich bitch." With her accent, it sounded like the Mexican Gnome had said *rish-uh bisht*.

"What?"

"Oh, Maria del Carmen always tell me of crazy old woman with the money. She clean house of this woman. Maria say the lady gonna put Maria del Carmen in her testament."

The Bible? "Testament?" I asked. Old or New Testament?

"Like the papers when you die and decide you give you money to some people."

"Oh, you mean a *will*. Who's the lady? Where can I find her?"

"I don't know. Maria del Carmen clean her house three times every week. She have a big house in the rich area, where all the *Judeos* live."

"You mean Jewish?"

"*Si*. I no think the *señora* is Yewish, but in that area."

"Is it in Forest Hill? Somewhere along Bathurst Street? St. Clair? Avenue Road?"

"Who knows? I tell Maria she have her head fulled of the clouds. All these *gringas* with money keep it with themselfs. Maids doesn't inherit from the rich folks unless in a movie starring Yennifer Lopez."

I gave the Latina Gnome my card and told her to call me if Mary Carmen came by.

Well, this was a twist. So, Mary Carmen also worked as a maid. I was starting to really feel sorry for this migrant girl whom I had never even met. All her gorgeousness couldn't prevent her life from becoming the cliché of every ethnic, non-English speaking woman to cross the border. Domestic work and prostitution, take your pick – either way you're fucked. Yeah, Canada might indeed have open doors, and may claim to welcome newcomers, but the fact is that power and agency still rest in the hands of WASPs. Just ask any visible minority taxi driver with a Ph.D. Diversity and multiculturalism be damned… though, to be fair, Canada seems more welcoming to Mexican migrants than other places like, say, Arizona.

So, who was this rich old lady and where did she live?

And how come no one else seemed to know about this other job?

Sunday, 2:30 pm

Next up: I wanted to find out more about Dave No Last Name and Mary Carmen's last booking. I probably should have chased the housekeeping lead, but it was too fresh and I needed to let it sift through my brain before I could figure out how to act on it. It was possible that the woman at El Topo had been mistaken, since I'd heard nothing about domestic employment from anyone else. Or maybe Mary Carmen had just lied to the Gnome about her career. Perhaps claiming to be a maid is less embarrassing than admitting to being a hooker. That's what I'd have said, and the way things sometimes go with the private-eye gig, it might someday be preferable to claim I clean other people's toilets for a living.

Oh, God, kill me now.

It was Sunday afternoon, and sunny, the perfect summer day. I walked from College Street as far north as Bloor Street, and then a few blocks east towards Yonge Street. I passed at least four churches along the way. One was Anglican, two were Catholic, and I think the other was Presbyterian. I saw families dressed in their Sunday finest, little girls in frilly pink dresses, little boys with their hair neatly combed. I could picture fussy moms dabbing spit on a Kleenex to wipe sticky spots off chubby freckled faces. Maybe the families had taken Communion during the service, maybe the kids sang in the choir, maybe they were all going out for ice cream cones after Mass. One certain thing was that none of them were en route to a bordello. I'm not even a little bit pious or holy, but it seemed sacrilegious to spend a bright summer Sunday afternoon inside a whorehouse.

"Okay, so how does it work?" I asked Candace. "How do you screen your clients? You must have a system of screening and some stopgaps to make sure you don't get pinched by an undercover cop."

"Clients have to give me a name, a referral from another client. I don't take bookings from anyone who isn't a friend of a friend. My initial client roster was made up of the more desirable clients from my street days, plus a few from when I was stripping."

"Okay, then what?"

"I take some personal information and ask for a credit card number."

"They give you a credit card number?"

"Yes, absolutely. No credit card equals no booking. The charge goes through as recreational consulting, event planning, or holistic therapy, all of which are vague enough to not make wives raise their eyebrows should they see a credit card statement not meant for their eyes. The credit card charges also sound legitimate enough for many of my clients to write off their visits here as a business expense. You've got to love that, don't you?"

"Priceless. Imagine if the taxmen down at the Canada Revenue Agency were to find out."

"Whatever, the clients are fine with it. My reputation precedes me. I gladly take cash, I don't take cheques, I declare all my income, and I pay all my taxes."

"How do you have four different ways to charge them?" I asked.

"You work for yourself, so you must know how easy it is to register a business name?" I nodded. "I registered the four I just mentioned to you as sole proprietorships. Then for each one I established myself as a merchant with Visa, American Express, and MasterCard. I rotate the business name under which I process the transaction. Keeps suspicion and potential problems to a minimum."

"Clever."

"As I mentioned before, this building is listed as a bed and breakfast, so that provides cover for people randomly coming and going."

"Got it. Okay, so what else?"

"All new clients are referred to me. If I don't get a good vibe from them, I say goodbye. I assign new customers a number for my records, but from that point on they're referred to by staff here by first names or initials only."

"So what about this call from Dave?"

"The girl working reception that evening took the call. Dave was already in the database, so I didn't actually speak with him that night."

"I think you said someone named Terra was on the phones," I said.

"Yes, Terra Kern. A relatively new girl."

"So she wouldn't have known Dave's voice. You know I'll need to talk with her."

"She's off today, but I can call her."

"By the way, what night did Mary Carmen work the reception?" I asked.

"She's an exception to the job sharing. Her English isn't quite good enough, so she's off the hook for phone duty, so to speak."

"And what about the thing I asked you about yesterday? About changes in any client's habits?"

"I've taken a quick look, but nothing leaps out yet. Give me a bit more time to check thoroughly."

Just as I was leaving Candace's establishment, a guy I recognized as the weatherman for the local news channel was ringing the doorbell. I tried to avoid making eye contact, but he was blatantly checking me out. Talk about a warm front moving in.

"Hey, gorgeous," he said, giving his lips a lupine lick. *Ugh!* "I haven't seen you here before. Maybe you should stick around." He winked at me, and I thought I'd vomit.

"Uh, I'm not… I don't… oh, look there's my cab."

A yellow taxi was cruising by, and I jumped in as fast as I could. I suspect the updated forecast for the meteorologist would now include a cold shower.

An hour later I was sitting on the sidewalk patio of a coffee shop in Yorkville. I knew who Terra was as soon as she arrived. Candace had described her as a buxom redhead oozing sensuality. I was thinking more along the lines of sultry hippie chick. It was all in the hair: wild, wavy, woolly, coppery red, long, and unruly. Something about her demeanour told me she was very good at her job. I'm not sure how I deduced that based on her tresses, but there you go.

"Hey, I'm Terra," she said, as she drifted into the seat opposite me. "Nice to meet you."

"Sorry to bother you on your day off," I said.

"Don't mention it. Man, we're having coffee at an outdoor café, the sun's shining, it's a lazy Sunday afternoon, I had a long walk in the park with my dog Daisy this morning, I'm happy and healthy, and man, what more could I ask for?"

Cue the saccharine soundtrack. Bring on the incense and peppermint. Smother me in patchouli oil. Terra had to be on drugs. No one could be this happy without chemical assistance. I kind of wanted to slap her.

"What kind of dog do you have?" I asked instead.

"It's called a schnorkie, a hybrid between a schnauzer and a Yorkshire terrier. Get it?"

"Yeah, it's a portmanteau."

"No, it's a dog." Clearly, Terra's was a case in which the synapses weren't firing in sync.

"I mean the word *schnorkie* is a portmanteau, which is the word for when you take parts of two words to make a new word that combines the meanings of both. Like *brunch* is a blend of breakfast and lunch, or *Brangelina* for Brad Pitt and Miz Jolie."

"Wow, cool, there's a word for words like that? So, I guess that means a *Dalmador* is a Dalmatian and Labrador."

"Yes, and a *Chihuashund* is a Chihuahua and a dachshund."

"Then a *cockapoo* must be a cocker spaniel and a poodle."

"Right. So, imagine if breeders crossed a cocker spaniel and a Maltese."

She gave me a blank look for a moment until it dawned on her.

"Man, that's funny."

Synapses one, patchouli oil zero.

"Anyhow, Terra, I don't want to take up too much of your time. I need to know about a call you took last week. A guy named Dave. He had a date with Mary Carmen."

"Yeah, I know. Candace told me what you're working on, and, man, I think it's cool, so cool. Maybe if I ever decide to get out of this life, I could do something like that. Is detecting hard? It sounds like fun. I bet you meet a lot of way cool people, and it must feel good to solve puzzles. That's what it's all about, isn't it?"

There should have been a halo of colourful butterflies flittering around her head, and she could easily have gotten away with a daisy-chain hair band.

"Uh, yeah, it's nice to find answers, and that's why I wanted to talk to you. What can you tell me about the call from Dave?"

"Well, I was working reception, greeting guests and answering incoming calls. This guy Dave called. Man, I didn't think twice about it because he was in our database. If he wasn't on file there, then, man, who knows where Mary Carmen would be now? Maybe she would be safe and—"

"We don't know for sure that anything's happened to her."

"It's just bad karma. It's—"

"Anyhow, so you thought this call from Dave was a regular... patron. How did you know who to match him with?"

"I sorta didn't. He was very specific. He wanted a Spanish girl, a tall girl. I put him on hold for a moment and mentioned the call to Candace. I knew Mary Carmen, of course, but I haven't been working there long enough to know all the girls off the top of my head, or all the clients either, so I asked Candace. She suggested Mary C. Of course, if I was better at working the computer, I would've seen that Dave has gone with Mary C before. Man, this is so weird. I'm not very tech savvy, you know. It's confusing. I bet you don't have to use computers much in your line of—"

"What did the guy sound like?" I broke in. "Any accent? A lisp? A cough?"

"Wow! Cool questions. Yeah, he sounded kinda like a Quebecker. You know how the French-Canadians drop the *H* on words that begin with it?"

"Like *'ello, 'ow* are you?"

"Yeah, man, just like that. That's what he sounded like."

"Interesting. So what did the call sound like?"

Terra blinked. "What do you mean?"

"Did it sound like a cellphone? Like long distance? Was the reception clear? Was there any background noise?"

"Man, the things you think of. Wow! No, it was just a regular call. Sounded like it coulda been from next door."

"What about call display?"

"Just about every incoming call is 'private name' or 'number blocked' or 'public telephone.' Sorry."

"What was he like? Polite, impatient, soft-spoken, assertive?"

"Maybe a bit gruff, not exactly rude, but I had a feeling he woulda snapped at me if I'd put him on hold again. Man, I just thought he was really horny and couldn't wait to get his rocks off."

"And he wanted an outcall?" I asked.

"Yeah, he said a hotel was more comfortable, more private, you know?"

"Is that unusual?"

"Nah. About one out of three of the guys prefer to see the girls off-site."

"No, I mean for this Dave guy. Did he usually see the escort on-site, or did he usually book a hotel room?"

"Man, I never thought of that. I have no idea."

"Don't worry about it. I can ask Candace. Anyhow, you suggested Mary Carmen and booked a room, guaranteeing it with Candace's card?"

"Yes. He sounded relieved when I told him she'd be in the lobby of The Grand Hotel at nine o'clock."

A few more minutes of conversation with Terra offered nothing new or relevant, but I did suddenly have an urge to go skipping through a field of wildflowers while playing a tambourine.

Man, oh, man.

The Dave call was obviously a fake. The guy I'd spoken with didn't have an accent.

That meant it was someone who knew Dave well enough to know he used Candace's services and who knew Dave's sexual preferences. That had to mean it was probably someone who had previously been involved somehow in providing such services to Dave.

So the question was: why did someone use Dave to get to Mary Carmen? There was obviously a connection, and even though Dave had been impersonated and somewhat compromised, he was clearly nothing more than a pawn. After all, he wasn't the one who was missing.

So, then, who wanted to get at Mary Carmen and why?

I was in no particular hurry, so I took my time walking down to Burrito Boyz on Queen Street. I popped into a used bookstore near Yonge and Wellesley and picked up a few titles on my must-read list, including a copy of *The Catcher in the Rye*, which I'd been meaning to revisit ever since Salinger died. I bought a bottle of water and a pack of gum at a corner store. I checked out the buskers outside the Eaton Centre. A huckster with a banjo and a white cowboy hat was strumming and singing as if out of spite. A street artist was drawing chalk murals on the sidewalk. Another artist, this one with pierced eyebrows and a Mohawk, offered to do a caricature of me for ten dollars, but I declined. My entire life already resembles an outtake from *I Love Lucy*. Panhandlers asked me for spare change, and I declined them, too. It was a typical afternoon walk down Yonge Street, and I would have enjoyed every minute of it if it weren't so stifling hot.

My feet were sore. I had developed a blister on my heel, and I was a sweaty mess by the time I got to

Burrito Boyz. I wasn't hungry but felt obligated to order something.

"I'll have an *horchata* please."

"*Si, señorita.* What size?" The guy behind the counter was short, dark, and handsome. Two out of three ain't bad, but he was also too young. Damn. I've always had a thing for the swarthy Latino type. Let me rephrase that: right now I have a thing for any guy with a pulse.

"Jumbo, please. With lots of ice."

Horchata is basically a rice water drink with a hint of vanilla and some cinnamon. The family I'd boarded with in Mexico had gotten me hooked on it. The Burrito Boyz version was pretty good, but it wasn't as richly flavourful as the ones I remembered from my days in Zacatecas. Sigh. *You can't go back…*

"Have you worked here very long?" I asked.

"It feels like it. Why?" His accent was almost negligible. He'd probably come to Canada when he was a kid.

"I'm trying to find one of your customers. I'm an investigator, and the girl I'm looking for has been missing for about a week." I passed him the photo of Mary Carmen.

"Yeah, she comes in sometimes, but not lately."

"What about the other staff?" I asked. Short, Dark, and Handsome called over his co-worker, an equally short dude with a ponytail, who was just as beautifully caramel-skinned, but not nearly as handsome.

"Hey Pancho, remember her? She been around lately?"

"Yeah, you can't forget a dime piece like that, but she ain't been in for a couple of weeks at least."

I wondered if anyone ever thought of me as a dime piece. If so, would I be insulted? And if not, would I be even more insulted? Or maybe guys think of me as a MILF? Or am I old enough to be a cougar?

"Here's my card," I said. "Give me a call if you happen to see her."

Well, that was a waste of time, and I had sore feet for nothing. At least the horchata was refreshing.

I decided to go home and take a nice long bath.

Sunday, 8:42 pm

I could have gone back to the cathouse, but I'd seen enough of the place for the time being. I knew there was still much to be gleaned from the girls and from the files, but I just couldn't stomach it, though that might have had more to do with tonight's supper.

After a dinner of macaroni and cheese from a cardboard box, wolfed down in silence in front of the television, I found myself back downtown. I was traipsing up and down Sherbourne and Church and Jarvis again, damn near melting in the thick humid night.

It had occurred to me that everyone comes from somewhere, everyone has a past. Fucking brilliant deduction, eh? Maybe next I'll come to the realization that water is wet, and what goes up must come down. *Stick around, you can learn from me.*

Mary Carmen must have had connections or acquaintances before she ended up in Candace's employ.

And her curriculum vitae most likely involved similar work. Someone along these streets must surely have been acquainted with her.

At least tonight I was wearing a comfy but oh-so-unsexy pair of open-toed Birkenstocks. The blister on my foot precluded any other kind of footwear for now. I marched up and down the hooker stroll: Jarvis Street, from crack-ho Queen Street at the south end, to transvestites and chicks with dicks north of Wellesley Street.

Many of the hookers were reluctant to talk to me, perhaps out of fear of their pimps who wanted nothing to interfere with the prostitutes' nightly quotas. Or maybe they thought I was a cop and spelled trouble, or figured I was bad for business, or they just weren't interested, or perhaps they were simply put off by my sensible footwear.

"She's fucking hot," said a rough-around-the-edges hooker with far too much makeup who had deigned to speak with me. "She could make a lot here."

"You don't recognize her?" I stupidly asked.

"No chance I'd forget a face like that. Maybe she worked farther up the street." She passed the photo back to me, and I noticed she'd left smudgy, streaky fingerprints all over it.

I gave the hooker my card, and walked to the next corner where I had almost the exact same conversation, followed by its carbon copy at the next intersection.

I wondered if I had hit the streets too early. I wondered if a Sunday night was off-peak for hookers hustling their trade. I wondered if there was some hierarchy about the corners they worked on. I wondered if some of the girls who might have been able to help me were currently servicing a client but might be back to chat an hour from now.

I handed out a few more business cards and told each of the hookers to call me if they had any information, no matter how seemingly trivial.

I expected most of them would throw my card in the trash, or maybe use it to parcel out a tidy line of cocaine, or possibly they'd use the corner of it to pick their teeth. Whatever. I had trained myself long ago to have low expectations, but it didn't sit well with me. My cynical affectations are forever in conflict with my inherent optimism, a combination that makes me either very good at or very ineffective at my job – I hope I'd never fully realize which.

I'd more or less batted zero with the streetwalkers, but wasn't ready to call it a night just yet. I was only a few blocks in any direction from any of the three downtown Toronto strip joints, so I took a moment to decide in which order to visit them.

The decision was sort of made for me. I waited for the light to turn green and for the little white pedestrian image to be illuminated. Then I began to cross the street, heading west towards Yonge Street. Even though he was facing a red light, an asshole in a black sports car heading north floored it as soon as I stepped into the intersection. I did a rather inelegant swan dive onto the hood of a Ford Taurus patiently obeying the red light in the southbound lane.

"Are you okay?" the Taurus driver asked.

"Yeah, no, holy shit, I'm fine. I think."

"He didn't hit you, did he?"

"Shit, what the fuck was that?" I sputtered.

"Probably a drunk driver. Do you want me to take you to the hospital? Call 911?"

"I don't think so. I'm shaken up, but he missed me. Just barely. Please tell me you got the fucker's licence number."

"Not a chance. It happened too quickly."

The cars behind the Taurus were now honking at us to get out of their way. I thanked the driver and sat for a few minutes on a street bench. The hit-and-run attempt had to be a drunk driver, right? No one was deliberately trying to mow me down, right? But it was hard to convince myself that it was a coincidence. BACK OFF BITCH. I sat for a few minutes longer, trying to decide whether to be scared or pissed off. I wish to hell I'd seen his licence plate. There was no way I'd ever know for sure if what had happened was deliberate or not. Damn.

Sitting around and thinking wasn't going to do me any good. Time to get back to work. I decided to change my route and walked instead towards Dundas and Sherbourne.

Filmores has been nicknamed both *Filthmores* and *Feelmores* by people who are sheepishly qualified to comment on the establishment's moniker and its personality. Either name seemed perfectly apt to me.

My eyes took a moment to adjust to the dim light, and the array of mirrors in the room disoriented me. I stumbled as I walked towards the bar and was momentarily worried I'd be thrown out for seeming intoxicated. But it was more likely I'd be thrown out for being an unaccompanied woman in a straight strip joint. I was pretty sure this place didn't exactly cater to the open-minded, experimental lesbian crowd hoping to add a bit of zest to their private lives.

I was only too glad to be in a licensed establishment. A shot of booze would go a long way toward calming me down. I ordered a gin and tonic, something you couldn't pay me to drink in the icy dark days of winter, but damn, nothing beats it in the hot, hazy days of a Toronto heat wave. Or on days when a sports car almost flattens me.

The bartender, a greasy Macedonian whose black vest and wrinkled white shirt would have been tight twenty pounds ago, seemed pleased to have fresh meat sitting at his bar. It would be hackneyed to say he undressed me with his eyes, but given that all the other females in the room were prancing around more than half naked, I guess fully clothed *moi* provided some new fodder for his lecherous imaginings.

"My name's Sasha Jackson," I said, holding out my hand.

"Call me Spiro. What brings you in here?"

"The extensive drink list and stellar service?"

"Nice try. You're not flashy enough or chesty enough to be looking for a job as a dancer." In some twisted way I know he meant that as a compliment. Maybe I'd have met his approval if I'd been wearing one of the skimpy, come-hither outfits from my days as a rocker chick belting it out on the music circuit.

Spiro moved to the other end of the bar where one of the dancers had just perched herself on a stool.

"What the fuck are you doing sitting down,

woman?" he barked at a lanky brunette.

"My feet are killing me. I'm just adjusting my shoes. I'm getting a blister from them."

Sister, I feel your pain.

"Hurry the fuck up, bitch! There's a group of guys over there and they don't have no broad entertaining them. Get a fucking move on."

The dancer tucked some tissues into the pointy toe of her come-fuck-me stiletto pumps and toddled off to a group of frat boys who probably didn't have enough cash between them to pay for even one lap dance.

Spiro came back over to me. "Gotta keep on top of things. The bitches slack off if you give them a chance."

I bit my tongue and nodded. "I understand. Listen, maybe you can help me. I'm a private investigator and I'm looking for a missing girl." It took all I had right now to be friendly and polite.

"Oh, shit, here we go." He momentarily took his eyes off my chest and looked at me with a constipated expression.

"I'm not here to cause any trouble," I said. "It's nothing to do with this fine establishment. I was just hoping someone from here might recognize this girl." I handed him the photograph of Mary Carmen. "I don't know if she ever worked as a dancer, but she does work as a call girl, and I thought maybe..."

"Broad's got a great face. What are her tits like?" He winked at me and studied my chest again.

The feminist in me was ready to jump over the bar and throttle the misogynistic pig. The detective in me held the offended self at bay. *Okay now, Sasha, remember why you're here. The ends justify the means. Focus on the big picture. Don't take anything personally. Remember your client. Think about the missing girl.*

I gave him what I hoped was a lecherous grin. "The broad's name is Mary Carmen; she's got great tits, a tight little ass, and she swallows. Mind if I ask around and see if any of your dancers know her?"

"Knock yourself out. Broad who looks like that and swallows would be a lot of bang for the buck, heh-heh. Get it? Bang for the buck?"

"Clever." I winked at him.

Not.

Schmuck.

I asked as many dancers as I could find about Mary Carmen and showed her picture around, but no one knew her.

Back at the bar, Spiro said, "If you find the bitch, give her my number. I'd love to have a poke at a piece like that."

The earlier hit-and-run attempt had given me an idea. I had a brief fantasy about running over Spiro, but since I don't really drive, I'd have to think of something else…

"No problem Spiro. When I find her, I'll tell her she has a client waiting in the wings. A word of advice, though. You'd be wise to stock up on Viagra. She's ruthless with guys who can't rise to the occasion." I winked as I said it. *Ha-ha, just a joke, you asshole – just a joke.*

"Hey, what's that s'posed to mean?"

"I'm just winding you up. Kidding. No offense."

I left ten dollars and my mostly untouched gin and tonic at the bar and walked out. If this had been another time and another place, and if the car thing hadn't unsettled me, I'd have thrown my drink in his face and then smashed the glass over his head and used the fragments to gouge out his eyes.

However, I had no contacts in the world of commercial sex, and it wouldn't be wise to burn any bridges yet. I never know who could turn out to be helpful, and duking it out with a sexist Neanderthal pig might have cut off my pipeline to a host of girls in the flesh trade.

Damn, life could be unfair at times.

The next strip joint, Zanzibar, was about as exciting and as useful as Filmores. Walking in, I felt every bit as objectified as I had at peeler bar number one, and I wondered once again how the girls could stand to work in this industry. I sat at the bar and ordered a drink, then gave the bartender the same *Reader's Digest* version of who I was and why I was there, just as I'd done with the oh-so-chauvinistic Spiro. This time, too, I accomplished little more than I had at Filmores, but at least I finished my gin and tonic.

As I was leaving, one of the dancers caught up with me and tapped me on the shoulder. I almost jumped out of my skin. Attempted hit-and-runs make me a tad nervous.

"Hey, want to grab a coffee? My shift just finished." It was hard to keep my eyes off the girl's chest. I hoped I wasn't making her feel as uncomfortable as Spiro had made me feel. She was wearing a red satiny nipple-less bra and lacy red panties with black trim. Her boobs were big enough to give me a complex, not only for their size but also for their perkiness. Had to be silicone, but I doubted any guy fondling them would have cared.

"Sure," I said.

"Give me five minutes to change and I'll meet you out front."

"I'm April," she said.

"I really appreciate your taking the time to talk to me," I said.

We were sitting in Fran's on College Street, just west of Yonge Street. Without a doubt, this was the most awful, overrated, low-end diner in the Greater Toronto Area. And it was an institution. Being the only authentic twenty-four hour greasy spoon in the downtown core had cemented its place in the city's popular nocturnal subculture. Everyone had a story about their drunken 4:00 am waffle excursion. Few actually remembered eating the waffles, which was good because, while biodegradable and recyclable, cardboard drenched in imitation maple syrup and slathered in artificial butter is not high on anyone's list of gastronomic delights.

April and I were both sweaty after navigating the few blocks up from Zanzibar. I'd been on full alert as we'd walked, my eyes darting from car to car. Nothing set off my internal alarm, though.

Even in the late evening, with the sun long since set, the humidity was unrelenting. It hadn't rained in days, and the air was bulky with locked-up moisture.

We'd ended up in Fran's because at this time of night it was unlikely to be busy, although I could have sworn I saw Julia Roberts and her entourage sitting on the banquette in the back. Must be the onset of heatstroke. Thank God this place was air-conditioned.

In lieu of the suggested coffee, we both ordered lemonade.

"Do you want something to eat?" I asked April. "A snack?"

"No, I have to be a lot hungrier than I am now to find the food here edible."

"So, you must know something about Mary Carmen? You recognized her picture?"

"I did. What's your interest in her?"

"She was working in an exclusive…"

"Whorehouse?" she finished.

"I see you don't mince words. Yes, she started working as an escort for Candace Curtis. It's a pretty slick operation. They service clients in an august old mansion near Rosedale and do some outcalls as well. Mary Carmen was sent on a call a week ago Thursday and hasn't been seen or heard from since. How do you know her?"

"More or less professionally. She did some street work, for a while, anyway. She came to Zanzibar with a john. He paid me for several lap dances. She watched, but seemed kind of bored." April sipped her lemonade. "I grinded away on his lap while she slammed back one shot of gold tequila after another. Didn't even bother with the lemon and salt and all that. I guess the john was turned on by having one woman watch as another aroused and fondled him."

"Whatever floats your boat, eh?"

With this case, unlike any other case I've ever worked on, or for that matter, any other situation I've ever been in, I was consistently at a loss for words, so thank God I could resort to clichés. I wouldn't describe myself as narrow-minded or parochial, but the sex trade world was really beyond my ken. And all the unveiled horniness of this case kept reminding me that I probably had dust bunnies down there. It's been so long since I've had sex that I should pick up some batteries on my way home.

"Turns out he was setting the stage for a threesome," April said.

"I thought you just danced. Do you turn tricks too?"

"Money's money. And believe it or not, this is paying my way through medical school."

There must be something witty I can say here about hypocrite/Hippocratic oath, or "Physician, heal thyself." *Gimme a sec … It'll come to me.*

"Good for you. That's awesome," I said instead.

"I'm going into second year in September," April told me. "I take the odd sex job if it appeals to me and the price is right. He and Mary Carmen stayed till last call. They had a limousine waiting for them. The guy had a lot of cash and rightly guessed that money talks. I got in the limo with them after work, we went to the Park Hyatt, and we got it on till the sun came up."

"Oh …"

"Easiest thousand bucks I've ever earned."

I darn near spat out my lemonade. "A thousand dollars? Really?"

"Yup. A cool grand. She and I took turns with him, then did each other while he watched. He had room service send up a couple bottles of champagne, which he poured all over our breasts and then licked off. It was the good stuff too, absolutely delicious, not some cheap horrible knock-off sparkling wine that even my tits couldn't save. Whatever he wanted, we did. A dream client. Too bad guys like him are so rare."

"Uh, so if you and Mary Carmen were, um, working all night, then how much talking did the two of you do?"

"Not much then. But the guy had the limo driver take us home the next morning. We talked a bit during the drive. She told me she was glad she'd scored the gig, that she was broke. She'd only been in Toronto a few weeks. Came here from Montréal."

Ding, ding, ding! Hold the phone, don't touch that dial, this could be a clue…

"And she was working the streets here?" I asked.

"Yeah, she said he picked her up on Jarvis somewhere."

"And she's from Montréal?" I asked.

"No, she's from Mexico somewhere but lived in Montréal a while before coming here."

Insert glowing light bulb above my head.

"So when was this?" I asked.

"Maybe five or six months ago? It was after Christmas sometime. There was a lot of snow. Probably early January."

"You have no idea how helpful this is."

I now knew that Mary Carmen had worked the streets in Toronto before climbing the corporate ladder and landing the job at Candace's cathouse. And I now knew she had lived in Montréal before relocating to Toronto. I could easily guess what kind of work she'd done in La Belle Province. This was still tenuous since Toronto and Montréal are two of Canada's biggest cities, but there most likely was a Montréal connection between Dave No Last Name and Mary Carmen. Hadn't he said he'd been in Montréal giving a speech at an environmentally friendly mining conference or something on the night she disappeared? And hadn't flower child Terra said that the alleged Dave caller had sounded French-Canadian? The Dave I had talked to had no discernible accent at all.

Hmmm… The plot was thickening, right on par with the muggy July night.

Strip joint number three was The Brass Rail, up near Yonge and Bloor. It was about a block from where my old office was, and I had a vague sense of melancholic nostalgia as I trudged along Yonge, continually checking traffic over my shoulder. I couldn't deny that this stretch of Toronto's main drag with its massage parlours and head shops is pretty seedy, and that my new digs, down by the St. Lawrence Market, are in a classier and safer 'hood. Yet I still had a soft spot for my old place. This was where my first office had been, the spot where I'd started my business. I was rather fond of it, proud of it, and even though it was very no frills, I kind of missed it.

I was also still resentful of what had happened there. The break-in and trashing of my furniture, files, computer, and everything else had been personal and hurtful, not to mention pointless and expensive. I pushed the potentially embittering thoughts from my little old brain as I neared the tacky, blinking neon signs surrounding the entrance to the next peeler bar.

The Brass Rail is on the second floor, but as soon as I entered the stairwell, I could hear the music blaring. They were playing Tuji Sanusi's "Sex Machine." Given the milieu, the horny tune was a fitting soundtrack.

Once inside, I didn't even get as far as the bar. As soon as I strolled in, a group of guys sitting near the stage whistled and motioned for me to come over.

Oh dear. Don't people refer to the seats in front of the stage as "perverts' row"?

"Hey gorgeous, I have to say it. What's a nice girl like you doing in a dump like this?"

Mick, my ex-boyfriend, pulled out a chair for me to sit beside him and called over the pencil-thin waitress.

"I could well ask you the same question, Mick. I didn't think you frequented places like this."

"Today's Bill's fortieth," he said, hoisting his glass and saluting the birthday boy, who was clearly not going to remember much of this night.

The waitress appeared with a round of Sambuca shooters for the whole table. We raised our glasses in a toast and a chorus of happy birthdays. Two of the guys at our table were all but drooling over the contortionist mulatto dancer currently defying gravity on the brass pole on the stage, and another in the group had found the object of his twenty-dollar-lap-dance affections.

"Listen, Mick, as much as I'd love to partake in the birthday festivities with you and the boys, I'm working a case." I gave him a thumbnail version of my current investigation, thanked him for the shot, and excused myself from the table.

At the bar, I had the same fruitless conversation as I'd had with Spiro and the barkeep at Zanzibar. My exchanges with the dancers were equally unproductive. I showed the picture, gave out business cards, and became increasingly frustrated at my lack of progress and even more unsettled by my surroundings.

I bought a round of shooters for Mick and Bill's table and made a beeline out of The Brass Rail before the bartender could tell me my Visa had been declined.

I toyed with the idea of walking home, but it was late, my feet were sore, and the humidity was suffocating, which is what I usually say about the subway. Claustrophobics like me tend to feel jumpy in subterranean metal tubes, even late at night when they're half empty. But the idea of walking across the Bloor Viaduct made me even jumpier. The viaduct would be a perfect place in which to run somebody down. So I threw a token into the turnstile. At least the subway cars are air-conditioned.

Mary Carmen

They worked right away, like all the times. No taste, no colour. Gracias a Dios *the* bastardo *didn't take my purse from me. He have no idea I drugged him.* Pendejo.

In twenty minutes he was a bit more tranquilo.

I fucked him again, porque *that is what the* puto *wanted, but he could hardly move by the end of it. I climbed on top of him and imagined the beach on the Pacific, near Mazatlán, where my grandmother have a house. I think of the beach and the waves and the ocean and no thinking of this animal here with me now.* ¡Chinga!

I twist on the top of his small penis, it made me think of a jalapeño pepper, but maybe the jalapeño is bigger. I pretend mariachi music is playing in the background. I kept my eyes closed and tried to think of happy thoughts. I tried to put my mind anywhere but here, anywhere but here with this bastardo.

But what I keep thinking is how much I hate this puta madre, pinche bastardo, hijo de puta *underneath me. So much I hate him. He ruined my life.*

Soon. I would go home pronto. *I miss my family* mucho. *I miss my country, my friends, my language. No matter how poor or* dificil *is the life in Mexico, I will never again complain one word. My life here in Canada is hell,* infierno, *since the first day leaving my country, since the day I first meet this son of a bitch.*

Dios, *just get me back to home. Just get me onto the plane.* Por favor, Dios, por favor.

I finished fucking the bastardo *and watched him quietly until he fall asleep.*

Then I picked up his knife.

Monday, July 20, 7:46 am

I woke up in a foul mood. An evening spent hop-scotching around Toronto's titty bars will do that to me. So will an attempted hit-and-run, if that's indeed what it was. Maybe it was just a drunk driver. And maybe BACK OFF BITCH was just the result of some crazy neighbourhood kids playing a prank. Maybe.

I was pissy about my lack of progress, and I was mad at myself for not handling this case as well as I should have. I was only three days into it but no further ahead now than when I'd first met with Candace, unless you count the one or two attempts to scare me off as progress. I was certain my approach was all wrong and that every action and every plan was a time-sucking bandit and a waste of Candace's money. All I wanted to do was go back to bed. I couldn't face another round of traipsing up and down the hookers' stroll.

There were probably more constructive and more obvious ways to handle this case, but for whatever reasons, they were foggy to me. For not the first time, I began to question my career choice.

Shane was in the kitchen when I dragged my sorry ass downstairs.

"Good morning," he said.

"Hmmph."

"So another night chasing down a missing hooker?"

"Yup."

"Think the hooker did the paint-by-number out front?"

"Unh-uh."

Shane shot me a sceptical look.

I didn't feel like mentioning the out-of-control car that had treated me like the last standing pin at a bowling alley.

"Any leads so far?" he asked.

"Unh-uh."

"Want me to make you some breakfast?"

"Nope," I said.

"Okay, well, it's been nice talking to you Sasha. Have a great day."

Shane somehow managed to tear himself away from my scintillating conversation and went upstairs. I poured myself a mug of java and buried my head in the newspaper.

The stories were all the same even though I hadn't

looked at a periodical in several days. Politicians breaking election promises. There's a shock. Another manufacturing company closing its doors in Canada. What a surprise. Some animal rights activists protesting at Queen's Park. Rah, rah, rah, militants! A professional athlete caught using steroids. What? Really? You don't say? And, Toronto's thirty-second homicide – a forty-one year old man from Montréal killed July 9 at the Camden Suites Hotel – was still unsolved. There were no leads, but police believed there was a possible connection to a Montréal-based prostitution ring.

Oh?

Prostitution, hotel, Montréal? *Hello.*

I reread the story.

Still No Leads in Hotel Slaying

Police Suspect Link to Prostitution Ring

Police still have few leads in the July 9 stabbing of Gaston Lalonde, 41, of Montréal, at the Camden Suites Hotel. Lalonde's naked body was found by housekeeping staff late Friday morning. He was pronounced dead at the scene, a victim of multiple stab wounds.

"The case remains open and we are investigating several possibilities," said Sergeant Quinty of the Toronto Police Service Homicide Squad. Lalonde allegedly ran a prostitution ring in Montréal and police speculate that he was killed by Toronto biker gangs to prevent Lalonde from cutting into their territory.

Funeral services will be held in Montréal once Lalonde's body is released from the coroner's office. An autopsy is being conducted.

Lalonde's family could not be reached for comment.

Well, tonight's agenda would be sure to include a visit to the Camden Suites Hotel. I had a feeling I was onto a lead the police would kill for. There was no point in going to the Camden this morning or this afternoon. If I were going to learn anything at all, it would be from the night staff, some of whom had hopefully seen Mary Carmen there during their shift on the evening of July 9.

Besides my newly formed plan for the evening, I recognized that I had some other interesting threads to pull on. This realization mildly lifted my waning spirits. The domestic worker angle needed to be explored. I hadn't had time yet – but hadn't forgotten about – checking into English classes. I still needed to fill in a few blanks about Dave No Last Name. And now there was also the Camden.

It hadn't escaped my notice that I was still supposed to be looking for a missing person. I had a cold feeling when I thought that. Nothing I'd discovered and no one I'd talked to gave me any reason to think Mary Carmen was still alive or still in town.

Shit. The little hairs on the back of my neck were standing on end.

This was my first 'big case' since The Case of the Fatal Fiancée, and I wasn't handling it with anything close to my usual confidence or even efficiency. I wondered if being shot in the boobs had robbed me of my normally abundant self-assurance. That, plus the BACK OFF BITCH and the car that tried to run me down.

I seemed now to be content chasing my tail instead of shaking things up. Usually, I make things happen rather than waiting for them to occur, but these days I seemed to be spinning my wheels. After berating myself a while longer, I looked at my horoscope, but there was little inspiration in it. In a nod towards being proactive I placed a call to a Mark Houghton of the Metro Toronto Police Service. Although Mark and I weren't close enough to be called friends, we certainly were solid acquaintances and had a healthy respect for each other professionally.

We'd also slept together once, long ago, and I'm sorry, actually, I'm embarrassed, to say I don't really remember the act itself. The memory lapse could be attributed either to his lack of prowess in bed or to reckless underage drinking, and I'm not sure which of the two is worse. I had dated Mark for a couple of months during my last year of high school. He was a few years older than me and was already in university. I remember feeling oh-so-cool that I was dating a guy who was doing post-secondary school – he was so much more mature than the Sweathogs my high school friends were dating. Mark was a very nice guy, at least I'd thought so, but after that one and only time we did the nasty, he never called me again. Life lessons learned early on.

However, we had casually reconnected about two years ago when I was in college studying to be an investigator. I'd long since forgiven him for stomping on my delicate teenage heart. My professor, Bryan Bessner, had invited Mark to be a guest speaker in one of my classes. Mark had recognized me right away but it took me a few minutes to dial back to my teen years and place him. The intervening years had definitely been kinder to me than to him. *Ha!*

Since that random reconnection, Mark and I have

sporadically kept in touch, usually with me calling him if I need the inside scoop from the cops.

"Please tell me you'd like nothing more than to join me for a coffee sometime this morning?" I said when Mark came on the line.

"Coffee this morning isn't going to happen, but an early lunch would work."

"When and where?"

"How about the Brownstone Bistro, Yonge and Gloucester? Say, 11:30?"

"I'll be on the patio waiting for you. Thanks. Lunch is on me," I offered.

"So you say, yet I have a feeling it's going to cost me something too."

"Well, since you brought it up… If you have any free time, you might want to brush up on the murder on July 9 at the Camden Suites Hotel. Gaston Lalonde of Montréal."

I made another coffee and threw a big-assed shot of Kahlúa into it. Who cared if it wasn't quite nine in the morning yet? I chugged it down, pulled myself up, and went to the upstairs bathroom where I jumped into a prickly, ice-cold shower. Time to grab the bull by the horns. One "can-do" attitude coming right up. Someone once said that if you can fake sincerity, you've got it made. Perhaps, though, it's better to say that if you can fake confidence, you've got it made.

Yeah, okay, pass the Kahlúa.

Monday, 11:30 am

The Brownstone Bistro has one of the best people-watching patios downtown. I got there a bit early and took the corner table where there was a good view up and down the street. After I ordered an iced cappuccino, I leaned back to enjoy a few minutes of sunshine. There was finally a wee bit of a breeze, although it was more or less ineffective against the cloistering mugginess.

Mark showed up a few minutes later. He was looking pretty flustered and definitely didn't seem comfortable in his police officer's uniform. Mind you, at six foot four, Mark doesn't look comfortable in a lot of things.

"I've only got about forty-five minutes," he said. "Busy day and it's all a matter of hurry up and wait."

"Typical."

"Since I'm pressed for time, why don't you cut to the chase and tell me what you're looking for?"

"Am I that transparent?" I asked.

"Most definitely."

"Let's at least order some lunch. I haven't eaten anything yet today. I was thinking of a grilled chicken wrap with a side salad."

"Sounds good." We flagged the waiter over and ordered.

"And a ginger ale," Mark said. "I'd love a beer, but I'm on duty."

"So what can you tell me about the dude who was stabbed in the Camden on July 9?" I asked.

"You want what's on the record, off the record, or purely speculation?"

"All of the above, please."

"I'll give you the scuttlebutt, but remember I work street patrol, not homicide, so none of this is first-hand."

"Got it. What can you tell me about the victim?"

"The papers have pretty much said it all, or at least implied it. The guy was a pimp from Montréal, a real dirtbag. Had a pretty long record for assaults, extortion, some minor drug stuff. The Montréal cops never pinched him for pimping girls, but he was well known to them for that. None of the Montréal cops are sorry he's gone. Why are you asking?"

"I can't tell you anything yet because it's all just guesswork at this point. He's kind of connected to a case I'm working on. Maybe."

"And?" Mark raised an eyebrow at me. The expression added a boyishly cute dimension to his ruggedly handsome face.

"Honestly, I'll tell you more when I can. I could be way off."

"You're going to owe me one, aren't you?"

"Buying lunch won't cut it?"

"Not a chance."

I sighed. "Okay. So what about the death itself? Time, weapon? Anything?"

"The weapon was left at the scene. He was stabbed more than a dozen times, mostly in the neck, with a double action OTF switchblade."

"A what?"

"OTF means 'out the front.' Regular switchblades flip the blade out from the side. Think of it like bending and unbending your arm at the elbow. 'Out the front' means what it says. The blade slides directly out the front, straight out from the handle, when a button, which releases the tension in the spring, is pushed. Double action means the button can extend or retract the blade."

"Okay, I'm with you so far..."

"Just so you know, the double action switch probably isn't as good as single action. The single action knife has a button to extend the blade from the handle, but has to be manually folded back in to close it."

"And that means?"

"Single action blades have a stronger spring. Basically, it opens harder and faster than double action, and it can lock into place more securely. It means business."

"I'll be sure to keep that in mind next time I go shopping for a murder weapon."

Mark grinned. "Anyhow, it was a nine-inch, stainless steel, serrated Smith & Wesson."

"Smith & Wesson? I thought they made guns."

"They have a line of knives, all kinds. Hunting, tactical, you name it."

"Holy smokes. Talk about diversifying your product line. I guess you won't be able to trace the knife?"

"Are you kidding? Knives like this are a dime a dozen. You can pick one up on eBay for less than twenty bucks."

"Jesus Christ. What about fingerprints?" I already knew the answer to that one, but had to ask anyway.

"Yeah, right. That would make it too easy."

"Anything else?"

"That's what we're waiting to find out from the autopsy. He was an average sort of guy, five foot eleven, one hundred and ninety-five pounds. It didn't look like he put up a fight, so the coroner's guessing he was drugged. My money's on Rohypnol."

"That's the date rape drug isn't it?" I asked.

"Yeah. Also known as roofies, ruffies, la rocha, R2."

"Wasn't it originally developed as a sedative? Or a sleeping pill?" I asked.

"More or less. It's in the same family as Valium and Xanax. It's illegal in Canada and the U.S., which doesn't mean you can't still get it easily. A little white pill, looks like it could be an Aspirin. It has no taste and takes about twenty minutes to kick in. It doesn't change the colour of the drink, and it makes the victim more or less a malleable rag doll."

"But this is still speculation?" I asked.

"Yeah. Coroner hasn't said anything conclusive yet."

"Time of death?"

"Around midnight, give or take."

"Anything else I should know?"

"Well, here's what's not in the papers. He got laid before he got iced. There was semen, and some pubic hairs mixed in that weren't his. Ironclad proof, if we ever find the owner of those dark and curly strands of DNA."

"Great, but not a lot of help right now," I said.

"There's something else. He had no luggage, no toiletries, and he must have checked into the hotel naked because there were no clothes found in his room. A ratty pair of Joe Boxers, socks and shoes, that's all. His wallet was still on the nightstand. No cash, but the usual plastic was in it. There's probably some missing jewellery. You can see a faint tan line on a couple of fingers. The investigators said he was probably relieved of his watch, too. There's a tan line on the left wrist too, but no watch at the scene."

"What about damage? To him or to the room?"

"Other than a bloody mess on the bed, the room was fine. No signs of a fight or a struggle. That's why Rohypnol fits."

"What about bathroom glasses… maybe there are fingerprints?" I asked.

"Gone. The killer took just about everything with him."

"Or her."

"Or her, yes. The knife was left behind. It was wiped clean of prints. Like all the doorknobs and just about every other smooth surface.

"Hmm."

Mary Carmen

I think maybe he no suffered so much, but I do not care. I did it fast and he was out cold, like they say. He never saw nothing coming, hardly made any sound. But I did. I saw what I did, what horrible thing I did. I was crying, probably not so very loud, but crying of the nightmare I was living in this moment, in the last months, all the moments since I left my country.

I killed a man.

Dios mio… Jesus Cristo… Santa Maria… *Help me. Forgive me.*

I just killed a man.

I took the pieces of my torn clothes and wiped all the things

I touched. I wiped the knife, the doorknobs. I took a shower to get all the bright red sangre *off of me. I wiped the faucet and the taps. I took the towels and the glasses and my ruined clothes and put all the things in the* plastico *laundry bag from the closet. I put on the jeans from the* pendejo *and his shirt. Is too big, but no one will see that this is same* señorita *from when I came into the hotel tonight.*

I think of the Mexican fiesta *called Day of the Dead, and think maybe this is some weird, turned-around version of it. Instead of bringing gifts to the dead, I took the gifts from him. He does not need his watch and rings anymore; he has no reason to need money. I took it all and put all the things from the dead* pendejo *in my purse. God help me. The sunglasses of the* hijo de puta *was too big for me and too dark for the night time, but I put them on anyway.*

I took the bag of towels and clothes and my purse and got the hell out of the hotel.

Chinga… *what am I going to do? God help me.* Perdóname, Dios…

Monday, 12:50 pm

"Holy shit. You weren't kidding about tossing them out by noon," I said to Agnes Pink Curlers Lynch. Her track pants du jour were robin's egg blue, and it looked like there were coffee stains on them. Not for the first time, I wondered how she could stand to wear fleecy pants during such a cloyingly sticky hot spell. I was in a pair of cut-off denim shorts and a navy-blue-and-white striped cotton tank top from The Gap. I was stifling and rather uncomfortably itchy. On my way here in the blistering humidity, I'd made a mental note to never again wear a thong during a heat wave. *Argh.*

"The Spic ain't paid up, so she's outta here," said the Slumlord with a Heart of Gold. "Twelve noon p.m., like I told you."

"Are you sure there isn't some misunderstanding? Maybe she's gone away?"

"Dunno and could care less, anyways. Rules is the same for everyone." Fritz the octogenarian guard dog growled to emphasize her point.

"So you're just going to leave her stuff out here on the lawn?" I was being generous with the term *lawn.* There was about three feet of dandelion-dotted, brittle brown grass on either side of the dilapidated, muddy brown front door. This was where Agnes was tossing cardboard boxes and environmentally unfriendly plastic grocery bags filled with Mary Carmen's stuff.

"I ain't got no use for it and I don't need no empty room. It's summertime and tourists are in town and I'll have the room rented by the end of the day."

Yeah, like there had been a mile-long line-up for the room I'd scooped up the other day.

"I understand," I said.

"No sense in me losing out on my income." She hoisted another box, and as she did, I saw deep, dark circles of perspiration on the armpits of her sweatshirt.

Oh, God, why did I have to notice that? Fritz began gnawing at the edge of one of the cartons.

"Listen, like I told you before, Mary Carmen's a friend of a friend, and I'd know about it if she were going to take off. How about if I cover her rent for her? I'd hate to see her or her stuff thrown out."

"You're gonna cover a week's rent for some Spic you ain't never even met?"

"Yes, and I think she prefers the term *Hispanic.*" Enough, already, with the ignorance. *Geez.* "I'm sure she's good for the money. That's what friends, or friends of friends, are for." I opened my frail, neglected wallet and peeled off five of the last six twenties in it. Agnes shoved the money into her waistband so quickly that I thought she'd take my fingers with it.

"There's no bloody way I'm hauling all this crap back up the stairs."

"I'm happy to do it," I said. "Good exercise."

"Well, okay. Here's a key to her room so you can take her stuff back upstairs, but you gotta bring it back to me right after, okay?"

"Sure."

Yeah, like not having a key has ever stopped me before.

I hauled the bags and boxes back up to the second floor and dug in. If I'd been expecting the mother lode, I'd have been disappointed. I poked through everything rather quickly. I knew Shrek in Sweats would be on my ass if I didn't return the key pronto. But I also knew I could easily break in later on and have a better look through Mary Carmen's things if I wanted to.

Her few belongings included a bunch of slutty outfits

and lingerie of every shape, style, colour and texture. There was something in a satiny turquoise that looked much more comfortable than the spiteful thong I was wearing. There were some racy, lacy things my ex-boyfriend Mick would have loved to see on me. I flashed back for a moment to my days with Mick. Our very active, wholly satisfying, and somewhat creative sex life was probably what had kept us together for much longer than we should have lasted. He'd liked seeing me in something sexy, something sheer, or something flimsy. And I'd liked wearing it for him – but not for long…

I shook my head to disperse the horny nostalgia.

In the next bag there were several skimpier underthings that surely must have been part of a bigger outfit, or maybe not. Perhaps the leather/PVC version of two Band-Aids and a cork was all Mary Carmen needed for her workaday togs.

There were a few faded Polaroid photos in a battered and creased envelope. I figured they were of her family back home in Wherever, Mexico. The woman I assumed to be her mother was long and lean and had her salt-and-pepper hair plaited into two long braids. Her face was worn and tired, with deep lines etched into her forehead. Despite age and whatever else wore her down, her sparkling green eyes had the same animation as her daughter's.

No address book. No mail or bills. No one-way plane tickets for destinations unknown. But I did find a battered copy of *English Grammar Made Easy! Level Two*, with property of ENGLISH LANGUAGE SKILLS INSTITUTE stamped on the inside cover along with the school's address near Yonge and Shuter. Yahoo! A solid lead at last.

Quick, Sasha, get a jump on this one and don't mess things up any more than you already have.

"Hi, my name's Sasha Jackson," I said, proffering my business card.

"How may I help you?" asked the stocky, middle-aged Asian man behind the desk who spoke flawless but deliberate English.

"I'm an investigator. I'm looking for Mary Carmen Ruiz Santamaria. I understand she's a student here."

"Yes. She's in our intermediate level, but she hasn't come to class recently."

"No one's seen her since a week ago last Thursday night."

"Well, she's only a part-time student. She has classes Tuesday and Thursday mornings." He consulted a binder filled with three-hole-punched, lined yellow notebook paper. "She attended two Thursdays ago, July 9, but hasn't come in since then. Maybe she'll come tomorrow."

"She hasn't been in her apartment in over a week. She hasn't shown up for work. Her employer hired me. No one I've talked to said Mary Carmen mentioned a vacation, or moving away or anything. She's just disappeared."

"I'm not sure what I can do to help you – "

"Well, if you don't know her very well, maybe some of the students do. One of her classmates might have an idea where she could've gone. Would you mind if I spoke with some of them?"

Thank God this was a fly-by-night language school.

Had it been a more official educational institute, I doubt I'd have gleaned even this much.

"Not at all, but her classmates aren't here right now."

"Duh, right. Today's Monday. What time does her class start tomorrow?"

"She has grammar and writing from 9:30 to 11:30 am and then speaking and pronunciation from noon to two."

"See you tomorrow then. You'll clear it for me to talk with her classmates?"

"I will, but please don't take up too much of their time. They really need the practice." *And what would talking with me be? Beginner Yiddish?*

I was just a few blocks from the Esplanade and the St. Lawrence Market, so I decided to pay a visit to my office and use it to pretend I really am a professional investigator doing real private-eye stuff.

A pile of junk mail was waiting for me, as were two dead plants. I put the advertisements and flyers in the recycling bin, and the erstwhile African violets in the garbage. Then I propped my feet up on the desk, turned on the computer, and wished I could have pulled a pint of Scotch out of the desk drawer so I could look really cool.

I decided to do some research, which in this case meant surfing the Internet. I Googled prostitution, commercial sex, and similar terms. I shouldn't have been surprised at the X-rated results and graphic pop-up ads that filled my screen.

After I refined the search terms, I had better luck. Some of the sites that came up were hosted by religious groups, others by the public health department, some by feminist groups – a couple of which were pretty damn militant and made no attempt to downplay their male-bashing. A few sites were run by human rights groups; another was run by a women's shelter. Two of the more interesting local websites were the Sex Workers Advocacy Group, SWAG, and the Coalition for Hookers' Equality and Rights, CHER. That, of course, made me think of Todd. Among all the sites there were several links to legal aid clinics, medical centres, Planned Parenthood, the Rape Crisis Centre, birth control options, and a number of blogs.

What I learned during the next hour of reading was heartbreaking, shocking, maddening, sickening and soul-destroying. Case study after case study detailed "bad dates," violent pimps, stories of physical and sexual abuse, tales of drug addiction, incest, homelessness, police brutality, exploitation, and on and on. There were all kinds of statistics illustrating just how grim and risky life in the sex trade really is. Some of the links I clicked on led me to other sites that detailed human trafficking and sex slavery, another gave graphic details of sex tourism, and the whole sordid exploration left me feeling as if I'd been kicked in the gut a few times.

I went back to the home pages of the local non-profits that served prostitutes and commercial sex workers in the Toronto area and made a few calls. What I learned during the next half-hour over the phone was even more tragic and horrific than what I'd been reading.

"Think of sex slavery as a reverse kind of Underground Railroad," said Tracy Dollois, a social worker with SWAG.

"Huh?" The analogy was totally lost on me.

"It's almost like the same kind of silent network of

secret hubs and covert movement of people. Except in this case they're moving away from freedom – albeit destitution in many cases – and into slavery. Not the other way around."

"Good grief. That's horrible."

"These girls have no idea what they're in for," Tracy said. "They think they're getting help sneaking into a First World country. They're told they have modelling jobs or nanny jobs or even waitressing jobs waiting for them."

"And then…surprise…"

"Somewhere along the way the girls have their papers – their passports and visas – taken from them, that is, if they had them in the first place. They're told they'll get a free flight home at Christmas, or after one year of service or something like that. The guys tell them they have to take their passports in order to process their work visas. Obviously that's a load of crap, but the girls don't know that. Hell, most of them don't speak or read English, and they have no idea what their human rights or their civil rights are."

"Then once they're here, they're trapped," I said. "Stuck. And I assume they have no money, right?"

"Right. Almost all of them left their countries with high hopes and magnanimous promises to send money back home to support their families, which they end up not being able to do."

"I have no idea what to say."

"In many cases they have no legal right to be in Canada in the first place. That's usually the case with girls from Latin America. Those ones generally work their way up through the U.S. With the girls from Eastern Europe and Russia, it's usually a case of a fudged foreign worker application or one that never gets filed."

"What becomes of these girls? How do they escape?"

"They don't. They get beat up. They turn to drugs. The pimps usually have a hand in that."

"Of course."

"Girls run away or try to. In many cases, the pimps at the receiving end have paid a lot of money for the girls they've imported. A lot of prostitution rings have taken to essentially branding their property. They tattoo the inside of the girl's thigh or between her breasts with the pimp's initials or some gang symbol. This ensures the girl doesn't go to work for the competition. And it ensures that runaways get returned to their owners."

"Holy shit!" I almost yelled. "That sounds just like cattle. You've got to be kidding."

"Sadly, I'm not."

I had already leafed through the current issues of *Billboard* and *Rolling Stone*, so I opened the online crossword and absently filled in the little blank squares while I reflected on my phone calls. I began to see the appeal of working in a setup like Candace's. It was less about the job itself – oldest profession and all that – than about the working conditions and occupational hazards. The girls in Candace's employ seemed safe, respected by her, and generally seemed content with their employer. I also started to get what Candace meant about being in control. Better that the girls work for her than become the chattel of some bastard pimp who keeps the lion's share of what they earn. For some hookers, maybe working for Candace was the lesser of two evils.

But in the words of Margaret Mead: "It may be necessary temporarily to accept a lesser evil, but one must never label a necessary evil as good." *You got it, sister!* I couldn't have said it better myself.

I continued to fill in the wrong answers to the puzzle until I was jolted out of my reflective moment by the annoying electronic *bleep, bleep, bleep* of my cellphone.

"Hey Sasha." Mick was on the line.

What had I been thinking about him earlier today as I'd poked through Mary Carmen's underthings? Oh yeah, something horny.

"Hola, what's up?" I asked.

"There's something I forgot to ask you last night."

"You were more than a little distracted. Did Bill enjoy his birthday? Better yet, does he remember his birthday?"

"We poured him into a cab not long after you left."

"I'm not surprised. He was three sheets to the wind. So what did you want to ask me?"

"How would you like to play a reunion gig?" Mick asked.

"Who's re-unioning?"

"Uh, the band, reuniting and playing at my old high school. It's our twentieth."

"Wow, does that ever make you sound old."

"Thank you so much."

"You know I haven't performed in ages."

"Doesn't matter. Interested?"

"Let me think about it," I said. "When's the gig?"

"The second week of September. Saturday the… I can't remember the date, but the second Saturday of the month."

"Would I just be singing?"

"Yeah, Brad said he'd play drums for the night and Cole will be on bass."

"Just like old times. I'll let you know in a day or two."

The thought of performing was appealing. The idea of a high school reunion – even someone else's – cranked me up. It's the kind of gig where everyone's just there for a good time and no one takes anything too seriously. The prospect of jamming with Mick and the boys was also enticing. So why was I hesitating? Because I knew that if I went anywhere even close to going back down that road with Mick, the old passions would probably reignite, sparks would fly, flames would smoulder, fireworks would burst... and my heart would soon be crushed.

Mick and I had always worked together exceptionally well when it came to music. We also had incredible physical chemistry – intoxicating, spine-tingling, pulsating chemistry. But when it came to a serious relationship, we just never clicked for very long. The nitpicking would start within a few days, the bickering and squabbling would begin inside of two weeks, and by the end of a month we'd be alternating mad passionate lovemaking with rip-roaring shouting matches.

Monday, 5:00 pm

"Okay, so now what? One sec." Jessica ran off to the other end of the bar to serve the two new customers who'd parked their asses on the fake leather upholstered bar stools of The Pilot Tavern, my favourite watering hole and Jessica's place of employment. I took advantage of the break in conversation to call Lindsey, and got her voice mail. I left a message and hung up, just as Jessica made it back to my end of the bar for some more aborted chit chat.

"I have no idea," I said. "I really hope I'll get some answers from the night staff at the Camden, but it's still too early to go down there."

"And now you also have to find out where she worked as a maid? And where she went to church? Hang on—" Jessica poured a couple of draft beers for the waitress.

"I could do either of those things," I said when Jessica had another moment to talk. "But I think it would be more productive to break into her room and really have a good dig through her stuff."

"Right, as if threats at your home and getting plowed down in the street weren't already enough to put you off." Jessica rolled her eyes as she said this.

"Well… nothing really happened. No permanent damage."

"Yeah, so why not tempt fate a bit more? You know you're crazy, right?" Sarcasm is so unbecoming in a good friend.

"Only a little," I said. "Besides, I don't know what else to do next."

"So, when in doubt, a break-in is always a good idea? Yeah, of course. Here, have a glass of liquid courage." Jess handed me an amaretto sour. I knocked it back in one long gulp.

Lindsey showed up about half an hour later and we moved to a quieter table in the back.

"So, you think this dead pimp from Montréal was the last guy to see her?" Lindsey asked.

"I'm sure of it," I said, "and I'd bet anything that Mary Carmen killed him."

"What would her motive be?"

"Pimp and hooker. You do the math. I read up on the sex trade on the Internet. Did you know that eight out of ten hookers are victims of assault with a weapon, usually at the hands of their pimps, and that eighty-five percent of hookers have been raped by their pimps? Of course, there are those who think there's no such thing as raping a hooker."

"Only a jackass would think that. Jesus. I guess the only good pimp is a dead one."

"Most hookers don't even bother to go to the police after an assault," I said. "They figure the cops won't believe them, or will think they asked for it. Talk about being victimized over and over."

We were both silent for a minute, then Jessica broke

the pregnant pause by dropping off two more amaretto sours.

"I hope these are on the house, Jess, because I have no cash," I said.

"Let me get this round," Lindsey offered.

"I love you because you always pick up the tab. But I'd still be your friend anyway."

"Thanks and go to hell." We clinked glasses and Lindsey continued. "Okay, so why would the pimp have tracked her down? Why would he have tricked her into meeting him?"

"I can make a lot of guesses. Pimps don't like losing their, uh, workers. My guess is she bolted on him, took off from Montréal and ended up here. He was trying to protect his property."

"His investment," Lindsey said.

"Whatever. Anyhow, I think the Dave guy maybe used Mary Carmen's services via this Montréal pimp. I think Dave probably still uses that pimp's girls when he's in Montréal. And I think Dave was the one who gave the pimp Mary Carmen's new location. He knows her here, he knew her there. That's got to be the connection."

Lindsey rolled her eyes. "Holy crap. So now what?"

"I still have to find her, only now I think she's hiding because she killed a man. That'll make her harder to find."

"Obviously."

"And based on everything I now know about prostitutes' lives, it was probably self-defence. Or at least justifiable homicide."

"Why don't you just take all this to the police?"

"It's all just theory for now," I said. "I don't have a lick of proof. Besides, I don't know where she is."

Monday, 7:56 pm

Well, I said I was going to break in, and that's exactly what I did. I was mildly worried about Fritz the guard dog, and Agnes, the sweatsuited bowl of mashed potatoes, but I figured I'd say I'd left the room unlocked, or that I thought I'd forgotten something in it, or whatever bullshit came to mind. I wasn't too worried about it since, after paying the week's rent, I felt kind of proprietary about the whole damn thing.

My skeleton key jigged open the door in less than a nanosecond. Mind you, that's no reflection of my skills as a cat burglar because the door was so bloody flimsy that a sneeze from a hamster could have blown it right off its hinges.

I found some of Mary Carmen's run-of-the-mill, everyday, regular clothes and shoes in one of the boxes. Her faded pair of Guess jeans were about the same size I wear, and her battered Nike runners would have fit me as well. A little zippered case had some silver and turquoise jewellery in it, nothing terribly fancy, but it was casually pretty, typically Mexican, like the stuff college kids buy as a souvenir of their spring break trip to Cancún. I found another envelope with a few more photos of people I assumed were family and friends back home.

There was a toiletry bag with Clearasil, Oil of Olay moisturizer, a toothbrush, waxed mint flavoured dental floss, spring-breeze scented roll-on deodorant, tartar control Colgate toothpaste, Aspirin, extra-hold hairspray, and the other mundane personal grooming accoutrements we all use every day. And if we use these things every day, then why hadn't she taken this bag with her? Elementary, my dear Watson. She'd left unexpectedly, and she'd left in a hurry.

Aha!

A battered manila folder that I'd missed on my first round seemed to contain all her official papers and important documents. Not surprisingly, the folder was pretty thin. There was a copy of last month's cellphone bill, which I very thoughtfully stuck in my pocket. That reminded me to try calling Mary Carmen's cell number again, something I had already done several times before. No answer. No voice mail kicked in.

There were rent receipts from Agnes the Slum Lord, a certificate from the language school for passing "Level One – Introductory English," with an eighty-three percent average. *Attagirl!* There was a receipt for birth control pills, dispensed at the Shoppers Drug Mart near Parliament and Queen. And there was an expired driver's licence from the state of Coahuila, Mexico. Even in a driver's licence picture, Mary Carmen was gorgeous. The date of birth on the licence was the same as the one Candace had in her files. There was a Torreón address on the licence but no phone number. Could Mary Carmen have just gone back to Mexico? And short of hopping on a plane, how could I find out?

The prize discovery, though, was some receipts from Western Union. Mary Carmen seemed to send about a thousand bucks back home every three weeks or so. The recipient's address, 601 Calle Santa Rosa, was the same as the address on her licence. The most recent wire transfer was for nine hundred and fifty dollars on July 8, the day before she disappeared. The stack of receipts showed that Mary Carmen had sent almost seven thousand dollars to her family. Hmm.

In the nightstand there was a well-thumbed, dog-eared Spanish-English dictionary, a hundred and sixty dollars, an econo-sized box of lubricated condoms, and an iPod with the latest and greatest of Spanish pop music: Paulina Rubio, Shakira, Ricky Martin, J-Lo, Menudo, Marc Anthony (is there *anything* sexy about him? *Anything* at all?), Christian Castro, Luis Miguel, and a bunch of others I'd never heard of before.

I found a bottle of Don Julio Tequila Reposado and was tempted to sneak a swig. Don Julio is without a doubt the Rolls-Royce of tequilas. Other than the booze, though, I didn't find anything else that was potentially mood-altering. There was nothing to make me suspect drugs. No rolling papers, no pipes, no cough syrup, no syringes, no little mirrors, nothing.

Besides not finding any indication of drugs, what was interesting were the other things I didn't come across as I snooped through Mary Carmen's personal belongings.

Unless you count the Western Union wire transfer receipts, there was no banking info or credit card stuff at all. No statements, no bank books, no ATM cards. There was no social insurance number or Ontario

Health Card. There was no passport or visa, no Ontario driver's licence, no library card, no record of landing or immigration papers, no citizenship application, permanent residence card, nothing official, nothing governmental.

The brilliant conclusion I drew from the absence of a paper trail was that Mary Carmen was in Canada illegally, even though I'd already assumed just as much.

Aha, the plot thickens. Okay, not really, but at least this felt something like progress.

Yo pienso, tu piensas, el piensa... I was conjugating Spanish verbs in my head as I walked down the street. I stopped at a convenience store and bought a prepaid long-distance calling card. As I trucked along looking for a quiet pay phone where I wouldn't be drowned out by traffic, I recited the alphabet in Spanish. Then I softly sang to myself the few Spanish songs I know: "La Bamba", "Guantanamera", "La Cucaracha."

I'd learned a fair bit of Spanish when I lived in Zacatecas, but that was years ago. It was rusty now from lack of use and I was talking to myself in Spanish to try to get into the right headspace to make some long-distance calls in *español.*

Mary Carmen's old cellphone bill had a bunch of calls to country code 52, which I knew was Mexico. Most of the calls were to area code 871, which I guessed was her hometown of Torreón. Three numbers had been called several times, and I assumed those belonged to her family or closest friends. I was about to call each of them now and ask matter-of-factly if I could speak with Mary Carmen.

There was no way I could determine if Mary Carmen was in Canada or Mexico, but I figured if she had fled for home, then maybe she'd come to the phone. Not bloody likely, but maybe. Of course, I realized that she could well be in Mexico and that the person on the other end of the line could lie and say she wasn't there. Once again I made my decision based on the options available, and not necessarily what would be most effective or foolproof.

"*No esta,*" said the voice at the number she'd called most recently according to this bill. *"Esta trabajando en Canada."* Translation, "she's not here, she's working in Canada."

The next two calls yielded pretty much the same results.

Okay, so my working hypothesis is that Mary Carmen is still in Toronto.

I hope.

Monday, 10:09 pm

The Camden Suites Hotel is classy, but not nearly as ostentatious as The Grand. I waited until the doorman had ushered a couple of guests into the taxi he'd hailed for them. Then I introduced myself and handed him Mary Carmen's photo.

"Jesus, who could forget a knockout like that? Not a chance."

The friendly doorman wore an ugly jacket with laughable gold epaulets and shiny buttons, a pair of stiff camel-coloured jodhpurs, and a pair of knee-high black patent leather boots with giant pewter buckles. Think Mountie meets Pilgrims meets an alpha male Hemingway matador. What goes through people's minds when they choose company uniforms? Do they want to humiliate their staff or do they try to choose work clothes they know employees won't steal?

"You're sure it was Thursday night, July 9?" I asked him.

"Yeah. Same night the guy got sliced. Why? Think she had something to do with it?"

"Was she alone?"

"Yeah. Strutted in like she owned the damn place. Didn't smile. Didn't say thank you. Just a gorgeous chick getting into the elevator. Totally aloof."

"I'd fall madly in love with you if you told me she got off on the same floor as where the murder happened," I said.

"Wish I could, but I didn't see where she got off. Actually, I think a couple other guests got into the elevator too, so who knows who got off where? Anyways, I already told all of this to the cops. Why are you asking?"

"I'm not with the cops, I work on my own, and I'm not actually interested in the murder here, except as it peripherally relates to my client, my case."

"Oh."

"Does the hotel have elevator operators?"

"Nope. Sorry."

"There would have been if this were a Hollywood black-and-white film circa 1940 starring Humphrey Bogart."

"Yeah, and the eyewitness would have led the cops right to the murderer," the doorman said. "Fade to black. The end. Too bad that ain't the way it really is."

"Did you see her leave?"

"Of course not. That would be too easy, wouldn't it? But she could've left after I called it a night. I turn into a pumpkin at twelve."

I pictured him dressed in a spherical orange felt Halloween jack-o'-lantern costume and determined that it was still sexier than the low-budget Beefeater livery.

"I'll be back after midnight to see your colleague on the graveyard shift."

Well, at least now I knew Mary Carmen had been here and, for me, that meant she had almost definitely killed Gaston.

Oh, dear.

I was still in my tank top and shorts, although earlier I had ditched my vicious thong in the garbage can of the ladies' room at The Pilot and was now going commando. I felt a bit uneasy at the prospect of traipsing along the hookers' stroll on Jarvis Street dressed as I was, so I stopped in the Camden gift shop and bought myself an oversized and overpriced I ♥ TORONTO T-shirt.

The girls on the street tonight weren't a whole lot more helpful than they'd been before. I wondered if I'd have better luck if I sweetened the deal by offering to pay for their time, but quickly dismissed that as being potentially too expensive.

A few of the prostitutes who deigned to speak with me remembered Mary Carmen from working the streets a few months ago. One claimed she'd seen Mary Carmen walking along Church Street earlier today, but she wasn't trawling.

"Yeah, Mary Carmen was around this afternoon, like before suppertime," said a skeletal prostitute with stringy hair who was so clearly jonesing for her next fix that I could put little stock into what she said.

"Was she working?" I asked.

"Nah, like I just seen her, like, go into some of the stores over there, ya know..." The prostitute indicated the string of pawnshops near the corner of Adelaide and Church.

At the risk of jumping to conclusions, I wondered about the likelihood of finding Gaston's jewellery in one of the pawnshops. That could be a dead end or a good lead. I didn't know which, so I filed it away for now, with the many other untouched nuggets.

"Look," I said, "there's money in it for you if you give me a lead that takes me to her. Here's my card. Call me right away if you see her again."

"What about a little gift, like a tip, for now? I could really use something to eat. I was, like, as helpful as I could be, you know?"

"Here," I said, handing her a twenty that would no doubt go up her nose or in a vein. "There's a bigger tip for you next time if you help me find her. Don't lose my card."

I felt strangely guilty for enabling this ho to get her next crack fix. Would it have been better to just take her to a diner and buy her a sandwich? Was giving her cash any better or worse than simply handing her a snort, or a spliff, or a syringe?

The next few girls who bothered to talk to me offered nothing. One hooker thought she'd seen Mary Carmen in conversation with one of the local pharmaceutical entrepreneurs a while ago, but I quickly dismissed that. Nothing I had seen or heard so far had given me any indication that Mary Carmen was a drug user.

I called it quits just after midnight and walked back to the Camden Suites to talk with the late night crew.

"Good-looking girl," the night-shift doorman said. "Is she an actress? Or a model?" This guy was rather short and bottom heavy, or what would euphemistically be described as having a low centre of gravity. The silly uniform looked even worse on him than on the afternoon-shift dude.

"No, neither one," I said. "Are you sure you haven't seen her? She's tall and slim. She was probably walking, or maybe looking for a taxi?"

"On my shift you have time to notice everything. I'd be sure to remember a woman like that. Never saw her. Sorry."

My visit to the Pumpkin Vigilant was a waste of time, but for the sake of elimination I had to do it. By now my feet were very sore, I was sticky and sweaty, and I was tired and frustrated. I decided to splurge on a taxi home. I know it's not smart, but thank God I'd taken a cash advance on my Visa earlier today.

Shane wasn't home yet, and the house was stuffy from being closed up all day. At least there were no surprises awaiting me. No unexpected paint jobs, no vehicles whizzing by. I cranked up the air conditioning, peeled off my clothes, and went straight to bed, where I tossed and turned and stared at the ceiling for the next couple of hours.

Tuesday, July 21, 9:26 am

"I'm sorry," I said. "I should've called first." I was with a teary-eyed Candace in her office on the third floor of the cathouse. The tears surprised me. She'd seemed so cool and composed the other times I'd met her that I was a bit taken aback by today's unexpected show of vulnerability.

"Don't worry about it," Candace said. "Tonya should have checked with me before sending you up."

"Do you want to talk about it?"

"The strangest things can set me off. I saw a commercial on TV this morning. I don't even know what it was for. Cereal maybe? Juice? Anyhow, the kid in the commercial looked just the way I picture Adam. I try not to think of him, but I can't help it. I think of him every day, several times, every single day. I know I did the right thing in giving him up, but I wish I knew where he is and what he looks like and how he's doing."

"I'm sure it's very hard." Yeah, you can always count on me for comforting words. Maybe I should write Hallmark cards for a living. "Is there no way you can track him down? Are his adoptive parents willing to talk with you?"

"He was never formally adopted. I think he's still considered a Crown ward, still part of the Children's

Aid system, or with foster parents or something. I don't know. I feel so ashamed. I was such a mess... still am... I couldn't face things when he was born and over the years, it's just become harder. It's like I'm paralysed."

"Why don't you call Children's Aid? Maybe a social worker could help you. Do you want him back?"

"No. I could never be a parent. Certainly not now. But I'd love to see him, just once. I can't help but wonder what he looks like, if he's happy. What his personality is like. Is he shy? Does he play sports? That kind of thing. I picture him playing on a little kids' soccer team, running after the ball and kicking it into the net. I don't even care for soccer, but in my mind's eye, that's how I see him."

"There must be a way for you to get some information."

"There probably is, but perhaps I'm too afraid to try. I wouldn't even know where to begin. Maybe I'm scared of what they'll say at Social Services. They can be hard-asses. They were somewhat less than impressed with me back then."

"Hmm..." I said, once again showing off my eloquence.

"I've been out of his life so long that I know they'll put me through the wringer if I ask to reconnect with him."

"You can't be sure of that. It's got to be worth a try."

"I think it's too late. Anyhow," she said, dabbing her eyes with a tissue and wiping away raccoon-streaked, mascara-stained tears, "you didn't come here to listen to me whine. What's up?"

"We have a lot, I mean, really a lot, to talk about." I gave her the lowdown on much of what I'd seen and said and done over the past few days. I kept a few details – mainly my suspicions about Gaston the dead French-

Canadian pimp – to myself. And the graffiti. And the runaway car. "I have to leave a few things out for now, but I think Mary Carmen is probably alive and is probably on the run. Don't ask me to explain that yet."

"I guess at times we both operate on a need-to-know basis," Candace said.

"Touché. Before I forget to ask, did Dave usually see Mary Carmen here on-site, or did he prefer a hotel?"

"He used her services here on-site. Always."

"Didn't it strike anyone as odd that he requested an outcall this time?"

"It would have if I'd known about it at the time, but, well…you've met Terra. I guess the request didn't seem odd to her, even if she looked at his profile."

"Alright, I need to know about cellphones and communications here. Do you supply the girls with a cellphone for business?"

"No. Cellphones would lead to too much of a paper trail, so to speak. And they make it harder for me to keep an eye on things. However, most of the girls have their own iPhones or BlackBerrys. I discourage them from using their cells with clients, but I can hardly stop them. Why?"

"I can't find anyone who claims to have seen Mary Carmen at The Grand that night. I think she was waylaid on her way there. I also think if she'd disappeared en route to meet Dave, he would have called here wondering where his date was, what the hold up was."

"We haven't heard from Dave since then, except to talk to you," Candace said.

"So it must have been a fake Dave and he must have tricked her into going somewhere else while she was en route to The Grand."

"Wouldn't there be a record on her cellphone if someone had indeed called her?" Candace asked.

"I'm working on that, but it's moot if it was from a pay phone or an unlisted number. The cops could probably get that info, trace incoming caller numbers, if it's even worth getting. But I don't have those resources. Besides, knowing what number called and when is only good for so much. Knowing that would tell us diddly-squat about what was said or who said it, and that's what I'd really like to know."

"I see..."

"I'd also like to know how this mystery guy knew to connect Dave and Mary Carmen," I said. "Even more, I'd like to know how Fake Dave got Mary Carmen's cell number."

"Maybe the two of them know each other?"

"Maybe. I think I should talk to Terra again. When is she in next?"

"She'll be in today at four o'clock."

"Can you keep her free till I get here?"

"Consider it done. So, what else should I know about?"

"Did you know Mary Carmen had a second job? I don't have all the details, but it was housekeeping or something domestic."

"I had no idea. I wonder why she bothered with something like that. It surely pays a pittance compared to her earnings here."

"Could have been a cover, or to save face. Maybe she wanted a job she could admit to? Part of an immigration application thing? Maybe she needed something more solid, something on the books? Who knows? You do know she's probably here illegally?"

"I sort of guessed so, but my way of thinking about something like that is akin to gays in the U.S. military," Candace said.

"Don't ask, don't tell. Got it. Okay. Back to the real client, Dave. How well do you know him?"

"Reasonably well, within the context of how I know him. He was a pretty regular client until about two or three months ago. Why?"

"I'm working on a hunch. Does he travel a lot for business?"

"Yes, as I recall, a couple of times a month."

"Where to?"

"Ottawa and Montréal usually, Vancouver sometimes. Why?"

"I really need to talk with Dave again," I said. "Can you arrange for him to call me? It's crucial. He's not involved, and I'll be discreet, but basically someone who knows a bit about Dave's, uh, preferences probably impersonated him to get Mary Carmen to go on that outcall that night."

I could easily have called Dave myself. I knew from the mining conference website where he worked, and I could get his work number in a heartbeat. But I knew if I contacted him via my magic powers instead of via Candace that he'd do the deer-in-the-headlights thing and clam up. *Nothing wrong with mixing metaphors.*

"I'll ask him to call you," Candace said. "Anything else?"

"Yeah, what about client changes or clients who have stopped coming around?"

"There are two that I've noticed haven't been in lately. Both were regulars, at least once a week, if not more. Neither one has been in for a couple of months. Why is that important?"

"It may not be, but keep the names handy. It might be something to follow up on later, but for now it's just a hunch." My gut had a hunch about blackmail, but I wasn't ready to put that on the table yet. Hunches can be wrong.

"Well, let me know if you need me to do anything to help with this," Candace said. "I'll do whatever I can, as long as I can protect my clients."

"Understood."

"Is that everything for now, then?"

"Yeah, that's about it, except for these reports. Here's a copy of the progress report. I've already told you pretty much everything in it. And here's an expense report. Sorry I don't have receipts for most of it, but that's the way it goes."

Candace skimmed through the pages. "I can reimburse you for this later today when you come back to see Terra. Is cash okay? I try to avoid writing cheques."

"Cash is fine."

Oh, yeah. Cash is fine. So very fine.

I had a wee bit of time before I was due at the language school, so I hit the pawnshops downtown.

AJ's Pawnbroker was a seedy, dumpy firetrap redolent of cats and marshmallows. Every inch of every shelf was covered with something tacky and dusty. Vases, candelabra, Royal Doulton figurines, pinwheel-patterned lead crystal decanters, silver teapots. Some of the *tchotchkes* and knick-knacks could have passed as antiques, but the majority of it was just old and junky. A glass-fronted display case that hadn't been touched by a spritz of Windex in years housed a collection of jewellery that all seemed dull and tarnished under the filthy glass.

"Can I help you?" asked a rotund old grizzly bear wearing acid-washed jeans and a threadbare Bart Simpson T-shirt. He had the gritty, gravely voice of a lifelong chain smoker.

"I'm looking for someone who might have dropped by here in the past few days." I pulled out the photo of Mary Carmen.

"A babe like that wouldn't soon be forgotten. I hope she does come in. She'd be a sight for sore eyes." He took a sip of coffee from a *Lord of the Rings* travel mug.

"Well, she might come in to try to sell some jewellery. She's mentally ill and wandered off. She needs medication."

I doubt he bought my story, but I gave him my card anyway.

The next pawnshop had a whole bunch of musical instruments and it almost broke my heart to see them lying there, homeless and ownerless. I couldn't imagine being so financially desperate that I'd ever hock my drums. A kidney or an ovary, absolutely, but never my drums. Not a chance.

The proprietor, an anaemic kewpie doll with a bushel of bright red hair, was struggling to open a well-taped cardboard box. I was surprised to see a woman working here. The pawnbroking gig just naturally seems to be a man's job, for some reason.

"Hand me that exacto knife, will ya?" she said.

I passed the ninety-nine-cent box cutter to her. She sliced across the seam and started to pull out a layer of bubble wrap, then dug through a bunch of those little white Styrofoam peanut-shaped thingies. I was itching to pop the bubble wrap.

"The way people pack up some of this crap is ridiculous. Look at this." She pulled out a wooden chest that held a set of silver cutlery. "The box is wooden. It ain't going to break."

"Maybe to keep it from getting scratched?"

"I know, I know. But still, ya don't need this much." She had a point. The cardboard box was about three times the size of the silverware set, and the rest was going to be landfill.

"Estate sales. Everyone thinks they're gonna get rich off of late Aunt Maisie. Well, I got news for them. Great Uncle Walter's cheap tin pocket watch ain't gonna pay off anyone's mortgage. Anyhow, what can I do for you?" she asked.

"Just wondering if this girl has been in here during the last week or so," I said. I should probably just tattoo Mary Carmen's photo on my forehead. It would save me a lot of trouble.

"Yeah, a few days ago. Why?"

"What was she selling?"

"She had some old lady jewellery she wanted a price on."

"Ladies' jewellery? Are you sure?"

"Yeah. A brooch and some necklaces, or something. Don't remember 'cause I'm not into jewellery. I told her I have enough baubles. The stuff sits on the shelves far too long."

"And you're sure it was this girl? About five foot nine, slender."

"It was her all right. Look at this 'hood. It's a dump. Look at the lowlifes who hang out here. Your chick stood out."

"You have a point. What about watches? Do you carry men's watches?"

"Don't care if it's men's or women's. I have a few bracelets, rings, and watches, and they sit on the shelf for a dog's age before I get rid of them. Not interested in any kind of jewellery. That's what I told her, and she left."

"Well, thanks anyway. If you see her again, please give me a call." I gave the kewpie doll my card and walked out.

Mary Carmen

My God, what am I going to do now? What I can do? I must get out of here, this hotel, this city, this life.

I can not go back to the Candace House. The policía *going to know I killed the son of a bitch.*

I can not go back to mi chingada *little room. The* policía *can find me in there. Even if my money is in there.* Mierde, *I cannot go to there.*

I can not stay around the streets. Some of the girls know me. I don't want no one to know where I am.

Only one place maybe where no one can find me. I should go to the casa *of the old lady. Si, in the* mañana *I will go to there.*

Just get through tonight. Stay moving. Stay quiet. Don't talk to no one. Don't let no one see me. Movomiento.

"One token please," I said to the fare collector of the subway station.

I go onto the Yonge subway line heading for north part of the city. I never seen the Finch Station at the end of the line, but I think is a good place to dump my bloody clothes. I can find some garbage can.

In the mañana *I can buy new clothes before I go to see the lady. Maybe she can help me.*

I think is a good thing I have the sunglasses of the bastardo. *No one can see me cry.*

Tuesday, 12:20 pm

Mary Carmen's classmates represented just about every member of the United Nations.

Pavel, a Russian student, didn't care for Mary Carmen and so had little to offer.

"Mary Carmen refuse date with Pavel." Pavel's voice was thick with perestroika and glasnost and pravda. *Da!* "Pavel make women swing on star. She lose chance with Pavel. Pavel don't waste more mine time on silly girl like her."

I always get a kick out of it when people refer to themselves in the third person. It's so obnoxious and pretentious. Besides, this scarecrow smelled like a distillery and had nothing to be pretentious about.

"I'm sure you would have rocked her world," I said. I kept a straight face, but I wouldn't date this clown even on a dare.

Hyung Sung from Seoul was shy and didn't really know anyone outside of class. Hyung Sung also sounded as if he should have been forced to repeat ESL level one. Francesca from Barcelona seemed more interested in gossip and speculation than in being helpful. The next few students also offered a whole lot of nothing. They all said Mary Carmen was a nice girl, upbeat, friendly, cheerful.

"Yes, sometimes she brings in Mexican candies and treats, strange stuff. I don't like most of it."

"Yeah, some of the Mexican candies she gets from the market are spicy, with chilli powder. Imagine a spicy candy? Yuck. And some stuff is sour, like those tamarind things."

"Yeah, those were awful, but she said they were her favourites since she was a little girl. And it was nice of her to bring in treats to share. She always thinks of other people."

"And she usually pays when we go for coffee after class. She is very generous. Very kind."

Everything people told me was warm and fuzzy. Great stuff if I were doing a Mary Carmen tribute, or an infomercial, or if I were on the beatification council, but it was all pretty much useless in terms of helping me find a missing person. I was beginning to think this exercise was yet another giant waste of time, and my ears were getting tired from trying to decipher broken English.

The turning point came when I spoke with Magda from Pragda, I mean Prague. She made my day, not with her warmth or her smile or her better-than-her-classmates English skills, but because of all the leads she effortlessly handed to me.

"Yes, uff course she working as maid. Like all inmigrant, she duz domestic job. I too work for rich Canadian family. But I am nanny also, am not just maid. I take care uff four children after school and do cleaning, all the house cleaning. So much work. Mary Carmen iz just looking only after one old lady, only just one person in big house."

"Do you know the name of the woman she works for?" I asked. "Where the house is?"

"Woman iz Miss Vivian. Vivian somethink. Her big house iz near to Avenue Road und St. Clair." Hmmm... That's sort of the same general area as the Gordita Lady had mentioned. "Somethink Hill Road or Somethink Hill Crescent. Maybe Drive? We take subway train to St. Clair West station together. Mary Carmen walk from station to her work. I take bus from station to my job."

"You have no idea how much help you've been."

"Tell Mary Carmen hurry back. I am needing conversation partner."

Okay, all I had to do was check Google maps for the St. Clair and Avenue Road area and find out the names of every street that has the word *Hill* in it. Then I had to find out which of those streets has a home on it belonging to a woman named Vivian, because of course all land registries and property titles are listed by first name only.

Sure, no problem. Hey, look! I just pulled this tiny, shiny needle out of that great, big, shaggy, old haystack. Sure I did.

I hit another pawnshop after the language school. Grossman's Buy and Sell, *We Pay Cash*, had an abundance of cameras and electronics. Most of the electronics would probably never find buyers, until fifty or sixty years from now when the junk cluttering this store was considered antique and collectible. There were black-and-white TVs, Betamax video players, slide projectors, transistor radios, and a whole bunch of Sony Walkmans, not even Sony Discmans, but the original ones that played audiocassettes.

"Are you looking for something?" The clerk was a freckle-faced kid with braces on his teeth and a chip on his shoulder. His demeanour didn't match his appearance – kind of like Alfred E. Neuman on meth.

"Do you work here full-time?"

"Yeah, mostly. It's my dad's shop, but he's kind of retired. Why?"

"I'm looking for a girl who might have come in here to sell some men's rings or a watch. Does she look familiar at all?"

Freckles looked at the photo and immediately said yes.

"Late last week. She dumped some jewellery. Aw, man, you're not going to tell me it's hot are you? My dad will kill me if I screwed up."

"Don't worry. It's not hot. Can you show it to me?"

"That brooch and those rings up there." He jerked his thumb over his shoulder to indicate the rather barren, wall-mounted jewellery case behind the cash register. "And the necklace." He indicated a number of women's pieces, all of which were old-fashioned and borderline ugly. I figured the rather gaudy brooch with red gemstones – garnets maybe – was supposed to be a robin or a cardinal, but it looked more like a bleeding mallard. It didn't seem sparkly enough to be made with rubies. The rings looked like opals in either white gold or silver settings, and the necklace was a double strand of cultured pearls. None of this would have been Mary Carmen's taste.

"I think there must be some mistake," I said. "She told me she was getting rid of a man's watch and a couple rings."

"Yeah, well, whatever." He was trying to maintain his jaded, tough-guy attitude but was having a hard time pulling it off. "Maybe she sold men's stuff somewhere else, but this is the stuff she sold to me."

Mary Carmen

The hijo de puta *had only two hundred sixty dollars in his wallet. I need more than that.* Mucho mas. *The plane ticket to Torreón is going to cost me eight hundred dollars even for a* pinche *one-way flight. I wish I did not send so much money to my* familia *back home last week.*

I need some clothings to wear. I can not go around in the asshole's jeans and shirt.

And I need to get me a new pasaporte. *How much is going to cost for that?*

I want mí madre. *I want* mí familia.

I wiped some more salty tears from my face. Chinga. *How did I get into this nightmare? Into this life? How I going to get out?*

"Can I please try on this clothes?" I asked the sales assistante *in Winners store. I am the first customer of the morning and I must shop quick and get new clothings.*

The sales clerk acted so importante, *and acted like I am a big interruption in her morning.*

*"No more than three items in the change room." The se-*ñorita *didn't even make eye contact with me when she spoke.*

"Is just one pants and two shirts," I say.

She gave me a ticket and pointed to an empty change room.

The clothings was very plain, almost ugly, but was cheap and not noticeable. A long-sleeved cotton blusa, *a pair of light pants and a short-sleeved* blusa.

"I will take this stuff. Now where is the place for underwear, por favor*?"*

The girl was again acting like I a big problem in her busy day. She pointed to the back of the store.

"Gracias," *I said, but the girl ignored me.*

I chose three pairs of cotton underwear and then went to the shoe department and found a pair of sneakers and some sandals.

All my own clothes, and even also all my money, was in the rooming house on Carlton, and there was no possibility to go there for my things. Maybe I would have took the chance if I have enough dinero *there for my plane ticket, but is not. I can live without all of my things. But I cannot live with any risk of the* polícia *finding me. I could never go back there. I could not say* adiós *to Todd or Carrie Jo, my first Canadian friends.*

I took my things to the cash register in the front of the store.

"Are you a member of our rewards program?"

"Rewards? ¿Que?*"*

"We offer instant approval on our Winners credit card. You get ten percent off your first purchase with it, and you get points each time you use it."

"No, gracias.*"*

"Okay, that will be $124.92 then please."

Chinga. *That's almost half of all the money I have. I gave the money to the lady and she packed my stuff in a* plastico *bag. Then*

I went to the public baño *and changed into my new clothings.*

I throw the clothes of Gaston in a garbage can in a park many blocks from the clothing store. But I keep his jewellery. I can sell it for some money for my plane ticket to home.

Tuesday, 2:26 pm

I decided to eat, since food is a great way of dealing with frustration and stress. Since I was already frustrated and stressed, I didn't see any reason to worry about calories. I picked up some Kentucky Fried Chicken and brought my cardboard boxed dinner for one, with a side of gravy and an extra order of coleslaw, to my office. This marked two consecutive appearances there, which damn near justified the monthly rent. I sat at my desk and enjoyed the silence. I had time to think and had turned off my cellphone. Bliss. Except for the coleslaw, I ate everything with my fingers and enjoyed every salty, greasy, deep-fried mouthful. I washed down my midday feast with a can of regular Coke, and then fired up the computer.

I was a bit underwhelmed at the thought of Googling maps of Toronto streets that had the name *Hill* in them, so I convinced myself it was okay to put that on hold as long as I was tackling other more important tasks. I took a quick look at my email and decided none of it was worth reading. Spam, spam, junk mail, update from

Dad, spam, recycled jokes. I deleted all but Dad's email.

I revisited some of yesterday's prostitution websites and bookmarked a few more pages. That became dull and depressing in no time at all, so I picked up the phone and reached out and touched someone. Okay, not exactly.

Something had been on my mind since my visit with the teary-eyed Candace this morning. I figured it wouldn't cost me anything to ask a few questions. I really wanted to find out what had become of her little boy, Adam. I picked up my new cordless business phone and dialled the direct number for Derek Armstrong, a professional acquaintance who specializes in family law.

Derek and I had worked together peripherally in some divorce and custody cases over the last while, and I always get a wee bit nervous talking to him because he is so damn sexy. Naturally, I disguise my nervousness by being brashly flirtatious with him, and Derek gives as good as he gets. He's incredibly gorgeous in a pompous, leather-elbow-patch-and-tweed-jacket professorial way. He's also very intelligent in a self-deprecating albeit slightly cocky way. And he makes my knees buckle in an I-really-want-to-throw-myself-at-him way. If anyone could take my mind off Mick, Derek certainly could.

"Hiya handsome. Guess who?"

"My favourite goddess? The singer with the voice of a black-winged angel?"

"Sorry, I must have the wrong number," I said.

He chuckled, and we danced through a few minutes' worth of social pleasantries before I got to the reason for my call.

"I know I shouldn't ask you this, and I really don't

want you to do anything that would compromise you professionally—"

"But you'd like to compromise me, anyway, right?" Derek said.

"Absolutely. And corrupt you. And lead you down the garden path and – never mind, you'd probably chicken-out if the opportunity ever presented itself."

"Don't be so sure."

"Aw, I'd probably be too wild for you. You wouldn't be able to handle it."

I almost felt like I was back in the Slut Mines, talking dirty to horndogs who called into the phone sex line where I had briefly earned a paycheque. Except in this case, I was the one who had initiated the call.

"Gorgeous, don't let your mouth write a cheque that your body can't cash," Derek said.

"Darling, that corny old line is beneath you."

"I know. That's why I said it."

"Listen, I need some information and hope you can help me get it."

I gave Derek whatever details I had about Adam, which admittedly were rather scant. I figured if anyone could help me get answers about Candace's son, it was Derek.

"Give me a day or two to see what I can find out," he said. "You need to understand, though, that I have to do this my own way. It could put me, not to mention you, in a difficult spot."

"I owe you one, Derek. Thank you."

"Don't thank me yet, but if I figure this out, you'll have to have dinner with me."

"Deal," I said.

After my call with Derek, I decided it was time to

invite Jesus into my life. I was searching for God, and Google led me to Him. I hit the jackpot before I even got through one Hail Mary. *Hallelujah!*

The blessed Archdiocese of Toronto website listed parishes alphabetically, or by postal code, or by language. Fourteen parishes offered Mass in Spanish. Of those fourteen, I easily ruled out six for being too far away from downtown Toronto. I was left with one St. Jude, two St. Thomas's, three Our Lady Someone's, a St. Augustine and a partridge in a pear tree. I looked each of them up on MapQuest and narrowed it down to five likely candidates for the place where Mary Carmen received her weekly Communion and confessed her daily sins.

Buttressed by this bit of what I loosely called progress, I kept plugging away at MapQuest. I pulled up the intersection of Avenue Road and St. Clair. I zoomed in and out, I panned north, south, east and west, then over to Bathurst and up and down some more. I found at least six streets that fit the general area, and a few more when I panned out. Forest Hill Road, Old Forest Hill Road, Chester Hill Road, Beacon Hill Avenue, Birch Hill Crescent and Cedar Hill Drive. And so on. Shit. Some of those streets were several blocks long. Damn it, there was no little flag or indicator on the screen showing "Vivian lives here."

I printed off a few maps and decided to put my cartographic sleuthing on the back burner for now. I had a hot date shortly with a space cadet call girl.

Mary Carmen

"What about this one? Can you tell me how many dineros *is worth?" I asked of the tall negro man in pawnshop. He took a close look at Gaston's watch and wrinkled his nose.*

"Ya, mon… the watch only be worth 'bout twenty bucks. Look how scratched it be."

"Okay. I'll take it. What about these rings? Is real gold."

These are the rings that make it hurt so bad before when Gaston punched and slapped me. I wanted to crush these rings, to burn them, or destroy them, but I think they maybe can be worth some money.

"This one kinda nice, mon. Fifty bucks?" The Africano *chewed on toothpick and looked like he was feeling not so interested with me.*

"That's all? What about this other one?"

Fifty dollars could not even get me a bus ticket to New York, not even to mention a flight back home to Torreón.

"How about I give ya a hundred dollars for the watch and both rings?"

"But the watch is Seiko, and the rings are real gold…"

"Best I can do, mon. Wanna sell 'em or not?"

"Sí. *I need the money."*

Tuesday, 4:33 pm

"You said something the other day about Dave being impatient, like he was pissed off when you put him on hold," I said to Terra at Candace's whorehouse.

"Yeah, man, that's right," she said. "You didn't even take notes and you remember that? Wow!" Terra was in work mode, but in a show of contrived modesty she had belted an emerald green satin robe around herself. It might have been more effective if her 38DD boobs hadn't been halfway spilling out of it.

"Walk me through the call," I said. "Do you remember how many times you put him on hold?"

"Not exactly. I guess once when I tried to open his file. I have a hard time with computers. I think I told you that."

"Okay, so he's on the phone, he's on hold, you open the computer program. Then what?"

Terra took her time answering me. I wish I knew if she were stalling until she could come up with a lie, or if she were simply trying to remember. She re-knotted her robe and then started fidgeting with her hair. When she brushed it away from her face, I noticed how glassy her eyes were. They'd been glassy the other day too, but nothing like they were today.

"I got back on the line to double check what time he wanted his appointment."

"Okay, then what?"

"Man, I just don't understand the whole database thing. I put him on hold and called Candace on the interoffice phone. She suggested I send Mary Carmen. I had to check if Mary Carmen was free for a nine o'clock appointment and I couldn't open the calendar."

"Okay, so eventually you got back on the phone and told him you'd booked the girl for him?"

"Yeah, and then I had to make him wait again while I booked the hotel."

"Okay, so he was getting edgy by then. That's three or four holds."

"Yeah."

"Can you remember anything else about the call? Anything unusual?"

"No. That was pretty much the end of it. I had to make him wait again while I looked for Mary Carm's cell number—"

Yes, oh, yes, oh yes! Another piece of the puzzle.

"You gave him her cell number?"

"Well, he asked for it. Said he had a new BlackBerry and hadn't copied his old address book. Why? Is this important?"

Oh darling, if only you knew how important. I wanted to kiss her but was scared off by the man-eating cleavage staring back at me.

When I left the bordello, I wanted to walk for a few blocks to digest everything that was beginning to come together, albeit foggily. Without thinking, I had walked downtown again, and was now just a few blocks from the Sherbourne Street pawnshops.

Since I was in the neighbourhood, I decided to wander into a few more stores to see if I could stumble across a big clue, or whip up a miracle, or something like that. The first couple of shops were more wastes of time, which was pretty much the leitmotif of this case, but I hit the jackpot at the third.

"Yeah, mon. She come in here last week," said a nasty-looking Rasta dude with a heavy but fake Jamaican accent and some serious dreadlocks. His red, green, and gold dashiki was a nice touch, but this Bob Marley wannabe was as middle-class, suburban Toronto as a golden retriever drooling out of the passenger window of a four-door Chevy Malibu.

"Was she trying to unload some jewellery?"

"Mon, she be successful in unloading it. Mon, that is one fine-looking lady. Felt kinda bad giving her such a low price, but she seem glad to get rid o' her stuff."

If he said *mon* one more time, I'd have to spark up a Jamaican gold fattie.

"Care to show me what it was?"

Rasta pulled out a balding black velvet tray with a man's Seiko wristwatch and a couple of gold bling-bling rings. "These t'ings."

"What'll it cost me for them? All three pieces?"

"For you, mon, I can go two hundred and fifty dollars, no lower, don't even be asking."

Yeah, *mon*, I be asking, we be jamming, and Rasta be scamming.

"Not even two hundred and forty?" I asked. "Pretty please?"

"Firm price, mon. Two hundred and fifty."

Between his *mon* and Terra's *man*, I was beyond irritated with pointless monosyllabic interjections.

"Do you take credit cards?" I asked.

"Yeah, mon. What kind of plastic you got?"

I said a quick prayer to St. Ganja and pulled out my emergency-only American Express. It was actually my dad's account, but he'd had a duplicate card issued for me to use only in life-or-death situations. I knew he'd be pissed at my using it here today, but he was out of town for a while longer, so I wouldn't get shit for this immediately.

Yeah, I'm in my early thirties and oh so proud.

Tuesday, 6:50 pm

Shane, wearing a bandana and a loud pair of Madras shorts, was tending to some giant prawns on the barbecue. Lindsey was in the kitchen making a spinach salad with toasted almonds, shredded cheddar and green apple slices. Tonight was Shane's night off, and I think maybe he and Lindsey had expected, nay, hoped, to have the house to themselves. *Surprise, here I am.* Luckily, I'd shown up just in time for dinner, and, luckily, they'd cooked enough to feed an extra person. Actually, they'd cooked enough to feed an army, but my dating life isn't that active yet. Hope springs eternal, though.

We were eating at the picnic table in the backyard.

It was hot as hell outdoors, but inside the house was no better. In fact, indoors was considerably worse. The central air conditioning had conked out sometime this afternoon, and we couldn't get a repairman to the house tonight for love, or money, or even gourmet food.

"So what's the update on the Hispanic Hooker in Hiding?" Lindsey asked. "Has she decided on a career in urban art instead?"

"Very funny. I don't think she's the one who spray-painted the garage. Anyhow, I've had a few eureka moments and I think I've solved the murder of that guy in the hotel last week. Hold still," I said as I smacked a mosquito off Shane's neck.

"Ouch! Not so hard."

"You should thank me. I might have just saved you from West Nile virus."

"I'm eternally grateful. So, sister dearest, will you be going to the police station, telling them everything you know, and letting them handle it from here? Or do you plan to be stubborn and risk being shot at again?"

Shane had a point. I would have easily avoided the whole bullet-in-my-bra debacle on my last big case if I had gone to the police. At the time, though, I didn't have any proof, and quite frankly, I was afraid the cops would have laughed at me.

"I will go to the police. Really. I will. But in another day or two. I still don't know where Mary Carmen is."

"And you think she was involved in that guy's murder?" Lindsey asked. "Rewind a bit. Give us all the details and bring Shane up to speed."

I filled our glasses with chilled Gewürztraminer

before I began. The bottle was slippery with beady condensation from the heat.

"As near as I can tell, this nasty dude was her pimp in Montréal. Apparently, she took off from him and ended up here. Somehow he tracked her down."

I pointedly omitted any mention of Gaston's watch and rings, which were now in a paper bag in my night-stand drawer. If Shane had known about that, he would have gone to the police on his own, right away, no matter what I said.

"The hooking world can't be all that big," Shane said. "He probably knew pimps here or hookers there."

"Yeah, probably something like that. I assume she left him and Montréal on bad terms. I assume the pimp knew Mary Carmen wouldn't be happy to see him. That's why he tricked her. Can you please pass the salad?"

Shane handed me the big bowl of greens and I scooped a generous portion onto my plate.

"How do you think he did that?" Shane asked.

"He must have called the whorehouse and pretended he was one of her regular clients. Mary Carmen agreed to an outcall at The Grand Hotel. He called her cell while she was en route and told her to come instead to the Camden. That's why no one at The Grand recog-nized her picture. She never went there."

"Wouldn't she have recognized his voice?"

"People can fake their voices. Or you can get some-one to make a call for you. Or you can hide behind background noises. Lots of ways. Besides, it would've been a quick call, in a language foreign to her – *meet me at this place not that place, blah, blah, blah*. It was probably of little interest to Mary Carmen. Just another john."

"Oh, shit," said Lindsey, jumping up suddenly. Her cotton dress was practically stuck to her with perspiration. "I forgot I have cornbread in the oven."

Shane and I paused the conversation until Lindsey returned with a very charred loaf. "There's no saving this, is there?" she said.

"Feed it to the squirrels," I said. I know squirrels are basically rats with fluffy tails, but in my next life I want to be a squirrel. They look like they have so much fun.

"What a waste," Lindsey said as she tossed a chunk across the yard. "It must be rather depressing doing all this work around hookers and strippers."

"It is. I find myself getting angry about so many things. I'm obviously influenced by the setup at Candace's brothel, and on that level it almost doesn't seem so bad, compared with what some girls go through."

"Are you saying you think prostitution should be legalized?" Shane asked me.

"I'm not sure. Some places – Amsterdam of course, but also places in Sweden and New Zealand – decriminalized it in the hopes of reducing other problems, like drugs, violence, and organized crime—"

"And STDs, too, right?" Shane said.

"Yes, health problems too. Anyhow, the theory was that other social problems would go away if hooking were legalized. Unfortunately, the reality didn't measure up to the theory."

"Do you think legalizing it would reduce coercion?" Shane asked. "I kind of think people should be allowed to do whatever they want as long as it's their choice. Nothing under duress. Think about it – how different is sex than a massage or something like that?"

"Brother dearest, I don't know if I want to nod in agreement or slap you upside the head for being a jerk. Are you saying that it's okay? How would you feel about it if your daughter became a hooker?"

"Well, it's never going to go away, so wouldn't it be better if it were legalized and regulated—"

"And taxed," Lindsey said.

"If we're going to get into this, think about all the different ways women prostitute themselves," Shane said. "How they use their looks or their bodies to get what they want, to make money. Models, waitresses, entertainers—"

I frowned. "Be careful where you're going with this."

"Well, you never went onstage in a woolly turtleneck sweater and baggy corduroy pants, did you?" Lindsey asked.

We argued about prostitution and commercial sex and the objectification of women for the next hour. Another bottle of wine made the conversation that much more spirited, but we accomplished nothing more than vacillating and contradicting one another and ourselves.

And swatting away mosquitoes.

And sweating.

"Damn. So, what do you think happened at the Camden Suites?" Lindsey asked, tossing another hunk of crispy cornbread across the lawn. Two black squirrels with bushy tails raced for it; the bigger of the two got it. Lindsey threw another piece towards the little fellow who had struck out on the last pitch.

"Well, the Montréal pimp formerly known as Gaston the Living became Gaston the Deceased. Could have been a fight, could have been self-defence."

"What about a crime of passion?"

"Maybe. Who knows? All I know is he's dead, and she's missing, which means she's probably alive. Cadavers have such limited mobility."

"So, what did this Dave guy, the real customer, have to do with everything?" Shane asked.

"I'm guessing he knew Mary Carmen professionally in Montréal. He often goes there for business. Then he found her here and probably mentioned seeing her to the Montréal people. He probably had no idea what kind of trouble that could have started. I don't even know if that's what happened, but it makes sense, and in the absence of a better explanation, I'll stick with it."

I offered to do the cleanup, since I hadn't helped at all with preparing the meal. There wasn't much to tidy, and at least the dishwasher was working fine, but I'd have gladly traded it for ten thousand BTUs of freon.

"We're going to head up to Baskin Robbins," Shane said. "Want us to bring something back for you?"

"Thanks, but no. It'd melt into a chocolate dairy puddle by the time you walked back here."

Tuesday, 9:47 pm

I've been known to go undercover before, and those who know me, know I will do whatever it takes get what I want or need. However, I still managed to surprise myself when I looked in the mirror. I'd worn some slinky outfits during my band days and I still have a lot of provocative clothes, but they're all just the right side of being utterly trampy – and tonight utterly trampy was the objective. If I'd been on the ball earlier today, I'd have purloined some of Mary Carmen's vestments.

An old, black denim miniskirt that had served me well onstage during my rocker days was too modest for Jarvis Street, so I took some shears from the kitchen and hacked off two inches from it. A push-up bra gave me the illusion of cleavage – although considerably less than Terra's. My fuchsia, satin blouse was knotted at the bottom to show off my flat tummy, which wouldn't be flat for much longer if I did the KFC fiasco and shrimp on the barbie extravaganza again anytime soon. My blond hair, normally long, loose, and wavy, was now teased, and sprayed. I looked like a honey-haired Peg Bundy. My lips were bright with shimmering magenta goop, and my eyelids were heavy with smoky, matte eye shadow and a lot of black eyeliner.

Shane and Lindsey came back from their walk and were suitably appalled by my appearance.

"You could get arrested in that outfit, sis."

"Did you use a paint-by-number kit to apply your make-up?" Lindsey asked. "You look like a two-bit hooker."

"Just two-bits? I've gotta be worth more than that. Think I'll blend in with the girls on the stroll?"

"I'm just glad Dad's out of town," Shane said.

I ducked my head downwards as I walked from my house to the streetcar stop on Gerrard Street. I could only imagine what my neighbours must be thinking, especially after the front door and garage incident. I could already hear them telling my dad what kinds of shenanigans his little girl had been up to while he was away. Here I am, in my early thirties and still worried about being grounded, and about my big brother or my neighbours ratting me out.

¡Ay, caramba!

Tuesday, 10:21 pm

This time I started on Carlton Street. I checked out the action near Allan Gardens. Most of the streetwalkers around here seemed to be hardcore drug users or transvestite she-male types, so I expected little.

I strolled west as far as Church Street and briefly thought about popping into Woody's, since it was just a block away, to see Todd's *Divas in Drag* show. I'd taken a shine to Todd during our brief encounter, but not enough as to want to suffer through campy drag queen covers of synthesized Eighties dance tunes.

The street was busy with cars and foot traffic. A cluster of teenagers stood smoking outside the Studio Café. A couple of bikers on obnoxiously loud Harleys roared by. For some reason I'd never thought of Mick's Harley as obnoxiously loud, but maybe that was because I associated his bike with straddling him. *Hmm.*

A dog walker scooted by, nervously looking from

side to side as he passed each doorway. A wino who looked as if he'd wet himself was sprawled on the sidewalk next to a mailbox. A bunch of drunken and entitled yuppie punks in a shiny red '65 Mustang convertible slowed down as they approached me.

"Hey bitch, I'll give you ten bucks for a blow job!" one of them yelled. Ten bucks? I didn't know whether to laugh or to be insulted, but at least it was better than the two-bits Lindsey had mentioned.

"Maybe the whore should pay us for the privilege of sucking our dicks," said the guy in the back seat.

Ever ready with a scathing retort, I yelled, "You can all fuck right off!"

"Oh, shut up and suck my cock!" said the driver before flooring it out of there. Well, that was a rather unpleasant exchange.

Prostitutes paced back and forth at every intersection, probably enduring the same kind of verbal abuse I'd just experienced. I couldn't imagine living this life. I toddled along in my impractical high heels, wincing occasionally at my not-quite-healed blisters. I approached every hooker I saw and wondered with each how she had come to be here.

I finally got a lucky break when I was around Church and Dundas.

"Yeah, she done gave me the rest of her pills. Said she don't need 'em no more." The hooker standing in front of me had a gold tooth and the biggest Afro I've ever seen.

"Pills?"

"We all use them. Girl would be a fool not to have them. They's protection, just like a rubber."

"You mean the morning after pill?"

"Y'all ain't never worked the street, did ya?"

"Sorry," I said. "I'm not a cop. I'm not going to cause any trouble. I'm an investigator and I'm trying to find Mary Carmen." I pointed again to the photo I'd drawn from my bag. "I think something bad has happened to her. She's been missing for almost two weeks."

"Well, I ain't seen her in a few days. Four days? Five days maybe? Or was it last week? I dunno. The days is all the same to me."

"So, what kind of pills?'

"Most of us what works the street carry roofies."

"You mean Rohypnol, right? The date rape drug?"

"You got it sister." *Aha*. This might explain the allusion to drugs from the skinny crack ho the other night. And it jibed with what Mark Houghton had speculated.

The Ho with the 'Fro continued, "Ain't just chicks at frat parties that gets fucked on roofies. Hos use it too if a john gets out of hand. Acts fast, no taste, and you can get out of a bad situation real quick if you can manage to slip it into the john's drink."

"And then make a run for it?"

"Good way to avoid a beating," she said. We talked for a few more minutes, but I'd already learned as much from her as I was going to.

So, Mary Carmen was generously giving away the tools of her trade. She had probably used the pills on the Late-But-Not-So-Great Gaston. Gold Tooth Afro probably had evidence related to Gaston's murder and not a clue about it. I didn't know what to do with the Rohypnol lead or nugget, whatever it was. So for the time being I decided to put it on the back burner with all my other un-chased leads, and I continued trawling along the blocks known as Hooker Heaven.

Nothing. No dice.

I crossed over to Jarvis and began to head north again. I would have taken off my shoes and walked barefoot if I hadn't been certain I'd step on broken glass or something worse. My come-fuck-me shoes were punishing the tender blister on my heel. I figured I'd give myself at most one more hour and would give up if I didn't get a break by then.

My lucky break emerged within a couple of blocks.

"Of course I recognize her. That's Tequila Girl." This adorable little Filipina waif was about the twentieth hooker I'd approached but only the fifth or sixth who was willing to talk more than briefly with me.

"I know you're busy, I know you're working, but I'll pay you for your time," I said. My reimbursement from Candace wasn't going to last long, I could tell. "I have a strong feeling you might be able to really help me. Can we take half an hour and grab a coffee?"

"Too hot for coffee, girlfriend. How about a cold beer at the Nag's Head on the next block?"

I strongly suspected this little *prosti-tot* wasn't quite legal drinking age, and I briefly worried about supplying a minor with alcohol. But what did the age of majority matter if she was old enough to be turning tricks? Then again, just how old is old enough to become a hooker? Might as well sidestep the moral conundrum, have a pint, and give my feet a rest.

"You're on. And please let me pay you for your time, okay?"

"My name's Cittin, sounds just like *kitten*, but I think it looks better spelled like this." She wrote out her name in a childish scrawl on a paper napkin.

"Cool," I said.

What other response was there, save for pointing out that there are no words in the English language beginning with **c**it that have a **k** sound. Something told me that linguistics or phonology or etymology or morphology, or whatever the hell the study of sounds and spellings is called, was of little interest to Kitten, I mean Sittin', I mean *Cittin*.

The Nag's Head is a dumpy wooden tavern, sparsely populated by unkempt old men lacking full sets of teeth and wearing checkered pants that were belted up somewhere just below the sternum. Meow Meow and I grabbed two pints of frothy draft beer from the cryogenically preserved bartender and took a seat at a table by the window up front. The window was open but there was absolutely no breeze. We allowed ourselves to enjoy the illusion of fresh air, but with the traffic coughing by and the steaming, fetid garbage bags out front waiting for the next day's pickup, the mirage quickly disintegrated.

"Yeah, I knew her for a little while on the Montréal scene," Cittin said. "Why? Did she end up here?"

"Yes, she came to Toronto a while ago. She works for a bordello madam but disappeared after going for an outcall almost two weeks ago. What can you tell me about her?"

Cittin took a healthy chug of her beer and damn near drained the mug. I was surprised at this Olympic power drinking from such a little pipsqueak. Not to be outdone, I took a healthy slug of my brew, and signalled the bartender for another round.

"I just seen her around the streets, you know?" Cittin said. "We hung on the same corner sometimes. I liked her, but wasn't too crazy 'bout working the same block as her. She's way, way, way too good-looking. I thought maybe guys would pick her over me."

"What kind of stuff did you talk about?"

"Shop talk, good scores, shared supplies sometimes. Warned each other about johns to avoid. The usual."

"What kinds of supplies?"

"Condoms. Hairspray. Maybe some breath mints. That kinda stuff."

"Pills? Roofies?"

"I don't think she was into using them. I always keep a few on me, just in case. She might have, but I dunno."

"How long have you been in Toronto?"

"Just about a month."

"You haven't connected with her since you came here?" I asked.

"Nope. Didn't even know she was here. Last time I seen her was probably about five or six or seven months ago maybe. I seen her at an all night drugstore in Montréal on Ste. Catherine Street, near St. Laurent, or maybe it was St. Denis? She looked totally, totally, totally beat up. I could tell by her puffy eyes she been crying a river, and her arms had some butt-ugly yellow bruises on them."

"Who do you think did it? A pimp or a john?"

"What difference does it make? Someone roughed her up pretty good. Come to think of it, I'm sure that was the last time I seen her. She musta split town after that."

"Do you know anything about her pimp?"

"Just that he was some French-Canadian asshole with a bad temper and a good right hook."

"Know his name?"

"She just called him Gas. I thought maybe he farted a lot or something. Stupid nickname."

Not so stupid if it's short for Gaston. Thank you Cittin with the stupid spelling.

My second pint of beer had magically been replaced by a third one, so I chatted a while longer with Cittin. "So what made you leave Montréal for Toronto?"

"One too many busts. I got picked up for soliciting again, and this time they found my stash. Bastard cops kept it too. I was supposed to go to court, and I knew I'd end up back in the slammer."

"You've done time?"

"Yeah, and it sucked. Done juvie a few times, and the real clink twice, but just in minimum security. I don't wanna go back there again, ever, ever, ever. So I fucked off. Skipped my court date and came here. I don't think I should show my face in Montréal again for a long, long, long time."

Wednesday, July 22, 8:35 am

I can think of few things that are more boring than digging through municipal records. I was up and dressed and out the door before eight o'clock, and I was the first one into the records room at City Hall when it opened at half past eight.

I greeted the bored civil servant with a warm smile. Fat lot of good it did me. He all but rolled his eyes at me when I told him what I was looking for. I smiled again and hoped that cute and friendly would serve me well. They didn't.

I silently waited him out. I had nothing better to do right now. Eventually, he grudgingly helped me check local birth records, but only after I accidentally dropped fifty dollars on the counter.

We did some digging for birth registrations and found that Adam Miles Curtis had been born at Mount St. Patrick's Hospital on Friday, February 13, 2004, at 2:38 pm. He weighed six pounds, one ounce, and was fifteen inches in length, a bit shorter and lighter than the average newborn. The effects of mommy's drug use, no doubt. The mother was listed as Candace Elizabeth Curtis. The father's name was left blank.

Candace could have told me all of this. My trip down here, like so much else I'd done in the last few days, was a big fat waste of time. However, I wanted to give Derek as much information as I could and I didn't want Candace to know I was looking into this for her. For all I knew, I might come up with a great big goose egg and I didn't want her to get her hopes up.

I toyed with the idea of going to the hospital to see if I could learn anything further, but knew as the thought came to me that it would be a dead end. Medical info is guarded like a fortress. And I didn't have enough money left to offer any incentives. Instead, I called Derek Armstrong. His voice mail kicked in, so I left a message with the few details I'd gleaned from this morning's wild goose chase.

Before I could make up my mind about what to do next, Dave, the purported last client of Mary Carmen, called me on my cell.

"Look, this might be easier in person," I said to him. "I'm near City Hall. Is there somewhere we can meet for a coffee?"

"I'd really like to keep this off the record," he said.

"That's why cells aren't a good idea. How about Java Joe's at Bay and Gerrard?"

"I'll be there in twenty minutes."

"I've got long blond hair, and I'm wearing a pastel-coloured peasant blouse and white capris."

"I'm sure I'll find you." He sounded less than happy about the prospect of meeting the World's Hottest but Most Underrated and Underachieving Private Investigator.

Wednesday, 10:12 am

"Look," I said, "I know you want to keep your name out of things. That shouldn't be a problem. But this isn't just about a missing hooker—"

"Please keep your voice down."

Dave glanced nervously around the room, but he needn't have worried. We were a few blocks out of the business district in a neighbourhood with an identity crisis. Chinatown was a couple blocks to the west and Ryerson University was a block or two in the other direction. On almost every corner, sterile condos rose like anaemic phallic symbols in every former parking lot that had been sold to developers. New Canadians, students and Gen-Xers all merged within these few blocks. The inter-city bus unloaded tourists, runaways, and commuters at the bus depot a block from City Hall. Panhandlers and hot dog vendors staked out the corners nearest the streetcar stops. All in all, it was safe to say that the pinstripe suit crowd doesn't often venture over to this part of downtown, so Dave should have just chilled out.

"Do you or did you frequent similar services in Montréal?" I asked. "Just tell me yes or no."

"I have on occasion. What does this have to do with anything?" His voice was even, but I could tell he was wound up tighter than a G-string on a Stradivarius. I couldn't quite put my finger on him in terms of a male specimen. He wasn't butt-ugly or anything, but he did have bad Einstein eyebrows, wavy salt-and-pepper hair in need of a cut, and a most un-masculine little button nose. He was tall and a little on the lanky side, with bad posture and worse fingernails and a lot of cut-rate dental work. But he was dressed to the nines in a Brooks Brothers suit and good shoes, and his wristwatch turned out to be a Rado.

"You heard about the dead guy at the Camden Suites almost two weeks ago?" I asked.

"I noticed it in the paper. Why?"

"As near as I can figure, he was Mary Carmen's pimp, Gaston." Dave's face paled when I said the name. "He's dead. She's missing. You're the only connection between them."

"Jesus. I had no idea."

"Care to fill me in?"

"I first met her in Montréal. She worked with – "

"With him? More like for him."

"Semantics. Through his, uh, enterprise, I became acquainted with her."

"Then you saw her here, right?"

"Yes. I just thought she made a change. New city. Last time I was in Montréal, I mentioned to him that I'd seen her here. The bastard blackmailed me." Dave's hand shook as he raised his coffee to his lips.

"Good grief!" I said. "I didn't see that coming."

"He made me tell him where she was working. I knew right away that something was wrong, that maybe Mary Carmen was supposed to be with him. Gaston threatened to ruin me professionally if I didn't tell him where to find her here. So I did. I can't risk my career – I'm up for a partnership at my firm. And my fiancée would kill me if she knew I'd played around."

"Hmm."

"I had no idea what the story was with him and her. I thought maybe they were lovers or ex-lovers."

"Of course. What boyfriend wouldn't want to pimp out his girlfriend, right?"

"I didn't think it mattered. He wanted to know where to find her, and I told him. I didn't think it was any big deal."

"Now that he's dead, maybe it's not. Unless you think murder's a big deal?"

Holy shit. So Dave, the horny client who plays hide-the-weenie in Montréal, boinked a gorgeous hooker there who later showed up in Toronto where he's also doing the horizontal boogie for a fee. Son of a gun. Dave's insatiable penis connected Gaston and Mary Carmen here. And Gaston must have had a lot invested in her or he wouldn't have bothered hunting her down.

Damn. Of course, being on the edge of making sense of this angle counted for diddly-squat in terms of determining Mary Carmen's whereabouts.

Even though Dave had tied up a loose end for me, my conversation with him presented me with a new set of questions. I had Gaston's jewellery from the pawnshop. Dave connected Mary Carmen to Gaston and Montréal. The faux Rasta in the pawnshop recognized Mary Carmen's photo, which connected her to the dead guy's jewellery, which only the killer would have had.

Yikes! I had accidentally solved the murder of a scuzzbucket pimp, but I still hadn't found my missing person. And being able to pin a murder on Mary Carmen was useless if no one knew where to find her.

On top of everything else, I knew that I was concealing evidence by not turning over Gaston's watch and rings to the police. I had no idea what to do about any of this, but I wanted first to find Mary Carmen before I made any decisions. Then I'd let the police handle the rest. Really. If I went to the cops now with a solution but no culprit, they might blow me off, or laugh at me, or even ignore me and the open case file, since solving the murder of a pimp is hardly at the top of any cop's to-do list.

Don't get in touch with the boys in blue, Sasha, until you have all the ducks in a row.

Quack, quack.

Wednesday, 11:31 am

Just before lunchtime I was back at the tenement on Carlton Street. I knocked on some doors, hoping I'd catch the tenants I'd missed the other day. Daria, a rather pretty twenty-something, answered right away. I introduced myself and asked about Mary Carmen.

"I know the chick you mean, but I hardly know her," Daria said. "I haven't lived here long and I'm normally not home during the day."

"I just moved here too. I'm from Calgary." Was that where I'd told the other tenants I was from? Shit, I have to keep my lies straight.

"I'm from Windsor. I came here to be an actress, but so far I'm mostly a telemarketer. I go to casting calls and auditions every day it seems, and I sell vinyl siding at night. Sorry, but I'm not around much."

"Well, if you do see Mary Carmen, tell her to drop by my room or call my cell."

Next up was Carrie Jo. I could hear snoring from the other side of the cheap plywood door, so I knocked very loudly.

"Yeah?" came a sleepy voice from the other side of the door.

"My name's Sasha Jackson. I'm a new tenant here. Can I please talk to you for a minute? It's about Mary Carmen."

"One sec. Let me put something on."

Her one sec was quite a bit longer than even the most generous version of one second. When she finally opened the door about ten minutes later, she looked so dishevelled I figured she'd spent the interim catching another forty winks rather than freshening up. Her bloodshot eyes were clearly being punished by the bit of bright sunshine streaming through the naked, filthy window.

"Late night. Sorry. Have a seat."

She indicated the only chair in the room, a lopsided wooden thing identical to the one in my room. Carrie Jo perched on the edge of her unmade bed, legs crossed yoga style. The soles of her feet were dirty and she had some nasty toe jam. In fact, she was pretty ripe all over. Even sitting across from her, I could smell the sour, fetid stench of a hard night's boozing.

"I'm sorry I woke you up. I've been hoping to catch you over the last couple days, but we seem to keep missing each other."

"Have you met Todd yet? The drag queen? I think you're on the same floor as him."

"Yeah, I met him the day I moved in. Why?"

"He's the reason for my late night. Todd's in the hospital. I was with him in the emergency until almost seven this morning."

"What happened?" I asked.

"He got rolled last night after his show. Had the shit kicked out of him."

I immediately wondered if this incident had anything to do with Mary Carmen. She and Todd were both sex workers and they lived in the same rooming house. Could some psycho be choosing victims based on where they lived? Was some nut-bar randomly assaulting hookers? I felt a chill wash over me. Until now I had considered Mary Carmen a runaway. All along I'd been thinking that wherever she'd gone, it was by choice. Now I wasn't so sure. What if she were lying dead in a ditch somewhere?

"Oh my God." I finally said. "Will he be okay?"

Carrie Jo picked at the toe jam and continued. "I hope so. He's still in the hospital. They had to wire his jaw. It got busted in three or four places. And his wrist got broke too. And also his ribs got fractured. They really did a number on him. Poor guy."

"Holy shit. Any idea who did it? Or why?"

"I think it was probably just shitty luck. A lot of hardcore junkies hang out in Allan Gardens late at night. Maybe they were mugging him. Maybe it was some nasty-assed gay bashers. I got no idea."

Gee, and I'd been traipsing around Allan Gardens last night dressed as a hooker. *Yikes!*

"How did you find out?" I asked.

"The guys who found him recognized him from Woody's. The people from Woody's know me and him are good friends. They called 911, and then one of them came and got me. I was just getting home from a night at Cherry Cola's. I was drunk as a skunk and ready for bed when they showed up. We were all in St. Mike's Hospital all bloody night."

I wondered what this latest development had to do

with Mary Carmen's disappearance. It was too freaky to be unrelated.

"God, that's terrible. I hope he'll be okay." Call me Captain Trite.

"Well, he sure as hell won't be singing Cher again for a while," Carrie Jo said.

I was actually sad to hear that, but only in terms of Todd as a performer and not in terms of his repertoire. I was kind of sorry I hadn't popped by his show the night before. Darn.

"Maybe I'll go visit him," I said.

"I don't think there's any point right now. They said they were probably going to do surgery on his jaw."

"Damn."

"I'll keep you posted. Anyhow, why do you want to talk to me?" She rubbed her temples in concentric circles as she spoke. I was more than familiar with that cobwebby hungover feeling, and was glad it was Carrie Jo and not me. I gave her my story about being new in town and about knowing Mary Carmen via a mutual friend.

"As I said, I haven't even met her yet, but she knew from a girl we both know that I was coming to town and it seems weird that I haven't yet connected with her."

"And?"

"Well, our friend, Monique, in Calgary, hasn't heard from her either." I told Carrie Jo about covering Mary Carmen's rent. She seemed impressed at my generosity, or maybe that was a look of incredulity at my stupidity. "Does she go away a lot? Do you know if she was planning a trip?"

"I don't think so. She's usually here almost every day

sometime. I know she works a lot of nights but I still see her mostly every afternoon, at least in passing."

"Can you think of any place she might go on her day off? Any favourite hangouts? I don't want to seem pushy, but Monique's getting worried about Mary Carmen."

"Works at night, some classes in the daytime – she's studying English. She's pretty much gone every morning and never gets back till sometime after lunch. Guess she has a lot of classes. I know she sometimes goes to Urban Nails for a manicure, and church every Sunday. And she usually goes out at night, especially like weekends. That's about it."

"Is she pretty close to the people at the church? She goes to one that offers Mass in Spanish, doesn't she?"

"I guess she might be close to some of them, 'cause, yeah, it's a Spanish congregation," Carrie Jo said.

"Too bad I don't know where her church is. Maybe someone from there knows what's happened to her."

"It's at Keele Street and Rogers Road. I had to show her on a map how to get there. She doesn't know the city very well yet." I could have kissed Carrie Jo right then and there, but the sour stench of alcohol and the dirty feet were off-putting.

Mary Carmen

Maybe the Señora *can help me. Maybe she can get me a plane ticket to home. She is a rich lady. Maybe she will be understanding of my problem, my homesick.*

Tengo miedo.

I say is just for a vacation. I say I am going to go only for two weeks. I tell her I miss my familia. *I hope the rich lady help me,* porque *I don't know what else to do. I have no one.*

Soy sola. Estoy sola. *Alone and afraid.*

Wednesday 2:08 pm

"I hope you can help me," I said to the jolly, rotund priest with the leathery face, hoping he didn't misconstrue my vague request as a plea for eternal salvation.

"Certainly," Father Ramiro said. "Have a seat."

I was kind of disappointed that he hadn't said, "yes, my child." They always do on television.

"I'm an investigator and my current case involves a missing person. She's one of your parishioners, Mary Carmen Ruiz Santamaria, a tall girl, absolutely gorgeous, from Mexico."

"Of course, I know Mary Carmen. Lovely girl, inside and out. You say she's missing?"

"Well, she hasn't been home in almost two weeks, and she hasn't gone to her English classes." She also hasn't been fucking strange men at the cathouse, I thought but didn't say. "No one seems to know where she is, and no one's heard from her."

"And what's your interest in her?"

"I'm kind of doing a favour for a friend, unofficially. Her landlord's a friend of my dad's and she asked me if I could sort of look into things." *Liar, liar pants on fire.*

Can you burn in Hell for fudging the facts with a man of the cloth? Even if it's for a good reason?

"Has she been going to work?" Father Ramiro asked.

"That's the thing. I know she works as a domestic. The landlord told me that. But she doesn't know who her employer is."

"Oh, I can help you with that. Our church set her up with the job. We have a weekly bulletin where people can place ads for jobs, items for sale, or places for rent, that kind of thing. It helps our parishioners. Most are new to Canada and they really need a hand getting settled. Give me a moment and I'll find the name for you."

Hallelujah a thousand times over. I could have kissed Father Ramiro right then and there, but I was pretty sure there was a commandment admonishing "Thou shalt not swap spit with priests" – unless you're an eleven year-old boy. Or something like that.

"Here it is. Mrs. Vivian Maplethorpe, 257 Chester Hill Road. She's not a parishioner here, but she called us a few months ago to place an ad for a part-time housekeeper. She's an elderly woman. I never actually met her, but from what I recall, she said she has trouble getting around, doing housework, and shopping. I believe she said she has arthritis."

"Sounds like a good part-time job for Mary Carmen. A little bit of money, some Canadian work experience." I only said that because I had no idea what else to say.

"Yes, getting that first job in Canada is an overwhelming hurdle for most immigrants. It's tough to get a break, to develop references, to build a work history. Everybody wants to hire people with Canadian experience even for manual labour or domestic jobs."

"As if sweeping, scrubbing toilets, or washing dishes differs much from nation to nation," I said.

We talked a few more minutes about the trials and tribulations of new Canadians, each of us commenting on the unfairness of the system. But at least Canada doesn't have a bunch of Tea Partiers praising the passing of xenophobic Juan Crow legislation. After a few minutes' more chat, Father Ramiro glanced at his watch, and I took the hint.

"Thank you so much for your help, Father Ramiro." I shook his hand and wondered if that was the correct protocol. Maybe I should have curtsied? "I'll get in touch with Mrs. Maplethorpe and see if she's heard from Mary Carmen."

"Please let me know what happens."

I practically danced out of the church and more or less sailed to the bus stop. In a matter of minutes I could, in theory, have all the answers to all my questions. I was heady at the thought of wrapping things up, but my upbeat mood was soon deflated.

The home at 257 Chester Hill Road was a red brick classic Edwardian, circa the 1930s. It was big and beautiful, with a mansard roof, dormer windows and a portico trimmed by a solid balustrade. I'd kill to have a home like this someday, although I must say it needed some imaginative landscaping. The east-facing front yard was nothing more than an expanse of trimmed grass – no shrubbery, bushes, or flowers. I could picture a velvety, mossy rock garden with lush, leafy perennials and some blooms thrown in for a splash of colour.

There was no answer at the home of Mrs. Vivian Maplethorpe. There was no car out front, but there might be one in the garage. I banged on the brass lion's head knocker a couple more times and rang the doorbell ever more insistently. No sign of life.

Maybe Mrs. Maplethorpe was out for an arthritic walk. Maybe she'd gone to the supermarket and was carrying home grocery bags in her gnarled and knotty hands. Maybe Mary Carmen was with her. Maybe they were in the basement and couldn't hear the door.

Maybe, maybe, maybe.

I went to the neighbours on either side and rang their bells. There was no answer at the house on the right, but the woman in the home to the left of Mrs. Maplethorpe's said she hadn't seen her in several days.

"Has her housekeeper been around?"

"The Spanish girl? Yes, I think I've seen her around recently. Why are you asking?"

"I'm an old friend of the family. Mrs. Maplethorpe and my grandmother grew up together. I told Grandma I'd visit Mrs. Maplethorpe when I had a chance this week. She's looking to hire a housekeeper too. We thought maybe Mary Carmen would be interested if she's available." At times it's a little worrisome that I can bullshit so quickly and convincingly. I wonder what that says about my character.

"Well, Vivian might be at bingo. That's about the only place she goes these days, besides doctor's appointments."

"Right, bingo. I forgot about that."

I said goodbye and I walked down the street as if I were leaving the area. I wanted the neighbour lady to forget about me.

Grabbing a coffee at a Starbucks on St. Clair Avenue, I killed some time doing the crossword puzzle in the air-conditioned café. The cool air was a welcome relief from the record-setting heat wave. I absently filled in squares with the wrong letters while I perused my case. On one hand, the Mary Carmen and Todd incidents seemed related, but on the other hand, maybe not. One was gay; the other was straight. One was ethnic; the other wasn't. One was a really hot chick; the other pretended to be. They wouldn't likely share the same kinds of clients. The rooming house could be just a coincidence. After all, not all the tenants there were employed in the sex trade. Maybe an uninvited visit to the Maplethorpe home would give me some answers.

When I finished making a mess of the puzzle – why didn't I use pencil? – and I'd downed my java, I hiked back to the Maplethorpe house. I approached it this time from the next block so I wouldn't walk past the neighbour lady again. I didn't need any witnesses for what I was about to do.

Slipping around the side of the house past the attached garage, I climbed over the cedar fence into the backyard. The back pocket of my white capris got caught on a wayward nail. Damn, there was a five-inch rip in the ass of my pants and my undies showed through. I was annoyed. Guess I should have worn a thong today. The irony is that I usually ruin white clothes within a week of buying them by spilling red wine or spaghetti sauce on them. But these ones had managed to escape being stained so far this summer. Now they were playing peek-a-boo with my panties. On the bright side, though, maybe now I'd finally get a guy to notice me, but hopefully not until after I completed the caper I had at the top of my agenda.

I ducked around to the back and peeked in all the windows. There was still no sign of life. No television blinking away in the family room, no lights on, no radio faintly playing in the background. Nothing. Was I dumb enough to do what I was thinking?

Yes, and the question was merely rhetorical.

I poked around a bit more, checking each of the windows and the patio door. The casement window to the main floor laundry room was amenable to my prying and poking. Within about two minutes, I was sitting on top of the washing machine, feeling as if I were in the spin cycle, listening to my heart wildly beating. I'd made more than an acceptable level of noise on this break-in, so I sat still for a moment, half-expecting someone to run into the room and zap me with a stun gun.

One thousand-and-one, one thousand-and-two, one thousand-and-three. I counted all the way to thirty and listened closely. I didn't hear a sound other than the stubborn up-tempo pulsing of my heart. After another moment, my blood stopped racing and I was fairly certain I was alone in the house. Okay, I'm in and I'm solo and God knows when someone will come home. *Get busy girl and find whatever it is you're looking for.*

I zipped through the living room, dining room and den on the main floor, giving each room a mere cursory glance. Then I hightailed it upstairs. I had a good poke around Vivian's sleeping quarters. The master bedroom was done in French provincial. The furnishings were tasteful and no doubt very expensive, but the room had little personality. The windows were covered in heavy burgundy brocade. The matching burgundy bedspread was neatly in place. There was a walnut chest of drawers with spindly cabriole legs. The jewellery box on top of it was mostly empty. There were a few costume pieces, but nothing of value. *Uh-oh*, that didn't seem to fit.

The bed, in what I assumed was the guest room, was a messy pile of sheets and pillows. Who's been sleeping in this bed? Goldilocks or Mary Carmen? A newish-looking splashy orange-and-yellow summery shirt was draped over a ladder-back chair. A pair of silver-and-turquoise earrings and a hair scrunchie were on the nightstand. A copy of *El Popular*, one of the local Spanish papers, with yesterday's date poked out of the wastebasket. Yesterday's date? It should have been in the recycling bin, but I didn't care. I was certain now that Mary Carmen was holing up here. I skipped the other two bedrooms, since I expected they'd reveal very little.

The bathrooms weren't particularly exciting. The ensuite in the master had a bunch of prescription drugs in the mirrored cabinet above the sink. I didn't recognize the brand names, but guessed they were part of the usual health-care routine for wizened old ladies. Other than that, there were eye drops, Poli-Dent, laxatives and other boring stuff.

I went back downstairs to give the kitchen a thorough look. In just about every home, the kitchen is the room that tells you what's going on in the household, which is why I always save the kitchen for the end of my searches since I know it'll take the longest. If you start in the kitchen, you might not have time to check out other rooms, but doing the other rooms of the house first takes mere minutes because people are so predictable. The top shelf of the master bedroom closet always has the important papers – wills, stock certificates – usually in a shoebox. The bottom drawer of the dresser has the jar of coins. The sock drawer always has a photo or two, plus a few pieces of the more valuable jewellery wrapped up in a pair of argyles tucked into the back (this one didn't). The nightstand has the sex stuff and maybe a rosary – often both, and often in the same drawer (this one had neither). And there is never anything hidden under the mattress except lint and maybe one of those scented dryer sheets.

The kitchen is always a gold mine, though. It's the room people go into first thing when they get home from work, when they get up in the morning, and several times throughout the day. The kitchen is the temporary dumping ground for mail and shopping bags, to-do lists, things that need to be dropped off when you go out. Calendars, appointment cards and reminders are stuck on the fridge with miscellaneous tacky magnets from Disney World.

Vivian's kitchen didn't really seem to match the rest of her house. It had obviously been renovated within the last couple of years, and it was a cold but sleekly modern showpiece. The countertops were granite, the floor was bamboo. There was an oversized stainless steel refrigerator and a chest-styled freezer, also stainless steel, off to the side. There was an island with a gas-burning range top and a wall-mounted oven behind it. A shiny set of stainless steel Lagostina cookware hung on a rack suspended from the ceiling. The pots and pans looked as if they'd never been used. In fact, the whole room looked like it had never been used. Every appliance and gadget appeared to be in mint condition.

There wasn't much food in the fridge. That could have meant the missus was on a trip, but then her neighbour would have probably said so. There was no blinking light on the answering machine attached to the phone on the kitchen counter. I hit redial on the phone and came up with a number I didn't recognize but I wrote it down so I could check it out later. Beside the phone was an address book with a picture of yellow tulips on the cover. I didn't want to spend my time flipping through it now, so I stuck it in my purse.

The oval, oak kitchen table had a bunch of mail scattered on it. Most of the envelopes were unopened – at least until I got my hands on them. There was a statement from an HSBC investment and trading account. Holy shit; the balance was almost half a million dollars, which was about half of what the house was probably worth. The cable bill was due next week. She has the basic cable package – no HBO or Playboy channels for Vivian. That's no fun. Then there was a statement from MasterCard and another from American Express. The balance on the former was $102.87; the balance on the latter $23.46. The only purchases seemed to be from drugstores, and not much else.

A couple of envelopes, one with the federal government logo on the upper left corner, were in the garbage can under the kitchen sink, along with an apple core, some dirty tissues, coffee grinds, and a wad of gum. *Hmm*... an annuity cheque and an old-age pension cheque. The latter is automatically given to those who have reached the golden age, even if they don't need the money. The direct deposit receipt was on the kitchen counter beside a statement from Mrs. Maplethorpe's bank. Last week she had two automatic deposits for her annuity and old-age pension, the first totalling $973.33 and the latter worth $538.76. Not really a lot of money, but for only one person it was plenty, especially if it was in addition to other income or assets. I wondered where her bank books and financial statements were. A quick look around the main floor produced naught. I'd now been in the house about thirty minutes and I didn't want to push my luck any further. I skipped the basement and the garage and got the hell out of there the same way I had come in.

Mary Carmen

"I just don't think it's a good policy to lend money to people, whether they are friends or family or employees." Mrs. Maplethorpe's dentures is loose and she make a funny clacking sound when she is speaking.

"Please, I no have nowhere else to turn. I really miss mí madre, mí familia. *Just a trip for two weeks. Please.* Por favor."

"Tell you what. How about if you earn some additional money rather than my giving you a loan? There's a lot of extra work you can do around here, things I cannot do myself."

"Si, *that is a good idea. I will be happy for some extra work and to earn some extra money."*

The señora *wrote a long list of extra works for me. Clean the basement, clean the attic, clean the garage, do the yard work, paint the bathroom, steam clean the carpets.*

Physical work. Hard work. Chinga.

"You can get all this done in a week or two. Why don't you

book a flight for the end of next week? Does that sound good?"

"Si, Señora *Maplethorpe. Is a fair list. Thank you for this opportunity for to earn some extra money."*

Bitch. Maybe I should have say mí madre *is sick, is* urgente *for me to go to visit her. Selfish rich bitch. Greedy old bitch.*

Wednesday, 6:06 pm

"Aha, you're off tonight," I said when Jessica answered her phone.

"Yes, why? Are we going to get into mischief?"

"Want to join me for a drink and hear about the latest break in my case?"

"I'm in. Where and when?"

"The patio at Café Diplomatico. I'm already here, so hop to it."

"Wow, you really expect people to jump for you, don't you?"

"Yeah, and can you bring me a pair of pants or jeans or something? I had a bit of a mishap and I've kind of been flashing people all afternoon." At least Jessica is only a bit shorter and a bit heavier than I, so clothes from her would be okay for the night, unlike if I were meeting up with Lindsey, who is much shorter and much curvier than I am.

"I don't think I could eat a whole one," Jessica said. "Can we just split it?"

We'd ordered a litre of house white wine and were looking at the menu. Both of us craved a panzerotto stuffed with prosciutto, goat's cheese and Portobello mushrooms, slathered in a robust roasted tomato sauce. The only problem is that the panzerotto at Café Dip are about the size of a football. Even when I'm famished, I can rarely eat the whole thing.

"Want to split a panzerotto and share a Caesar salad with it?" I suggested.

"Perfect."

I filled Jessica in on what I'd learned and what I'd done this afternoon.

"Part of me thinks the Todd and Mary Carmen incidents are related, but part of me doesn't. I'm going to hit the stroll again later tonight and ask around about both of them. Someone must have seen or heard something," I said between bites of the panzerotto.

"Good luck with it, but be careful. Maybe you shouldn't go alone. I can tag along if you want."

"Thanks, but I prefer to go solo. It'll probably be another waste of time, and it would either be boring as hell for you or depressing as hell."

The waitress came by to check on our meals and dropped off some more paper napkins. There's really no elegant way to eat a panzerotto, but there weren't many cute single guys on the patio, so decorum mattered naught."What did you find out when you broke into the house?" Jessica asked as she dabbed a splotch of sauce from her upper lip.

"The last phone call made was to Continental Airlines."

"Sounds like someone's literally getting ready to fly the coop."

"Probably, but I think she'll have a hard time getting out of here," I said.

"What do you mean?"

"Well, her hometown is Torreón in northern Mexico. Assume it was she who called Continental and not Mrs. Maplethorpe. And assume she was looking into booking a flight, and assume the destination was Torreón."

"Okay, I'm assuming all of the above."

"Well, all the Continental flights between Toronto and Torreón connect in Houston, Texas. American Airlines makes the connection in Dallas. I'm ninety-nine percent sure Mary Carmen doesn't have a passport. You can't cross a border these days without one. Especially not if you're going through the United States."

"Is there no way she can fly there directly? What about a charter flight?"

"No charters."

"How the hell do you know all this? Is your brain hard-wired to the Travelocity website or something?"

"No," I said. "I learned about flights there the old-fashioned way. I stopped by a travel agency on my way here."

"Aha. Elementary, my dear Watson."

"Yup. Almost every option the travel agent looked into makes a connection somewhere in the U.S. Besides, even with the flights that don't have a connection via the States, like the Air Canada routing via Mexico City, you still can't get on a plane these days without documentation. I'm unsure about the whole customs and immigration thing, but Mary Carmen might need to show a tourist visa or something when she leaves

Canada, and I doubt she has that. I know Mexicans need visas to come in to Canada, but I'm not sure if they need it upon departure."

"Wow, you've covered a lot of ground in a short time. Good for you."

"Well, there's a bit more, but I can't say anything about it just yet."

The empty jewellery box at Casa de Maplethorpe was really bothering me, especially in light of the conversations I'd had with the various pawnbrokers. Nevertheless, I considered the day a victory of sorts. In less than a week, I had scored a major lead and more than a few breaks on my missing person case. I had also pretty much figured out a murder and was on the verge of taking the whole package to the police. As well, I was confident that within a day or two I'd see Mary Carmen face-to-face. I had a feeling she was getting ready to leave town, but my gut told me she wasn't going anywhere immediately.

The waitress cleared our plates and offered dessert menus.

"No thanks, I'm stuffed," Jessica said.

"Maybe a coffee or another drink?" our server asked. Before I could answer, my cell bleeped to life.

"What are you up to?" Mick asked. I kind of wish I'd looked at caller ID before picking up. There once was a time when seeing Mick's number on my call display would have brought a smile to my eyes and butterflies to my tummy. But after two years of a heaven-and-hell relationship, I was now apprehensive whenever I had anything to do with him. And besides, last night I'd had the female equivalent of a wet dream, starring none other than Derek Armstrong, the lawyer. I'd woken up this morning with a strange case of afterglow and a craving for a post-coital cigarette.

I have no doubt that Mick loved me when we were a couple, and that in a way he still loves me. I have no doubt his intentions were always the best. But we are either just too different or maybe just too much alike to be romantically involved. It had taken several teary break-ups and just as many passionate but short-lived reconciliations to finally muster the resolve to say "no more." That happened about two years ago, and since then I had avoided seeing him whenever and wherever possible.

Then, back in the spring when I was tracking down a serial killer, Mick had come through for me, stood by me, and selflessly helped me, even to the point where he had put himself at peripheral but considerable risk, although I'm the one who ended up getting shot.

He'd been in the hospital room with my family when I regained consciousness. I remembered being happy to see him there. During my recuperation, he'd practically waited on me hand and foot. But as I got better I started putting some distance between us. I had started to feel myself slipping into comfortable, old, familiar patterns, and I knew where they would eventually lead.

"I'm on a patio with Jessica," I told Mick now. "Just finished a delicious dinner and debating what to do next."

"How about hopping in a cab and coming to Brad's place? We're doing an impromptu jam session tonight and want you here."

"This is really a rehearsal for that reunion gig you told me about, isn't it?"

"More or less."

"I didn't agree to the gig yet."

"I realize that. But you know you're going to."

"Damn you. I can't make a late night of it, though. I have to do some work later tonight."

"No worries. Just come by for a bit and leave when you have to."

"I'll be bringing Jessica with me. She can pretend she's a groupie. Is Cole still single?"

Wednesday, 8:50 pm

Brad lives in a super-funky old loft in what used to be a cookie factory on Sauroren Avenue in Toronto's west end. At times I am convinced that I can smell chocolate chip cookies almost ready to come out of the oven.

His pad is huge, and as a bachelor and a musician, Brad lets his home reflect his passions and his personality. There's nary a domestic or homey touch in the place – no bric-a-brac, no family photos, no plants. The fridge rarely has anything in it but beer, and there's a fifty-fifty chance as to whether or not there would be toilet paper in the washroom. Every potential girlfriend who saw this place must surely have projected ahead to customized window coverings, decorative throw rugs, and scented votive candles.

Every musician who saw the place turned green with envy. The living room was a state-of-the-art recording studio and rehearsal space. There were mixers, equalizers, headphones, consoles and reel-to-reel recorders. There were stands with acoustic and electric guitars and basses, and even a beat-up old banjo. A warped metal shelf had just about every kind of small instrument on it: maracas, castanets, a flute, two tambourines (they made me think of Terra), some triangles, a cowbell and a collection of harmonicas. Propped next to the shelf, he even has a didgeridoo which I've never seen Brad or anyone else play.

If I were even a bit materialistic, I'd have thrown myself right at Brad solely for the purpose of being closer to all his equipment, and I don't mean equipment euphemistically. However, I'm not quite that shallow, and besides, I know better than to ever again get involved with a band mate. Also, Brad's girlfriend du jour might have objected.

Brad's drums were set up in the middle of the room. Mick was plugged into his Marshall amp and Cole was hooked up to a new five-hundred-watt, twelve-band Peavy. The microphone stand was forlornly waiting for me to make use of it.

"Have you guys given much thought to your set list yet?" Jessica asked.

"It's a reunion gig for the class of '89, so we'll be doing the top of the charts from back then," Mick said.

"But no Milli Vanilli," Brad said.

"Too bad," I said. "I really liked those songs regardless of who actually sang them."

"So that means glam rock and hair bands," Jessica said.

"And we'll throw in some of our originals, too," Cole added.

For the next two hours Jessica drank beer and tapped her foot to the music as we plugged our way through Poison, Bon Jovi, The B-52s, Aerosmith, Guns N' Roses, Tone Loc, Extreme, Def Leppard, Fine Young Cannibals and more Bon Jovi.

"I can't believe I still remember all the words to any of those songs," I said. "I feel like I'm stuck in a time warp."

We were taking a break. I can only go a couple of hours before my voice starts to feel worn out, and I know the guys wanted to give their hands a rest.

"How many people do you expect at this gig?" Jessica asked Mick.

"Maybe three or four hundred. The party's open to anyone who graduated between 1988 and 1990. And some of them will bring their spouses or dates, although I can't imagine anything more boring than attending someone else's high school reunion."

"But it's okay for me to sing at it?" I asked.

"Of course."

Cole went to the fridge to grab a few beers. "Who's ready for another?"

"Count me out," I said. "I have to go to work in a little while." I had too much going on to allow tonight to tailspin into an "alcoholocaust", which was an all-too-frequent outcome of any get-together among us.

"I'll have one," Jessica said. I took that as a cue to move down the couch away from Jessica so Cole would have to sit next to her when he returned.

"Do you have any gum?" Jessica asked me. "That Caesar salad was way too bloody garlicky."

"No gum, but here's an Altoid. Actually, keep the pack."

We sat around and shot the shit for a little while.

The guys entertained us with exaggerated tales of their goofy high school exploits.

"I still laugh whenever I think of the black shoe polish on the mouthpieces of all the horns in music class," Cole said.

"I had to do something to liven things up," Mick said. "Mr. Goebel was dull as dishwater and probably turned a lot of kids off music." He switched to a deep, glottal German accent. 'Vun-two-three-four, vun-two-three-four. *Fo*cus, people, *fo*cus.' Mr. Goebel had no soul, no creativity. He was clearly in the wrong job. Should've been a math teacher."

"Well, the nerds in the marching band didn't find the shoe polish gag very funny," Brad said. "Every single one of them had a shiny black stain around his mouth. It took a few days to wash off."

"You were in the marching band, weren't you Brad?" I asked.

"Yup."

"Nerd," I said.

I got up to help myself to a glass of water. Cole moved a bit closer to Jessica while I was in the kitchen. She surreptitiously gave me a thumbs-up. Good. Mission underway, if not yet accomplished.

Brad's current squeeze, Cheyenne, showed up a few minutes later, and suddenly the dynamics in the room changed from a group of friends hanging out to three *couples. Uh-oh.* Cheyenne was sitting on the arm of the chair where Brad was holding forth, talking about hanging out at the local drive-in theatre during his teen years. "We always had a scam. Someone always got in free, either by crawling under the fence or by hiding in the trunk."

"You did that with me once," Mick said. "I really didn't think you were going to let me out."

"I shouldn't have," Brad said. "I could've had a better chance at scoring with the girls if I'd left you in the trunk."

Cole's hand was now on Jessica's knee. I was tired of standing, so I moved over to the loveseat and Mick immediately slid into the empty seat beside me. The awkwardness was palpable to me, if not to him. Mick tried to put his arm around me, but I faked a coughing fit and stood to leave.

"Are you sure you don't want to hang around a while longer?" Mick asked. "The night's still young."

"No. I really do have to get to work."

"It's almost midnight."

"I thought you just said the night's still young."

"I meant from a social perspective. Anyway, do you really think you're going to get much work done?"

"This is actually the perfect time for me to hit the streets. The hookers will all be out and about now. I have to see if any of them can tell me anything about Todd or Mary Carmen."

"Sure you wouldn't rather come to my place?"

"I'd love to, but I can't. My client's anxious for an update."

"Too bad. It's been fun hanging out with you again. I've missed you." Mick leaned forward to kiss me and I launched into another hacking fit. *No, no, no, no! Don't play with fire, Sasha.*

"You'd better not," I said. "I think I'm coming down with a cold." I bloody well knew he saw right through me.

"Alright," Mick said. "I'd give you a ride downtown,

but I've had too many drinks."

"No problem. I'll hop in a taxi."

During the ride to Church Street, I kicked myself and almost told the driver to turn back. Behave Sasha. Behave. *You're just pumped after a good jam session.*

Yes, Mick is sexy, but he's toxic. Don't go there.

Thursday, July 23, 12:12 am

My objective for tonight's misadventure was she-males and trannies. I had to find out if there was any connection between Todd and Mary Carmen even though my gut told me there wasn't. However, the chicks with dicks might offer leads I hadn't yet considered.

The first gender-bending hooker I approached looked like a young Elizabeth Taylor with a five o'clock shadow and a prominent Adam's apple.

"Of course, I know Todd. Isn't it terrible what happened to him?"

"Yeah, and that's why I'm asking around. I'm an investigator and I've been hired to find a missing hooker who lives in the same rooming house as Todd." I gave Miss Taylor my business card.

"Well, Todd's not missing."

"I know, but he was found beaten to a pulp in the park. Maybe my girl was beaten up too, and left somewhere, and hasn't been found yet."

"I see," the she-male said.

"So what's the word on the street? Have any of your, uh, colleagues been assaulted or harassed?"

"It happens from time to time, but there really hasn't been anything lately. Nothing of concern, you know? The worst is a client who gets serviced and then doesn't want to pay, but that happens sometimes, and what can you do? You get used to it." La Liz was eyeballing a compact mirror while she spoke with me. She smoothed her raven hair and touched up her pearlized lipstick.

"Is it likely your colleagues would hear the gossip from the straight girls?"

"The sex trade in this town's a pretty small network. People play on both teams; people switch teams; people team-up. So, yeah, we'd hear about it if someone was targeting hookers. Word travels." Miss Taylor added a coat of clear lip gloss over her crimson lip colour.

"And what's the word on Todd?" I asked.

"As far as I know, he did the drag show last night, had a few drinks, and then hit the streets looking for a score."

"Did anyone see him with a client or anything?"

"Not as far as I've heard, but you might want to walk down to The Corral and ask the folks around there. Todd was pretty popular with the leather crowd."

"Thanks."

The Corral is a pretty rough country and western bar that would best be described as heaven for a sado-masochistic, gay Marlboro Man. The outside is rough-hewn wood with a sign painted like the kind seen on ranches in the Old West. There's a wide set of bull's horns over the doorway, and a few nasty-looking dudes in leather chaps were having a smoke out front. I have never before approached a cluster of tough-looking gay men, so I decided to be ballsy.

"Hi guys. My name's Sasha. I'm an investigator working on a case involving a missing hooker. My case might relate to the guy who got beat up last night in Allan Gardens, a transvestite working the stroll." I paused to see if there was any reaction and was greeted by stony silence and undisguised disinterest. "His name's Todd. He looks like Cher. He's in the *Divas in Drag* show at Woody's every week." Two of the guys flicked their cigarette butts onto the ground and went back inside without even acknowledging me. A third shrugged and followed the other two.

"Yeah, I heard about it," said a guy wearing a leather vest and faded Levis. "Whaddaya wanna know?"

He didn't have a shirt beneath the vest, and I could see that both nipples were pierced. Ouch. He was holding hands with a balding, older guy dressed in red from head-to-toe, right down to his red snakeskin boots and belt.

"I'd love to know if Todd's beating was just a case of wrong place, wrong time, or if it was an angry customer, or..." I left the question hanging.

"I've seen the Cher queen around a few times," Leather Vest's boyfriend said.

"What about Tuesday night?" I asked.

"Sorry. We weren't around that night. Dinner party at home."

"Well, if you hear anything, please give me a call."

I continued my pointless perambulations for another half-hour and then gave up. The she-males had nothing new to add, nor did the straight hos on the next street. The heat was getting to me, my feet were sore again, and I was beyond tired. I walked a block south and caught the Gerrard streetcar.

When I arrived home, I was exhausted and didn't even bother brushing my teeth. I climbed right into bed, alone once again, and wished more than anything that Mick was beside me. When I finally drifted off to sleep, though, I had another very vivid and very erotic dream about Derek Armstrong.

Mary Carmen

I need some time to get organizada. *Maybe an extra week of waiting and an extra week of work is not so bad. I must get my* pasaporte. *The* bastardo *Gaston took it from me in Montréal, and I will never see it again.* Hijo de puta.

I was washing the draperies when the señora *came into the laundry room.*

"We need to discuss room and board. If you plan to live here all this week and part of next, then we need to adjust your pay to reflect meals and lodging."

Is this chingado *woman crazy? Is this* pinche *woman making a joke with me?*

"Whatever you decide is fine with me, Señora *Maplethorpe."*

"I think ten dollars a day for food and ten dollars a day for sleeping quarters is fair. Are you agreeable to that? I assume it will be for seven days at least."

"Is fine with me, señora.*" What choice do I have? She has the control. She has the money. I hate this* pinche *fucking place.* Chinga. *Get me out of here and back to Mexico.*

Get me back to my home. "Is only one thing I worry about, señora. *I need some time to go to* El Consulado Mexicano. *I must have a new* pasaporte. *Mine is lost.* Perdido."

"Sure, I understand. Just keep track of the time you're off duty and we can adjust your wages."

Thursday, 11:05 am

Well, there she is. She's even more beautiful in person than in the photo from Candace. Mary Carmen opened the door just enough to reach into the mailbox and scoop up the day's delivery. My case could have, and probably should have, officially ended right then and there. I had found the missing girl. By all appearances, she was alive and well.

The fact that she was alive and well made me rule out a connection between her situation and Todd's. She didn't seem beaten, bruised, or broken. So what did the assault on Todd have to do with this case, if anything? I couldn't spend too much time thinking about that. My client was paying me to find Mary Carmen. Candace probably had no interest in Todd, especially if his story was unrelated, but I'm getting a bit ahead of myself.

Most of the dumb things I do seem even dumber in retrospect, like yesterday's break-in. It was foolish to have done that in broad daylight, and stupid to do it so impulsively. Most of the dumb things I do are generally harmless, only occasionally risk of long-term damage, and are rarely inherently dangerous. On the "Dumb Things I've Done" scale, this morning's action was only about a four or a five, so it really wasn't so bad. Not like yesterday's break-in caper, which I'd rate as a nine-plus on the Dumb-o-Meter.

Once I had the address and name, it had been easy to look up Vivian Maplethorpe's phone number, which the priest had neglected to give me. I'd called the Maplethorpe house a couple of times yesterday evening, and again a few times this morning. No answer. So the next step, of course, was to keep an eye on the house and see when or if Mary Carmen or the Matron emerged.

Surveillance sucks. It's boring. It's like reading a vegetarian cookbook just for the prose. Surveillance is usually a waste of time. It's hard to do covertly. It's hard to stay awake. And it's one of the reasons I try to avoid missing persons or cheating spouse cases, since both of those almost automatically mean surveillance work.

If the investigating life was anything like big-budget Hollywood movies, there would be a team of operatives renting the house across the street from the object of their surveillance. Some more operatives would be disguised as telephone or cable repair men, and there would be a couple of guys in stiff blue-collar uniforms pretending they were from the gas company or the city's road maintenance crew.

On a TV detective show, surveillance usually means a lonely investigator sitting in a parked car across the street from the subject. He goes to the location armed with a Thermos of coffee to help stay awake, and he usually brings along a milk bottle to pee into when his bladder can't hold any more of the rancid java he's been sipping on all night.

Aye, there's the rub. The parked car, that is, not the milk bottle, though, really, how easy is it for a woman to aim into one of those?

I don't have a car and I don't exactly drive. I think I can figure out how to drive, but that's an assumption based on many hours observing others behind the wheel. I'm sure driving ability requires a degree of hands-on experience, but I had nothing else to go on, so I just hoped I wouldn't mix up the gas pedal and the brake.

The gas pedal is on the right, yes?

Shane was still sound asleep when I decided to steal Dad's car out of the graffiti garage. I'm sure he would have brained me if he'd known what I was doing. At least Dad's four-door sedan was generic enough for surveillance. I was kind of surprised at myself for never having thought to do this before. I drove very slowly and very cautiously to Forest Hill. I signalled with every turn, obeyed every stop sign, stayed a few clicks under the speed limit, and took my time getting there. Now I was parked about three houses down from where Mary Carmen was staying and I was bored stiff. *Veni, vidi, Velcro. I came, I saw, I stuck around.*

I'd now been watching the house since just after nine o'clock. Montessori moms in yoga pants had walked their precious little angels to school. A cyclist had zoomed by. A few cars had pulled out of their driveways, and one or two had returned home laden with grocery bags. *Boring, boring, boring.* I read the paper, guzzled two coffees, and now had to go pee, and my MP3 player was just about out of juice.

After seeing Mary Carmen check the mailbox and

go right back inside, I should have gone straight to Candace and wrapped up the case. But I didn't. I couldn't. My interest now was mostly personal, mostly curiosity, and mostly an obsessive desire to tie up all the loose ends. I had no intention of billing Candace for any more of my time, but I had to piece everything together. Why was Mary Carmen in this house? How come she hadn't said goodbye to the bordello folks? Why had she taken-off from the rooming house without bringing her stuff? What did she have to do with the dead pimp, besides everything? Where was Vivian Maplethorpe? I was so lost in thought that I damn near jumped out of my skin when my cellphone twittered to life.

"You'll never guess what's happened," Jake, the perky blond bordello receptionist, said. "I'm still in shock."

"About Mary Carmen?" I was momentarily confused. I was sure Mary Carmen was still in the house. Of course, she could have left by the back.

"No. It's Candace. She was shot."

"Oh, my God! What? How? When? Is she okay?"

"Yeah, maybe, I don't know. She's in the hospital, in intensive care."

"How did it happen? Where was she shot?"

"At the house, the bordello," Jake said.

"No, I mean, where on her body, oh, God—"

"She was shot in the shoulder and somewhere low, like the pelvic area. I dunno where exactly, but thank Christ it wasn't in some vital organ, like her heart or something, you know?"

"Do they think she'll make it?" I asked.

"I think so. She's at St. Michael's Hospital."

It struck me as conveniently coincidental – and

coincidentally convenient – that she was in the same hospital as Todd, the beaten-up drag queen. At least I could make a two-for-one visit.

"How did you find out?" I asked Jake.

"I had an outcall last night that lasted until almost four this morning. I was on my way back to my apartment when I realized I'd left my house keys at the bordello. So I had the cab driver make a detour. When I got to the bordello, the front door was open and I knew right away something was wrong."

"Jesus."

"Candace was in the billiard room, sprawled out face down on the pool table, covered in blood. I heard someone run out through the back door, but Candace was lying there bleeding."

I have no idea why I focused on the trivial, but my first thought when I heard that was that the bloodstains would never come out of the green baize table covering.

"My God," I murmured.

"Yeah, I checked to see if she was breathing and I thought about getting a compress to stop the blood, but there was just too much. She was moaning, so I called 911."

"That's horrible. I can't believe it. How did it happen? Who do you think did it?"

"I have no idea. I didn't see the guy. At least I think it was a guy. The glass was smashed on the gun cabinet. The gun was left right there on the table, next to the cue ball."

Fuck! The cops would be all over the bordello now. I had to think about how I'd move forward with Mary Carmen and the dead pimp. Maybe it was time to hand it all over to the Boys-in-Blue. Did Mary Carmen go to the bordello late last night and try to kill her erstwhile madam?

"So Candace was there alone?" I asked. "There was no one else on duty?"

"Not that late at night, they were all gone home by then. Besides, last night wasn't very busy."

"Did the cops take your statement?"

"Yeah. I talked with some guy in a uniform until about eight this morning."

"How did you explain the house?"

"I said what Candace told us to say when we get hired. If ever there's a problem, we stick to the story that the place is a bed and breakfast. Fuck, do you think the heat's going to be on us?"

I didn't think for a minute that the cops were dumb enough to believe the bed and breakfast claim. Not a chance.

"Did you tell them about Mary Carmen's disappearance?" The fact that I had just seen her didn't need to be mentioned at the moment.

"No. I really tried to tell them as little as I could. I don't need them charging me with anything, you know?"

"I think all of you girls are on an unexpected vacation as of right now."

"You don't have to tell me twice. I've already called a couple of the other girls."

"Who have you talked to?"

"Terra, Tonya, Michelle, Dawn, Liz, and Nancy. I left voice mails for the others."

"Good. Was there any other damage besides the gun cabinet?"

"Yeah, the computer at the front desk was smashed. Actually, the whole desk was trashed. The drawers were emptied; papers were tossed all over the place. The computer screen was on the floor in a bunch of pieces, and the box with all the discs in it was gone."

"Holy fuck! Listen, I'm going to need to talk to you girls. This is getting way too fucked up. Do you feel like calling your co-workers again and arranging for us to meet?"

"Sure. When and where?"

"How about four o'clock this afternoon at my office?" I gave her directions. "Try to round up as many of them as you can."

Jake said she'd do her best, then hung up.

My instincts told me that Mary Carmen probably wasn't the culprit. From what I'd learned and surmised, she had killed Gaston in self-defence or justifiable something or other. But, I couldn't think of any reason for her to try to kill Candace. If anything, the madam was probably more useful to her alive than dead.

So then who did it and why? How does this relate to Mary Carmen? Or does it? The obvious guess was a burglar, but I didn't think so. From what I'd heard, there wasn't enough stolen to pin it on a burglary gone wrong. The missing discs told me it was client related, not staff related. From what I'd learned of the bordello set-up, none of the girls would resort to violence to get client info, since they all had access to it when they worked the front desk. By deduction, I figured it was a client, and by further deduction, I was ready to put my money on Dave. He'd been blackmailed once by Gaston, and who knows what else might be going on in his head? Given his position and his fiancée, he certainly wouldn't want his name to come to light in any of this. Would he resort to violence to protect his reputation?

I decided to give up on surveillance. It seemed unproductive to be hiding in a parked car. Besides, I really had to pee. I hit the ignition and headed back towards my end of the city. Briefly, I wondered if Dad would notice the miles on the odometer, not that I'd driven very far. I must have been on nervous autopilot, because in no time at all I found myself doing what could generously be called parallel parking a couple blocks down the street from the cathouse. I nudged backwards and forwards several times until I was more or less in place, although the rear tire was up on the sidewalk. Oh, well.

A Toronto Police car was parked directly opposite the house. I knew – despite my hopes – that the cop in the unmarked sedan wasn't Mark Houghton. That would have been too perfect. The Asian officer sitting in the driver's seat was sipping a coffee and eating a doughnut. Thank goodness I can always count on clichés. A small crowd of cops and gawkers were milling around out front. The house had been sealed off with yellow crime scene tape. I stood next to the cluster of the curious and eavesdropped on their gossip and speculation. None of it was useful. I desperately wanted to get inside the house, but couldn't even contemplate it for now. Damn.

Gently, I edged the car out of its spot and drove south. Several other drivers blared their horns at me each time I had to make a left turn. Next time, I'd avoid the stress and just make three rights. My destination was St. Michael's Hospital. Luckily, I found a pay parking lot nearby, so I didn't have to fake my way through parallel parking again. I stopped at the gift shop near the entrance and bought two bouquets of the least browned and wilted flowers I could find.

"These will make a lovely bouquet together," said the matronly cashier, who looked like she should be hosting a cooking show rather than ringing up sales for people visiting sick friends.

"Actually, I'm visiting two separate people. They don't know each other, but both ended up here in the last couple of days."

"I hope they each recover quickly. Did you want to pick out a couple of get well cards too?"

The elevator doors opened right onto the nurses' station on Candace's floor. A hostile Amazonian nurse at the helm, whose name-tag ironically said she was Felicity La Joie, was adamant about not letting in any visitors.

"The patient is resting. She's still very weak. Only immediate family are permitted in, and at that they can only stay for five minutes at a time." The woman's brassy orange hair was so tightly pulled back into a bun that her face looked as if she'd gone too far with Botox injections.

"I told you, she's my cousin," I said.

"Uh huh."

"Well, has anyone else come to see her?"

"Not so far."

"That's because I'm the only relative she has in town. Please let me at least pop in for a moment to drop off the flowers."

"I really shouldn't."

"I just want to see her so I can tell her parents she'll be okay. They live far away. In Ohio." Couldn't I have said Paris or Hawaii? If I'm going to lie, I might as well be sexy and exotic about it.

"Of course they do. Okay. Five minutes." She made an obviously painful attempt at a weak smile, and I thought her face would crack from the effort.

Candace was out cold. The window blinds were drawn and the room was chilly. I set the flowers on the nightstand, dug through my purse, and found a pen. Then I scribbled a message on the card I'd picked up in the gift shop. What does one say to an HIV-positive madam who has been shot? *Pip, pip, darling, chin-up, it's not so bad. You'll be right as rain in no time.* I wrote a generic "get well soon" message and signed the card from "the girls".

The woman at the nurses' station on Todd's floor was much friendlier than Krusty the Krankenschwester downstairs. The wholesome little nightingale's name-tag said she was Edna Schwartz, which seemed more suited to the battle-axe on Candace's floor.

She beamed at me. "You can go in, but don't expect much. He can't talk yet."

"I understand. I just want to see him, even for a minute."

"Room six-fifty, end of the hall."

When I entered Todd's room, I said, "So, I guess we won't be singing a duet anytime soon, eh, Todd?"

"Ummphh." I took that as a no.

I really felt sorry for the guy. He looked like absolute hell. His eyes were drawn and vacant, his jaw was a mottled blend of purple and yellow, and he seemed wholly uncomfortable draped in a blue hospital gown and propped up on the hypoallergenic hospital pillows.

"Too bad. I had my heart set on us doing "I Got You, Babe," although I must admit I'm not thrilled about singing the Sonny Bono part."

"Ummphth."

"I don't want to tire you out, so just listen, okay?"

"Ummgth."

"I'm not really a friend of Mary Carmen's. I'm a private investigator." I gave Todd the whole story, and he grunted now and then in acknowledgement. I filled him in on everything, right up to seeing Mary Carmen this morning, and to Candace being shot and ending up in St. Mike's, too. I figured, since he couldn't talk, that there was no risk in being completely upfront with him. He wasn't in any position to spill my secrets, such as they were.

"I have to wrap up a bunch of loose ends on this case, and I think you can help. I need to rule out a few things, okay?"

"Unnph."

"How about if you blink once for a no and twice for a yes?"

He blinked twice.

"Did you recognize whoever it was that beat you up?"

One blink. No.

"Was it a client?"

One blink.

"Did the beating take place right there at Allan Gardens?"

Two blinks. Yes.

"Were you trying to score when it happened?"

No reply. Hmm, try a new line of inquiry.

"Did you and Mary Carmen ever work together?"

One blink.

"Did you ever have any of the same clients?"

One blink.

"Do you work for a pimp?"

Another no.

"Do you think what happened to you had anything to do with what happened to her?"

One blink.

"Do you know any of the people from the bordello where Mary Carmen works?"

One blink.

"Was Mary Carmen relatively happy with her job at the bordello?"

He blinked yes.

I wanted to ask some more questions, but Todd seemed to be fading.

"Get some rest. I'll visit again soon."

Thursday, 3:41 pm

I left Dad's car in the parking lot by the hospital and walked the few short blocks to my office. Jake-Jackie and Terra were already waiting out front for me. Terra had her little schnorkie, Daisy, with her. We were silent as we entered the building, though, of course, I had a lot I wanted to say. However, I preferred to wait until I had the whole captive audience.

"Who else is coming?" I asked.

"Nancy and Michelle, for sure," Jake said. "Tonya said maybe. Maxine can't come, and I left voice mails for the rest of the girls."

"I don't have enough chairs."

"I don't think that'll really matter. We can sit on the floor."

"I didn't think this through very well. Besides not having enough seats, I can't offer anyone a drink. I don't even have a coffee maker here yet."

"I can do a coffee run if you'd like," Jake offered.

"Thank you." I opened my purse to hand her some money.

"Please. It's on me."

Jake and Terra left Daisy with me and went out for java while I tried to collect my thoughts. Ideas and conclusions were still floating randomly around my brain when a couple more girls showed up.

"We'll get started when Jake and Terra get back," I said, just as Terra opened my office door. We all busied ourselves for a moment, opening paper envelopes of sugar and stirring in cream. Daisy got excited by all the new faces and had a poop on my carpet, which seemed somewhat metaphoric. "Okay, girls, you all have to promise to be frank with me," I said. "I mean it. Candace has been shot, and one of you could be next, so don't bullshit me."

There was a round of murmurs in agreement.

"Have any of you had a bad date lately?"

No's all around.

"Do any of you take on any side work, any clients off the books, any freelancing?"

There were a couple of uncomfortable looks, but everyone answered in the negative.

"Whoever broke into the bordello wanted one thing and one thing only – the client records. That could mean a john is trying to cover his tracks, or it could mean someone's planning to do some blackmailing."

"Holy shit!" Michelle said.

"I never thought of that," said the girl I'd seen on my first visit, the brunette in fishnets whose name was Nancy.

"Well," I continued, "the records that went missing have info on all the clients. Anyone getting their hands on that could have a field day."

"What do you mean?" Terra asked.

"Like I said, blackmail. Anyone wanting those records kept secret might go to great lengths to do so. So don't bullshit me. Have any of you kept copies?"

"No."

"Uh-uh."

"I wouldn't dream of it."

"Do any of you have clients who've seemed nervous lately?" I asked. "Have any of you been threatened?"

Once again, they all said no. Between Todd and the hookers, no seemed to be the word of the day.

"There's a lot of nice stuff in that house, a lot of valuables," I said. "If it were just a burglary, a lot more would've been taken."

"I agree," Maxine said.

"Who was on reception last night?" I asked.

"Tonya," Jake answered.

"How come she isn't here now?" I asked.

"I dunno. I told her we were meeting, and she said she'd try to come."

Thursday, 6:58 pm

I was lying naked on my bed at home, deep in thought about what had happened to Candace and Todd. The air conditioner was still on the fritz and the humidity was making my already stressed-out and anxiously cranky self even more stressed-out and more anxiously cranky. I couldn't stop thinking about Candace and Mary Carmen and Todd and Gaston and Terra and Dave and the rest of the crew I'd met during this case.

All the connections and coincidences I'd encountered along the way made me uncomfortable. Seemingly insignificant, incidental details had directly or indirectly led to a murder and an attempted murder. All these apparently unrelated things had converged in an ugly, bloody mess and I was unsure what to do next. Son of a bitch. What other inconsequential details would unfold to yield such horrible results? What other non-starters would become ends, dead ends, or at least severely beaten ends?

I was also starting to obsess about Mary Carmen's boss at her housekeeping job. My gut told me that Vivian Maplethorpe wasn't out of town. My gut told me that something had happened to her, and despite the temperature, I felt a chill run through me. Arthritic old ladies don't just take off during a heat wave. And part-time housekeepers don't just make themselves at home in their place of employment. It seemed odd that Mary Carmen was on the premises when the old lady wasn't.

I had to come up with a better plan for tomorrow, but I dismissed each idea as soon as it came to me.

I wasn't thrilled at the prospect of spending another day sitting in a parked car slowly going mad, but what alternatives were there? It also occurred to me that perhaps it was a good thing Mary Carmen hadn't ventured out today, since, if she had, I would have needed to figure out a way to tail her. My driving skills were sub-par enough to know I wouldn't have been able to discreetly zigzag in and out of traffic. More importantly, what would I have done if she'd headed for the subway?

The shooting still weighed heavily on my grey matter. I was certain Dave had done it, but I couldn't prove it. Maybe that was the one thread I would just have to let go and have the boys in blue take over. I had enough to deal with. I was just about to pick up the phone to call Mark Houghton when my cellphone bleeped me out of my frustrated reverie.

Derek Armstrong.

Ah, if anyone or anything could lift me out of my funk, it was he.

"Can you have a late dinner with me? I need to talk to you."

"Absolutely," I said. "What did you have in mind?"

"Do you know Le Paradis? It's on Bedford Road."

"One of my favourite places. I'm a sucker for their *confit de canard.* What time should I meet you there?"

"*Confit de canard.* Classy. How about if I pick you up at eight-thirty?"

"I'll be ready." I gave him my address and jumped into the shower.

I lathered up with lemon-mint body wash and smoothed some honeydew body oil over my freshly shaved legs. I had no idea if tonight's dinner was business or pleasure, and I couldn't decide what to wear. Four dresses were tried on, accessorized, then taken off and tossed onto the bed. Finally, I let the weather choose my outfit for me. I slipped into a buttercup-coloured linen sundress with a halter neckline and a tapered waist, touched up my toenail polish, and donned my favourite pair of sandals. My hair was out of control thanks to the humidity, so I pinned it up in a loose knot. A pair of dangling silver earrings completed the look, and I was ready for anything when the doorbell rang promptly at eight-thirty.

Thursday, 9:31 pm

"How about another bottle of Les Chailles?" Derek said to the waiter. It was a medium bodied Syrah-Grenache blend with a bold cherry undertone and a light finish. We had sucked back the first bottle a bit too quickly to do it justice.

"Certainly, monsieur."

We'd worked our way through a plate of mussels Provençal and a decadent order of pâté de foie gras. Derek was clearly enjoying his main course – veal kidneys with fresh herbs in a port sauce. I had decided to forgo my usual duck in favour of trying a new dish. The braised lamb shanks were delicious, but after the appetizers, I didn't think I'd be able to finish the meal.

The conversation was even better than the food. Derek entertained me with stories of shit disturbing pranks during his university days.

"The neighbours started it, a house full of giddy girls in first year. It probably began as a weak attempt at flirtation. They put a FOR SALE sign on our front lawn. We got back by putting them on ultra-right-wing mailing lists. That kind of stuff. Mostly harmless, mostly clever. Back and forth."

"You're a brat," I said. "Sexy as hell, but still a brat."

"Well, the prank war with the neighbours came to a halt when we did the ice sculptures."

"I'm afraid to ask."

"It was winter, and they had a bunch of clothes out on the line to dry, which was kind of stupid to do in January. We took all the bras and panties off the clothesline, stacked them in our front yard, and ran the garden hose over them. Their Wonderbras and underwear were frozen solid on our snow-covered lawn until spring thaw."

I laughed and shook my head while Derek topped up my glass of wine. Then, as if someone had flipped a switch, the mood changed from social to professional. Damn.

"I've found some of the answers to your query about

Candace's son, Adam," Derek said.

"You're kidding," I said, showing off all my rhetorical skills.

"You're right. This is all just a ruse to get you on a date with me. Of course, I'm not kidding, but I can't tell you."

"What do you mean you can't tell me?"

"The particulars of Children's Aid Society cases are kept confidential, including the very name of the kid in question. That's why case reports only use initials and try to leave out identifying information."

"So…?"

"Listen up. I have the information. And – " Derek fumbled in his jacket pocket for what appeared to be a folded piece of paper " – I wrote it all down."

"Great. So give me the—"

"No, no, no. Play along. You have to do this my way."

I hadn't yet mentioned Candace's shooting to him and decided right here and now that I wasn't going to. Whatever Derek had to tell me tonight would remain unchanged by the fact that someone had tried to make Swiss cheese out of Candace's torso last night. Besides, I could tell him everything later on if I had to.

I had no idea where he was going with this mystery paper route, and I was getting mildly weirded out by all the cloak-and-dagger stuff. Derek put the sheet of paper on the table, then checked his watch.

"Ah, yes, that time. I have to make a call." He reached into the inside pocket of his jacket for his cellphone.

So much for pleasure as opposed to business. Damn.

"So…" He gave me a meaningful stare over the rim of his glasses, and I was momentarily taken back to the principal's office in grade three. "I'm going to step outside for a moment to make this call. I've had a fair bit of wine, so I might forget that I've put that piece of paper on the table. I probably wouldn't even notice if it were somehow to disappear." And with that he stood up and went outside.

Got it! And here's what I pieced together. Adam had been in a short-term foster home until he was about six months old, then he was placed permanently with a middle-aged couple, and—

Derek came back in.

"So the people he's placed with—"

"What people?" Derek cut in. "Who?"

"The hypothetical people that a kid in Adam's situation might be placed with." Even after too many glasses of France's finest squished grapes, I eventually catch on.

"Oh," he said, "*those* people." And there was that damn, lopsided, knowing grin. "Often in these situations, the typical couple can be middle-aged and have waited too long to have kids. By the time they're ready to put their careers in the back seat and start a family, they've missed the boat."

"So they adopt?"

"Depends. In the hypothetical family situation I'm thinking about, they're still foster parents, albeit long-term ones. They haven't adopted him, and I don't know or care why not. The bright side is this scenario can make it relatively easy to trace the kid. Adoption records, on the other hand, are sealed pretty tightly."

"So, what does that mean? Permanent custody?"

"Well, they might apply for custody, but if a kid had special needs, or some medical condition that required extra attention and resources that some people couldn't afford, it would more likely be a Crown wardship, which means the social workers do periodic checks when things are still in limbo, so to speak. If things look smooth, and it's a good fit, they can grant permanent custody as a way of closing off the case and having one less file to worry about. But for any number of reasons, this doesn't always happen."

"So how is a Crown wardship different from adoption?" I asked.

"The foster parents still get a stipend from the government to cover some of the child's expenses. The birth mother can still walk back into the picture. In fact, depending on what the court order says or doesn't say about access, the birth mother can still be involved."

"Or the father."

"Right."

"Could either of the birth parents try to regain custody?"

"They could certainly try," Derek said, "but they would have to convince a lot of people. Child psychologists, social services, a family court judge. It's a case of what's in the best interests of the child."

"So Candace could get an update on him if she wanted. Does she have the right to visit him or anything?"

"Hypothetically."

There was that damn sexy grin again.

"Wow. Thank you. This is so helpful. I could kiss you."

And with that, Derek leaned over and kissed me like I have never been kissed before. All the simmering sexual tension and electricity of all the times when we'd flirted shamelessly was unleashed in a kiss that sent me to the moon. I dropped my fork, and it clanged to the floor where a fleet-footed waiter scooped it up and quickly returned with a new one, but I really didn't care. Food was about the last thing on my mind.

Derek's mouth and mine remained locked for a very long time. I was absolutely lost in the gentle smoothness of his velvety lips and in the teasing flicker of his tongue against mine.

Wow!

I have never wanted a kiss to last as long as I wanted that one to.

Wow!

We finished the second bottle of wine but hardly touched the remainder of our plates. His hand kept finding its way to my thigh, and I was playing a heated game of footsies with him. The waiter brought the check as soon as Derek signalled for it. I'm surprised the waiter didn't say "Get a room" when he placed the bill on the table. The pheromone level of the dining room dropped exponentially as we made our exit.

We silently held hands as we left the restaurant. Derek checked to make sure his car was locked, then hailed a cab for us. He held the door for me, then walked around and got in the other side. We both knew as we climbed into the taxi that we were on our way to his condo, even though we hadn't said a word about it. I suddenly forgot about work and hookers and pimps and shootings and drag queens.

Nothing else mattered right now. Nothing at all. I could hardly wait to feel Derek next to me.

Our clothes fell off in a horny, hurried heap the second we were inside his front hallway. Derek kissed my neck and shoulders and nibbled behind my ear, then he worked his way lower. I swear that at that moment he could have asked me to do anything – chop off my right arm, commit treason, sell crack to school kids, you name it – and I'd have said yes. Everything I was feeling, both physically and internally, was new and raw and exciting and wonderful. We had urgent, heated sex on the living room sofa, followed by slow and tender lovemaking in the bedroom.

We drifted off for about an hour, then stirred back to life and stayed up till the wee hours. Derek and I shared a deliciously leathery Cuban cigar, sipped peaty single malt Scotch, and listened to music. It felt as if we'd been doing this every night for years, but that every night was a new discovery about each other's minds, ideas, and bodies.

After exploring every inch of each other once again, we talked for a while longer. Derek refilled our glasses of Bowmore and put on Miles Davis. When I finished my drink, I pushed him back onto the bed and spent the rest of the night treating his body like an amusement park ride. When it was over, we high-fived each other.

Wow!

When I slowly came back to life just before six in the morning, I was heady at the feeling of his arms wrapped tightly around me. It felt as if I'd woken up in his arms every morning since forever ago. It felt right, like I was exactly where I was meant to be. I curled up closer to him and was more content and more comfortable than I've ever felt before. Ever.

Derek stirred to life a few minutes later. He began kissing my shoulders and slowly worked his way along my back and down my arms, then back up to my neck, and before long he was rocking my world again and taking me to heights I'd never dreamed of.

Wow!

Mary Carmen

Why I am doing this? I lift another one of her heavy box full of junk and take it down to the garage. My back is so sore, so achy. Why I am taking all these heavy boxes of shit from the attic of this old bitch? This attic is so hot and is stinky. Muy *stinky.*

For this week and the next week, I going to earn about half of the dinero *I can earn in one weekend at the house of Candace or some few nights on the street. But I cannot go on the street, and I cannot go back to the* casa de *Candace.*

The policía *for sure is looking for me. I'm illegal in this country. I would not get a fair trial. I would go to the jail. I would not see my* familia *ever again. I cannot take any chance that the* policía *sees me. I must keep hiding.*

Just a week or two. Then I am going home. ¡Mexico. Viva Mexico!

Dios, ayudame, por favor. *God help me.*

Friday, July 24, 7:42 am

It's probably not a good idea to break into a place that already has crime scene tape around the perimeter, but I wasn't about to let a trivial detail like that call a halt to my latest plan. Of course, I wasn't capable of rational thought at the moment. I was still walking on air – or strolling bowlegged, take your pick – after my morning and my night with Derek.

Wow!

Eventually, we'd pulled ourselves out of bed, made some coffee, and slowly drifted back to reality. I was too deep in this case to play hooky for the day, as much as I might have wanted to. I felt a brief pang of guilt for taking last night off, but it was worth it. Oh, so very worth it.

"I'd give you a ride home, but my car's still at Le Paradis," Derek had said.

"That's fine," I had replied. "I'll just call a taxi. Do you want to hitch a ride with me? We can drop you at your car."

"I'll get it later. I think I'll work from home today."

I was supposed to be heading home, but I impulsively told the cabbie to take me to the bordello and asked him to drop me at the end of the street. My plan was to commit another illegal entry. I had bed head, and the sassy little dress that had looked so good last night seemed very out of place this morning. And then there was the smile on my lips that refused to go away.

Wow!

Maybe the intoxicating afterglow had left me feeling invincible or cocky, but whatever the reason, I had no misgivings at all about what I was about to do.

After the taxi driver took off in search of his next fare, I walked up the road to the bordello. Other than the yellow crime scene tape, you'd never know there had been a shooting here a little more than twenty-four hours ago. There was no cop car out front, no doughnut-eating officer standing sentry by the entrance.

Bingo!

I went around to the back of the house, treading carefully in my strappy little sandals. I found a small rock, and hoped the noise I was about to make would blend in with the other early-morning sounds of downtown Toronto. Plus, I was counting on the passivity of people who don't want to get involved. Just in case, though, I faked some loud sneezes as I broke the window of the back door just enough to reach in and grab the doorknob. I was smart enough to put a Kleenex over the knob before touching it.

Once inside, I was careful to step over the shards of glass littering the floor by the kitchen door. I didn't waste any time peeking into the reception desk or nosing about in any of the main floor rooms. A brief look in the billiard room made my stomach do a flip-flop. The blood on the pool table was dried up, and the room had an acrid metallic smell to it.

Yuck.

I peeled my eyes away from the bloodshed and ran up to the third floor where Candace had her office. She was too well organized and too professional not to have had copies of any and everything from downstairs up here, as well. I wasn't about to take time digging around, so I went to her desk and grabbed the few discs and the USB memory stick and got the hell out of there the same way I had come in. For the record, breaking into a crime scene rates about an eleven on my Dumb-o-Meter.

Friday, 9:48 am

There was no way I could do surveillance at the Maplethorpe place in anything but a car. This was a residential neighbourhood. There was no coffee shop where I could sit unnoticed for hours as I pretended to read the day's paper. There was no park bench across the street where I could absently while away the hours feeding the pigeons.

So, here I was again in Dad's stolen car. I had dashed home for a quick shower and change of clothes after the bordello break-in, and I was back to work right after that. This time, I'd planned ahead and had a fully charged and fully loaded MP3 player, but I hardly paid any attention to it. My mind kept replaying scenes from last night, and I couldn't wipe the goofy grin off my face. No guy has ever made me feel the way Derek did last night. Not even Mick. Not even close.

This morning I had, surprisingly, been organized enough to remember to bring along my laptop. I was skimming through the files I had taken from Candace's office, while keeping one eye on the Maplethorpe house. The eye on the computer, though, was damn near popping out of my head in shock.

If I ever decided to give up investigating, I'd ask Candace for a job. Okay, maybe not a job, but at least a partnership or a franchise. The files I'd just looked at contained info about her net monthly revenue. She cleared way more in a month, even after expenses, than I did in the whole of last year. Significantly more. The bordello was pretty much a license to print money. Even the call girls' pay records were impressive. They were making a killing, too.

I thought I saw a flicker of movement near Vivian's house, so I peeled my eyes away from the computer screen. I sat still and alert, waiting for I have no idea what. Nothing happened. Maybe I'd imagined it. After a while – minutes, hours, millennia, who knows? – I brought myself back to the present time and place.

No action at the Maplethorpe domicile.

I checked out some more computer files. The next disc I inserted had all the top-secret, super-duper confidential client info. *Tee hee.* I was about to learn everybody's secrets.

The johns were listed alphabetically in an Excel spreadsheet. I scrolled down to Dave Bowring's dossier. Not much in it was new to me, and none of it surprised me. What did surprise me, though, was the name listed directly above Dave Bowring. It was Belham. Emery Belham.

Well, way to go, you old coot.

Emery Belham was Candace's and my mutual client.

I knew Mr. Belham from the world of corporate finance. I routinely did corporate background checks for him whenever he recruited new fiscal talent. In my last case Belham had helped me understand financial flim flams, and now here I was reading about his sexual proclivities.

Belham, who is about a hundred and sixty-eight years old, seems to have the appetites of a frat boy. *Veni, vidi, Viagra.* He likes to be handcuffed to the bedposts, and prefers a copper-haired Celtic lass to be on top and wearing something satiny. Oooh, bad mental picture. I felt like I'd just seen my grandfather having sex. *Yikes!*

I closed the file. Too much information. I wondered if I'd be able to make eye contact with Belham the next time we did business together. I couldn't shake the image of wrinkly old Belham and a slutty Anne of Green Gables. *Argh!*

Enough for now. I shut down the computer and shoved it under the front passenger's seat, then tucked the USB memory stick and CDs into my purse for safekeeping. There's no way in hell I'd let any of this stuff out of my sight.

I shuffled in my seat and wished I'd brought a cushion. Moving the seat a bit farther back so I could stretch out my legs, I took a few sips of my now-cold coffee and wondered how prisoners in solitary confinement coped with their circumstances. Small spaces, nothing to do, and no mental stimulation were enough to make any sane person crazy. I fidgeted some more and moved the seat back up. Finally, I found a comfortable position once I'd tilted the steering wheel upwards and shifted so I was sitting sort of sideways, leaning against my door. I sat there and waited.

And waited.

The silent ennui gave me free rein to indulge in some more horny daydreaming about Derek. I blushed as I replayed scenes from last night in slow motion. Just as I was about to mentally relive the best orgasm I've ever experienced, Jessica called my cell and jolted me out of my X-rated reverie.

"I went out with Cole again last night," she said. "What a great guy. He's almost perfect."

"Perfect? You mean he has an eight-inch tongue and can breathe through his ears?"

"Yes, of course. No, seriously, he's so funny and so sweet."

"Gimme details," I said.

"None yet, but soon. He's taking me out again tomorrow night."

"Ohhh… hot date. What are you going to wear?"

"I don't know. I'd rather think about what I'm not going to wear. How come you never introduced me to Cole before?"

"He had a girlfriend for a while. A real bitch. He finally ditched her a few months ago."

"Gee, I hope I'm not a rebound. I really like him. He's just my type."

"Play it cool and see what happens," I said.

"Well, it looks like I have a much better chance of getting laid sooner than you do."

"Actually, that's where you're wrong. I fell on a penis

last night. Several times." There was a great big grin on my face as I said it.

"What? Whose? Mick's?"

"No, someone new. You've never met him. His name's Derek Armstrong and he totally rocked my world."

Friday, 11:45 am

The mailman appeared on the horizon, walked up and down each driveway, and deposited envelopes in all the mailboxes on the even numbered side of the street. Then he crossed over and did the same for all the houses on the other side. Mary Carmen poked her head out the door just enough to collect the day's post. Still no sign of Vivian.

A few minutes later Mary Carmen emerged. She was dressed in summer slacks and a thin blue cotton blouse. When she took a right down the street, I assumed she was on her way to boarding public transit.

Decision time. Keep an eye on the house or follow the hooker?

No brainer.

I locked Dad's car and left it parked there, hoping it wouldn't get towed later in the day. Briefly, I worried about the laptop, but all my files from it were backed up at the office, and the files from Candace were safely tucked away in my purse. Up and at 'em. I trotted a bit to catch up enough to keep Mary Carmen in view, but hopefully not enough for her to notice me.

Mary Carmen

With eighty-six years of age, Señora *Maplethorpe has lived a long and good life. It's time for her to go. It's not too soon. No more arthritis, no more glaucoma, no more diabetes. No more pain.*

She will go peacefully and soon be with angels. In the heaven, she will be happy; she will be back with her husband and all the old amigos *she have lost over the years. No more of loneliness.*

Why she didn't just give me money? If I had money to escape, maybe she will still be alive.

I can not make her suffer. A cheap lady, a mean old bitch, but she still should not suffer.

I make the dinner for her. Same boring gringa *food today as yesterday. Chicken, mashed potatoes and cauliflower. No colour, no flavour, nothing* picante. *But she can not taste the roofie pills. She going to be like a rag doll very quick. Very fast.*

She have a long and good life. She can now go in peace, no suffer, no pain.

And no mas problemas *for me.*

Friday, 12:15 pm

We turned onto St. Clair Avenue and walked a few short blocks to the subway station. At the corner, just before the transit entrance, Mary Carmen stopped at a bank machine. I stayed back a few steps and feigned interest in the headline stories on the newspapers in the coin-operated boxes on the corner. I couldn't see Mary Carmen well enough to tell what she was doing, but it struck me as odd that she was doing any banking at all. How could she have a bank account if she were here illegally? And why hadn't I seen any banking info when I'd searched her room?

When she finished her business with the ATM, she darted into the subway station and headed down to the southbound platform. I followed suit. There were enough people milling about, waiting for the train, for me to get lost in the crowd.

I sat in the same subway car as Mary Carmen did, but at the other end. More than anything I wished that I had some accessories to alter my appearance – a baseball hat, a pair of sunglasses, a windbreaker, a rubber nose, or a fake moustache. Damn, why hadn't I bought a newspaper while Mary Carmen was at the bank machine?

Once again, poor planning on my part.

We got off the train at St. Andrew Station at the

corner of King Street West and University Avenue, the heart of the downtown core. Concrete and glass skyscraper territory. Head office of this and that. Granite and steel. Banking. Law firms. Insurance companies. Corporate HQ. My definition of Hell.

I followed her up to street level where she waited at the intersection for the red light to turn green. The streets were busy with the office crowds out grabbing their lunches and a few minutes of sun before heading back into their air-conditioned high-rise labyrinthine cubicles. Everyone seemed cloned. The men were all in summer suits with their ties loosened, the women were all in cotton, wrinkle resistant skirts with bare legs, and open-toed shoes. Everyone marched around like zombie rats under remote control from some giant malevolent BlackBerry hidden behind a steel curtain on the penthouse level of the tallest building. *Ugh.* Every reminder of why a nine-to-five office gig would be a death sentence for me.

Despite the crowd of corporate clones, I was getting very nervous that Mary Carmen would realize I was following her, so I held back and didn't cross when she did.

I saw her turn into the building known as Commerce Court West. I waited for the next light, then crossed and entered the same building. I didn't see her waiting by the bank of elevators, but that was okay. I looked through the building directory in the lobby and saw that the Mexican consulate had its offices on the forty-fourth floor.

Okay, so now what?

I did the only thing I could do now. I bought a Blue Jays baseball cap at a nearby souvenir shop, picked up a pair of cheap sunglasses and a newspaper at a drugstore, and went back down to the subway. Sticking a token in the slot, I pushed through a creaky turnstile. For someone who is claustrophobic and therefore deathly afraid of subway trains, the idea of subterranean subterfuge was about as appealing as shaving my head with a cheese grater.

Downstairs on the northbound platform where I hoped Mary Carmen would eventually catch her train home, I sat on a bench and waited. And waited. I turned on my MP3 player and cranked up the sweet soul sounds of Aretha Franklin. *Belt it out, sister!*

I popped a piece of bubble gum in my mouth and tried to blow bubbles, but they burst almost immediately. As the trains went by, I counted them. I checked out a few men in suits. Yummy. The hot men in Armani reminded me of Derek, and then I was once again off in a goofy-grinned afterglow. I replayed scenes of my night with him over and over. I could still feel the way he touched me, still remember how he tasted, how he smelled, what his skin felt like next to mine. Shivers ran up and down my back and the inside of my thighs.

Wow.

I wondered when I'd be seeing him again and hoped it would be soon. I already knew exactly what I wanted to do to him. I was thinking along the lines of a mechanical rodeo bull.

The grunting of the next train – the seventeenth since I'd been sitting here – jolted me out of la-la land. I popped another piece of gum in my mouth and chewed it noisily. The tunes were going on my MP3 player, so I couldn't hear myself, and I was beyond caring what strangers thought of me. A punky teenager with the waistband of his jeans somewhere down near his shins stepped on my foot as he ran to board the train before its doors closed. Maybe the dude with the low-lying jeans should get together with the crazed old gummers at the Nag's Head whose pants hovered up somewhere near their rib cages. It seemed there could be some sort of cosmic balance in merging the two crimes of fashion.

After about two years of sitting there and slowly decomposing, I was beginning to wonder whether I'd missed Mary Carmen, either in the stream of people coming and going, or during my quick excursion to buy a makeshift disguise. I switched my playlist to a selection of AM radio one-hit wonders of the 1970s and 1980s – Barry Manilow's "Copacabana", Rupert Holmes's "Escape (The Piña Colada Song)", followed by some very boring James Taylor, the troubadour of choice for the L.L. Bean set.

How did these formulaic, trite, easy-listening, canned pop songs make it onto the charts when everything I'd ever written remained unknown, unreleased, the music world's best-kept secrets? I told myself for probably the thousandth time that life just isn't fair. At least the cheesy tunes I had blaring away were irksome enough to keep me from falling asleep.

For all I knew, Mary Carmen could have plans to spend the rest of the afternoon – hell, the rest of the evening and the night – downtown. She could be shopping. She could be going to a movie. She could be turning tricks. I could slowly become fossilized sitting on this damn bench. A team of archaeologists or maybe emergency medical personnel would have to use chisels to chip my solidly petrified body away from this red plastic bench. *Yikes!*

Then, just as I was contemplating donating my body to science, there she was, coming down the escalator. She didn't look happy; in fact, she was downright scowling. Even so, she was beautiful.

Mary Carmen walked to the front end of the platform with her head held high, shoulders back, with all the poise of the latest *Vogue* supermodel. More than a few heads turned to look at her, and almost as many checked out her ass once she passed. Almost none turned to look at me or my ass, which I am pleased to say is rather firm, despite my recent dining misadventures. *"Hey, look at me!"* I wanted to shout. *"I'm cute, too!"* This was something of a kung-fu kick to my self-esteem.

I stayed about thirty or forty feet behind Mary Carmen and jumped into the subway car behind her just as the doors were about to close. The ride back up to St. Clair West station was uneventful. I kept my distance as I followed her home. She let herself into the Maplethorpe abode without ringing the bell. I walked a few houses down the street and sat in my dad's stolen but un-towed car. I checked under the seat to see if the laptop was still there. It was.

Now what?

What would I do if I were a hooker, living in a country illegally and I had recently killed my pimp? I'd bolt. I'd get the hell out of there. I'd be on a plane in record time.

Obviously, Mary Carmen had gone to the Mexican consulate to do something about her passport. I had no doubt that she had entered Canada illegally, and if she'd had a passport with her upon arrival, it most certainly was no longer in her possession. As it was a Friday afternoon and she'd looked decidedly unhappy after her visit to the Mexican consulate, I was pretty sure she was stuck in Canada for the weekend.

However, I still figured she was getting close to making her escape. The call to Continental Airlines convinced me of that. If she could have taken off right now, I'm sure she would have, and I had no doubt she would at the first opportunity.

I rolled down the window and let the humid air in. Believe it or not, the muggy day was actually much more refreshing than the stuffy interior of the parked car. Just for fun or for the sake of due diligence, I hit *67 on my phone to block out my number and punched in the number for the Maplethorpe residence. After five rings, the answering machine clicked on, and I hung up.

I wondered what to do next. Not next as in a moment from now, but big-picture next about Mary Carmen and her situation. I believed, rightly or wrongly, that Mary Carmen had had valid, justifiable reasons for killing the scumbag pimp. The world suffered no loss at his premature departure.

As far as I could tell, Mary Carmen hadn't had an easy life, certainly not since coming to Canada. And her situation in Mexico must have been grim as well, or she wouldn't have chosen to leave. She seemed desperate, and I wondered what I would have done in her shoes.

I was certain after my search through Candace's computer files that Mary Carmen had nothing to do with the attempt on Candace's life. The finger for that pointed squarely at Dave. I'd pretty much decided how I was going to handle him, but it couldn't be done today. I knew I'd need help for what I had in store for the self-preserving bastard horndog, and I was pretty sure Mark Houghton would be willing to give me a hand, official or not.

Maybe I should just let Mary Carmen go – get her passport, get on a plane, and get out of here. I had absolutely zero right to be judge and jury about this or anything else, but unlike the situation created by Dave, it seemed pointless to rat Mary Carmen out to the police. By all accounts, she was a nice girl and not a violent criminal or likely to be a repeat offender. I should keep my mouth shut and let her walk away.

So why didn't I?

I was getting a very bad feeling about Vivian Maplethorpe – that's why. For once, I knew exactly where to go to get my questions answered.

I started the car and drove downtown.

Friday, 4:00 pm

This whole driving thing was pissing me off. I'm an unlicensed driver and nervous as hell at the best of times, but the crowds of downtown Toronto traffic on a Friday afternoon in summer are enough to irritate even decorated Formula One drivers. I had several near-death experiences with bicycle couriers and taxis, and several pedestrians gave me the finger. Biting my tongue, I made my way to the same parking lot as yesterday, pulled into the farthest corner, and gladly locked the car. I paid for overnight parking because there was no way in hell I felt like tackling rush-hour drivers any further.

I was en route to the pawnshops where the clerks had said that Mary Carmen had come in to sell women's jewellery.

The rotund grizzly bear hadn't seen her again, though he seemed happy to see me. I had the feeling his shop didn't get much foot traffic, and I rather doubted he'd be in business much longer.

The shop with the freckle-faced kid whose daddy owned the store was my next stop.

"You're back," he said when I entered. "Still looking for your friend, or did you find her?" The little puke was still vacillating between Opie and a bad-assed homeboy.

"Uh, yeah, I did. She was in an accident. Got hit by a streetcar and she's in the hospital. That's why she never came back to get her jewellery. I told her I'd pick it up for her."

"Well, it's still here. The way things are going these days, I don't have a lot of people wanting to buy." He gave me a well-rehearsed look that attempted to combine apathy and attitude. Unfortunately for him, his face was way too Boy Scout wholesome to pull it off.

"In this economy, most people are selling their stuff in order to try to keep a roof over their heads."

Opie shrugged. "Hmm, I guess." He obviously still lived with Mommy and Daddy.

"So how much to get back the brooch, the two rings, and the pearl necklace?"

"A thousand dollars."

"What? She told me you only gave her a fraction of

that when you bought them from her." I had no idea how much she'd been given but I could tell when I was being screwed, and this freckle-faced punk was giving it to me up the ass.

"Sorry, lady, but that's business." He switched demeanours from sour apple-pie boyishness to Russian black market trader. I had no idea how to finesse my way out of this, other than by paying a thousand bucks. Maybe now was a good time to go apeshit. I had nothing to lose.

"C'mon, we both know this junk isn't worth that much. It's ugly, out of style, dowager jewellery, for crying out loud."

He rolled his eyes. "A grand. Take it or leave it."

"You'll never get that much for it, from me or anyone else. You know it yourself. No one's buying these days."

"But eventually the economy will pick up and I'll make a mother of a profit on this."

All my frustrations from the few days bubbled to the surface. I made a deliberate effort to keep my voice level.

"Six hundred."

"A thousand."

"Seven hundred."

"A thousand."

"Oh, for fuck sake's be reasonable. Seven hundred, you little fucking puke, and you'll take it, or I'll go to the cops and tell them half this shit is hot and that you're fencing it all."

"That's a load of crap and you know it."

I wanted to punch this little puke so hard his freckles would fall off.

"That's right, I do, but the cops could make your life a living hell, tearing through everything, checking your records, checking burglary and insurance reports. Then they'd probably involve the taxmen, who would poke around and probably find things they shouldn't."

"Okay, eight hundred," he said. "Cash."

And that's when I lost it. Totally. Surprise attacks are always such fun.

I reached over the counter and grabbed the collar of Freckle Face's shirt. I twisted it and pulled it down until he was looking right into my eyes. He gasped and jerked around, and that made me yank a little tighter.

"No, fuckwad. The price is now two fucking hundred dollars and here's my American Express."

"All right, all right," he sputtered. "Let go. Jesus Christ, you crazy bitch. What are you trying to do? Kill me?"

"No, I just don't like being screwed."

I signed the bill and got the hell out of there at warp speed. I was seeing red – financially and figuratively.

Mary Carmen

After maybe twenty minutos *she was loose and easy to move. She tried to talk to me, but the words came out all slow and sleepy.*

"I think I had better lie down, Mary Carmen. I feel rather weak," Mrs. Maplethorpe said.

"Si, señora. *May I help you upstairs to your room?"*

"Please do."

I pulled out her chair for her and helped her to stand up.

"I don't think I can make it upstairs. I feel a bit light-headed. Take me to the sofa in the living room. I need to lie down. Maybe you should call a doctor."

"Si señora. *I will call the* médico. *First you should get*

comfortable." I put a cushion under her head and took her shoes off her crooked old arthritic feet. "Maybe I can get for you a glass of water?"

"Yes. Water would be good. But not too cold. It hurts my gums."

Friday, 5:40 pm

"Please tell me you're free?" I said when I got Lindsey on her cellphone.

"I am, more or less. I just had a showing near Yonge and Eglinton. What's up?"

"I'm downtown and need either a sounding board or a drink."

"How about both?" she asked.

"Even better."

"When and where?"

"Well, if you head down from Yonge and Eglinton, and I head north form where I am, we should end up at The Pilot around the same time."

"Sounds good. Their rooftop patio should be rocking right about now."

It certainly was. At any other time The Pilot's rooftop oasis near Yonge and Bloor would be the starting point for a wild evening of drunken debauchery. Often it was the end point, as well. However, tonight I planned to behave. I had too much weighing on me and needed to walk through it with Lindsey before I acted on anything.

I got the last empty table and ordered a couple of gin and tonics and a plate of pad thai. My stomach was loudly reminding me that I hadn't eaten a thing all day. I had intended to have the other gin and tonic waiting for Lindsey when she arrived, but I accidentally drank it right after I'd downed the one I'd ordered for myself. The waitress, Heather, was on the ball and showed up with two new drinks just as Lindsey arrived.

"Jessica's not working tonight?" Lindsey asked me.

"Unh-uh. She's on a hot date with Cole. But I don't want to talk about her. My hooker case has spun right out of control."

"What's going on?"

Between mouthfuls of deliciously spicy Asian noodles, I filled Lindsey in on everything. I didn't leave out a single detail.

"I haven't seen hide or hair of the old lady, and I just picked up some of her jewellery at a pawnshop."

"Which means what exactly?"

"I think Mary Carmen killed the old bird. Mary Carmen probably has no money and is desperate to get back to Mexico."

"The jewellery doesn't necessarily mean anything," Lindsey said with an utter lack of conviction.

"I saw Mary Carmen use a bank machine today too."

"So? Everyone does."

"I don't think she has an account here. She's here illegally. The old lady gets a direct-deposit annuity and old-age pension. I think Mary Carmen's financing her return home courtesy of Vivian Maplethorpe."

"How would she get into the old lady's account?"

"People are stupid about their PIN codes. She probably has it written down somewhere, or Mary Carmen has accompanied her to the bank. Something like that."

"I really hope you're wrong." Neither of us said anything for a moment.

"What are you going to do?" Lindsey finally asked between bites. The waitress had dropped off another set of chopsticks, and Lindsey was helping me finish the mound of noodles.

"I don't know yet, exactly, but it'll come to me. I have several ideas."

"Are any of them legal?"

"This time, surprisingly, yes, actually."

"What about the other part of this story? The madam, Candy?"

"Candace."

"Whatever. Does her shooting have anything to do with the Mexican hooker?"

"No, well, yes, indirectly, sort of. The guy I think pulled the trigger on Candace was one of the bordello's clients. I don't think Mary Carmen was involved. I doubt she put him up to it or anything like that."

"So why would he have shot Candace?"

"I had a coffee with him on Wednesday, and he was practically shitting bricks by the end of it, after I told him about the dead pimp."

"Who was killed by Mary Carmen," Lindsey said.

"Right. Methinks Dave the horndog was perfectly content to fuck whoever he could pay for, and to him it was no big deal as long as he got his rocks off. Just a sexy game to him, just a piece of tail. But the stakes changed when someone died, and he was eager to distance himself and his clueless fiancée and his precious career from the whole thing. I'm still not really sure about everything, but I think that's what happened."

"You've got to go to the police. This is bigger than you."

"I will, really, I will. But first I need to find out about Vivian Maplethorpe."

Mary Carmen

When I came back into the living room, she looked like almost asleep. I took another cushion from the armchair and held it over her face. I pressed down on it for many minutos. Señora *Maplethorpe did not even make one sound.*

Then I took a look under the cushion and I think she is dead. I didn't hear any breathing, but must be sure. I pushed the pillow over her mouth and nose again and hold firmamente *for several more minutos.*

When I lifted it again, I was sure there was no breathing, no pulse in the neck or in her wrist.

God help me. Angels, look after Señora *Maplethorpe.* Dios, *look after her soul.*

Dios, perdóname.

I have killed another person.

God help me and please God forgive me.

Friday, 8:45 pm

"Hi, my name's Sasha Jackson, and I'm trying to get in touch with Vivian Maplethorpe. I understand you're a friend of hers." I was at home in the den with my feet up on the desk, cleaning out my purse as I made a number of pointless phone calls. I stuck the USB key and computer discs with Candace's records in the bottom drawer.

"Pardon?" said a creaky old woman's voice.

I repeated myself.

"Just a minute, dearie. Let me turn down the radio." I heard some shuffling, and when the woman came on the phone again, I introduced myself a third time.

"Well, now, I haven't seen Vivian in a few weeks, but she doesn't come to bingo when her hands are really bad. Why are you looking for her?"

"Um, I'm an old friend of the family."

"A what?"

For God's sake, Grandma, turn up your hearing aid.

This old bat was about as helpful as the two I'd spoken with previously. I'd been calling all the names listed in Vivian Maplethorpe's phone book. It would have been easy if she had listed people by first and last name, even easier if family had all been listed under "Maplethorpe."

Who says life is easy?

So I'd spoken to Adele Watkins and Annabeth Rice, and then to Beth Brady from bingo. I heard voice mail kick in when I called Cheryl Freedman, who apparently was Mrs. Maplethorpe's physiotherapist. Denise McDonald from down the road usually only sees Vivian once a month or so for tea and neighbourhood gossip. The outgoing message at the number for Eleanor Digby indicated she was some kind of insurance agent who may or may not have kept her face in a jar by the door.

I caught a break when I got to J.

"Yes, I'm her son," said Jerry from area code 604, Vancouver. "What's going on?"

"I'm a private investigator, and I'm looking for Vivian in relation to a case I'm working on. She was a witness to a traffic accident, but I haven't been able to reach her." Liar, liar, pants on fire. "One of her neighbours said she might have gone out west to visit you. She gave me your number."

"Well, Mom's due to visit, but not till later this summer. She booked a flight on August 15 so she could be here for my fiftieth birthday."

"Have you talked with her recently?"

"We spoke about a week ago. We usually talk every couple of weeks. Why? Do you think there's something wrong?"

"No, no. I don't want to alarm you. Maybe my timing's just been bad. I'll call her again and leave a message."

I kept plugging away through her phone directory, mostly to no avail. I did stumble upon a nugget when I got to *P*, though. There was a listing for Pin, just Pin, nothing to indicate whether that was a first name or a surname. The fact that there was nothing more than four digits written next to it told me almost certainly that it was the PIN code for her banking. The banks all say you're not supposed to write down your PIN. *Why, oh, why don't people ever trust their own memories?*

I can't recall a time when I've ever said I needed a drink. I've wanted one many a time, and on occasion, I've longed for one or craved one. But I don't think I've ever *needed* a drink before. Until tonight. The gin and tonics at The Pilot hadn't taken the edge off.

The air conditioner was still out of commission and the heatwave hadn't subsided. I had all the fixings for a mojito – white rum, soda water, lime, sugar, and some mint leaves I picked from Shane's herb garden in the backyard. I downed the mojito in one long, cool, refreshing slurp.

Then I made another.

How to handle this?

I knew who had killed Gaston, but so far I'd kept that mostly to myself. And I probably would never have said a word about it, if Mrs. Maplethorpe hadn't been killed too, and I was sure she had been. A dead pimp is no great loss, but a little old lady… that's someone's mother, somebody's grandmother, someone's bingo buddy. There was no forgiving that, no justifying that.

But if Mrs. Maplethorpe is dead, then how come no one seems aware of it yet? And if Mrs. Maplethorpe is dead, then where is her body?

And what about Candace? I was thinking about her parents and her son. Should I try to call her folks? Would they want to know what had happened to their daughter? Would she want to see them? And what about her little boy Adam?

I was confused by all of this, so I pulled myself back to the here and now. Priority number one: Mrs. Maplethorpe. I drained my glass and decided to have yet another. Sitting on the back step, I turned everything over in my mind. I gazed at the night sky, as if expecting to find answers there. A funereal, translucent blanket of smog washed out most of the night, but I could distinguish the silvery glow of the waxing crescent moon. Or was it waning? I'd probably had too many drinks, but I could have sworn I saw a shooting star. As it twinkled its way behind the horizon, the *whats*, *whys*, and *hows* of my conundrum slowly shifted into place.

Going back into the den, I got my digital camera. I shot several quick pictures and downloaded them to Dad's antique desktop computer right away. Then I made a strong cup of coffee and steeled myself for the call I was about to make. Even though it was after 11:00 pm local time, I picked up the phone. Vancouver is three hours behind Toronto.

"Hi, Jerry, it's Sasha again. The investigator from Toronto?"

"Hello. What's up?"

"Listen, I wasn't straight with you before, but I lied because I don't want to freak you out. I could be wrong."

"About what?"

"Have you got email? Can you go online while we're on the phone?"

"Sure. Is my mother okay? What's this about?"

Jerry gave me his email address, and I immediately sent him a message with some digital photos attached to it.

"Do you recognize that jewellery?"

"Yes, it's my mother's. That's the ruby brooch Dad gave her for their anniversary. Their twenty-fifth, I think? What's going on? Should I come out there?"

"I'm sorry, Jerry. I really don't like doing this on the phone. Obviously, I think something has happened to Vivian."

"What does this jewellery have to do with anything?"

"I bought all those pieces at a pawnshop. Does it make any sense that your mother would be hocking her jewellery?"

"A pawnshop? Not a chance. My mother's loaded. Cheap as hell, but loaded. And she'd never sell anything that Dad gave her, especially not the ruby brooch. It's worth too much to her, both financially and sentimentally. No way."

"I think you'd better book a flight to Toronto."

Saturday, July 25, 9:28 am

I had taken a cab downtown this morning to the lot where I'd left Dad's car. Between the parking fees and the taxi fare, I almost would have been better off renting a limo. I drove back to Forest Hill and parked a few doors down from Vivian's house. I would rather have shoved bamboo shoots under my fingernails than do another round of surveillance, but what choice did I have?

It was hot and boring, and I was antsy, but not for long. Mary Carmen, wearing the orange and yellow shirt I'd seen draped over the chair in the guest room, emerged around 10:30, and this time I wasn't interested in following her. I needed to find out about Vivian Maplethorpe and was afraid of what I'd discover.

I waited a few minutes until Mary Carmen was down the block and had turned the corner. When I was sure she was gone, I made my move.

I entered the house the same way as before, via the casement window in the laundry room. My shoulder bag got caught on the handle, and I stumbled as I hopped down from the washing machine. *Shit!* Too much noise.

Hold still. Listen.

No sounds.

The house was quite warm, and I wished I were wearing something backless or cotton, something that would breathe, instead of this royal blue crinkly rayon shirt, even if it did match my eyes.

Poor planning once again.

Unlike last time, when I had no idea what I was looking for, this time I had something definite in mind. I was hoping – well, not actually hoping, more like expecting – to find a dead body.

I went straight upstairs to the bedrooms and checked under the beds and in the closets of each room. *Nada.*

Hightailing it down downstairs, I searched around. The basement seemed to be more of a giant storage area than anything else. It was very tidy and well-organized, unlike the war zone in the basement of my house. Here, boxes of old clothes and books were neatly stacked and labelled. An artificial Christmas tree was packed in a clear plastic bin. There was a set of matching luggage that looked as if it had never been used. Lots of interesting stuff, but no dead body.

Back up on the main floor, I did a cursory examination of the living room and dining room. Neither seemed to have anything big enough to hide a corpse in or behind.

The kitchen did, though. I had saved this room for last, not because of my usual theories on searching a house, but because my instincts were telling me this would be the place. I was hoping to stay in denial for as long as possible. The chest-styled freezer was big enough for a body, and I knew before opening it what I'd find.

And there she was.

Vivian Maplethorpe.

Dead as a doorknob.

She looked like a mannequin or a statue. I didn't even register what I was looking at. It was surreal. She was half folded into the freezer, balanced on top of a rump roast and a package of boneless chicken breasts. Her thin lips were about the same shade of blue as her tightly curled hair. She seemed so peaceful and calm that she could have been sleeping. If I hadn't known better, I'd have thought this was some kind of twisted, macabre prank, something from Ashton Kutcher's *Punk'd*.

Vivian Maplethorpe was fully clothed, and there was no blood or other visible signs of a fight. She looked just like an old woman who had died peacefully in her sleep.

But people who die peacefully in their sleep don't end up in stainless-steel freezers in gourmet kitchens.

Time to call 911.

I closed the freezer lid and—

"Back away! Don't come near me, *señorita.* Don't make even one sound." Mary Carmen's face was expressionless.

Oh, shit!

The twelve-inch stainless-steel blade pointing at me convinced me not to do anything rash, but I couldn't keep quiet. I never can.

"What are you doing back so soon? You just left."

"Shut up," she said.

"Mary Carmen, I'm here to help you. My name's Sasha. Candace hired me—"

I glanced at the butcher's block on the counter opposite me. The knife Mary Carmen was holding came from that set.

"It does not matter. You know too many things; you saw the *señora* in the freezer."

She took a step towards me. The knife was pointing straight out in front of her. Both of her hands were gripping it. I took a small step backwards. "Please. I understand what you've been through, what you're going through." My voice was quavering, and I was almost numb with fear. Mary Carmen had already killed two people. Was I going to be the third?

No fucking way. Think, Sasha, think. Is she close enough to stab me or can I put up a fight? Could I try to wrest the knife from her hands? Is there any way to create a distraction?

She'd have to stab me in the right spot – my heart or my lungs. She'd have to use enough force to pierce my clothes and my skin, and drive the knife in deep enough to do some damage. She'd have to aim the knife just right to get through my rib cage.

Or maybe she'd try for my stomach or neck. Painful,

and a bloody mess, but probably not instant death, unless she went for the jugular. The blade was pointed too low for my neck and a bit too high for my stomach.

Fuck! I don't remember signing up for this.

I was taking baby steps backward, away from her. What the hell could I do to get myself out of this daylight nightmare? This is a kitchen. There must be something I can use as a weapon.

"Keep your hands up over your head where I can see them," Mary Carmen ordered. "Both of them." Her knuckles were almost white around the handle of the knife.

I did as I was told. I had to create a diversion. But what?

"Please, Mary Carmen, let's talk. I know about Gaston. I know what you've been through. Don't make things worse for yourself." I was almost boxed in now by the granite countertop island. *Fuck!*

"You have no idea what hell I went through. You have no idea of the tears I cried, so many. That *bastardo* was an animal." She took another step towards me, and I backed into the gas stove.

"He's gone now, Mary Carmen. Don't fuck up your life. You don't want to go to jail. Don't do this."

Create a distraction. Get her to drop the knife.

"I can not stay here in this country. I will not get a fair trial. I almost ready to go back to my country and you will not make *problemas* for me. I have my ticket. I will get on a plane next week as soon as I get my *pasaporte*, and say *adiós* to this horrible life here."

"I can help you. We can work through this, really."

"Work through this? Are you making a big joke? Since my first days in Canada, I try to make it work. Modelling job? Was a lie, was a big lie. I never thought

I will work as a prostitute. I never plan to sell my body. I was a *virgen*. I come here to work in the fashions as a model. To work with a photographer. I did not come here to have sex with *pinche* men for *dinero*."

I tried to step back a bit more, but there was nowhere to go. I'd pretty much boxed myself in. *Fuck!*

"I know you didn't, and when you tell your story in court—"

"The *polícia* here will not be just. I am a foreigner, I am illegal."

"Don't make it worse…"

"You are the only one who knows about the old lady. You are the only one who knows my secret and can make it worse for me. I don't want to go to jail."

I had backed into the fancy gourmet stove. Nowhere to run. I shuffled a few inches to the side and felt the knobs and buttons of the stove poking into my butt. Mary Carmen took another step towards me. The knife was way too close for comfort.

"You won't go to jail," I said. "I won't tell anyone. Just let me go and you can go back to Mexico. I won't say a word. Honest."

"I do not trust you. I can not trust anyone here."

I leaned my ass against the ignition button for the stove and wiggled my cheeks against the dial a bit to get the flame up. Perhaps that was a bad idea, but desperate times required desperate measures.

In a second I could feel the heat from the flame of the front burner, and in another second I could feel the flames on my back. I was too close to the stove. The bottom edge of my blouse was on fire! *Jesus fucking Christ!* Rayon is so fucking flammable or inflammable or… why doesn't one of those words mean the opposite of the other?

"Oh, my God, help me!" I jumped away from the stove.

The flames shot right up the back of my shirt and into my hair. I threw my purse behind me and ripped off my flaming blouse and bra. My purse landed on the lit burner and almost immediately shot up in flames.

Kaboom!

There goes the travel-sized bottle of hairspray at the bottom of my bag.

I dropped to the floor and rolled over to smother the flames on my head. "Fuck, help me!"

Mary Carmen was still pointing the knife at me. She hadn't moved, hadn't said a word, but her eyes looked hotter and more dangerous than the fire.

"Holy fuck! Do something! Help!" I rolled over again.

The smell of my burning hair set off the smoke detector. *Beep, beep, beep* – the alarm was going non-stop now.

"Get me some water! My fucking hair's on fire!" I rolled over a few more times, screaming from the pain, screaming from the heat. Then I jumped up and grabbed a four quart saucepan from the rack hanging above the island and stuck it over my head.

Smother the flames.

I left the Lagostina pot in place for a moment, making sure the flames were out.

The smoke detector was still bleating away.

Mary Carmen dropped the knife and ran out the front door.

My hair was no longer burning but was at least a few inches shorter now, and my hairdresser was sure to say something to me about split ends.

I took a deep breath and ran after Mary Carmen.

The neighbours from both sides, plus the ones across the street, were all standing in their doorways. No doubt they'd heard the *kaboom* and my screams; no doubt they'd heard the fire alarm. All of them looked confused and curious about what was going on. The man across the street had a cellphone in his hand. The woman two doors down was peering out her kitchen window.

"Help me!" I cried. "Don't let her get away!"

Mary Carmen was about halfway down the street. I chased after her, still clutching the stainless-steel saucepan as if I were a slapstick character in a low-budget French comedy. Off in the distance, I could hear a siren. Someone must have called 911, thank God! I was winded and I doubted I'd be able to catch up with Mary Carmen.

And to make it all the more special, I was racing down the street topless, my charred blouse and bra now a pile of ashes on Vivian Maplethorpe's kitchen floor. My boobs were out there in the open for everyone to see. Jesus Christ, does it get any better than this? Maybe the neighbours were calling 911 to report a perverted lunatic arsonist running half-naked down their street.

"Don't let her get away!" I screamed. "Call the police!"

Two boys on skateboards scooted up beside me.

"Yo, lady, what's going on?" one of them asked. "You need help?"

They pretended not to look at my boobs, but they couldn't help staring. I bet mine were the first real ones these two prepubescent boys had ever seen.

"Of course, I need help! Don't I look like I need help? Get that woman! Catch her, please! Don't let her get away! Stop staring at my boobs and get that woman! She's a killer!"

They gave each other confused but excited looks, shrugged, and skateboarded off towards Mary Carmen. This afternoon's tomfoolery would sure make for an interesting "How I Spent My Summer Vacation" essay when school resumed in September.

Two fire trucks came up the street, followed by an ambulance. I ignored them all, though they surely noticed me. I threw the saucepan onto someone's front lawn and ran after the skateboarders, who were gaining on Mary Carmen. A couple of Mrs. Maplethorpe's neighbours were chasing me. I hoped one of them had thought to bring me a shirt.

Just before the next block, the boys caught up with Mary Carmen, did a kick-flip on their skateboards, and rolled right into her. Neon-coloured skateboards flew up into the air, two preteen boys landed on top of a drop-dead gorgeous killer, and a police car rounded the corner.

"Don't let her get away!" I yelled. "She's killed two people and tried to kill me!"

"For crying out loud, Sasha. Put some clothes on."

I don't think I've ever been so happy to see Mark Houghton of the Toronto Police.

A middle-aged man ran up to join our little clusterfuck of absurdity. He had huge circles under his eyes and a tote bag slung across his shoulder. "What the hell's going on around here? Why are all those fire trucks in front of my mother's house?"

"You must be Jerry," I said. "Took the red-eye flight from Vancouver, did you? I'm Sasha." I placed my left arm across my boobs and stuck out my right hand for him to shake.

Saturday, 1:30 pm

The next few hours were insane. Someone had found a shirt for me to put on, but I was momentarily topless again.

"You're very lucky," the paramedic said. "It could've been much worse."

"I don't feel very lucky. Look at my hair." Sections of my hair were now just below shoulder length instead of halfway down my back.

"As I said, it could be worse. Anyhow, at least the burns on your back are all superficial. Put this ointment on three or four times a day. You don't want to get an infection. Keep the area clean, sleep on your stomach, and you'll be fine soon."

"Thanks, but I don't think so. There was a dead woman stuffed in the freezer. A dead woman…"

A whole bunch of men in uniforms were milling about. Collectively, they were all pretty damn sexy, especially the firemen. Buff, broad-shouldered, and tall, they all looked like they'd been sent over from Central Casting. Most of them were getting ready to leave now, though. The fire hadn't spread beyond the kitchen, so it was now just a matter of writing up the report.

The police, coroner, and crime scene technicians were taking over the rest.

Mary Carmen had been cuffed and was taken into custody. Yellow crime scene tape had been put up around the perimeter of the house. It did little to jazz up the bland front yard. A couple of guys from the coroner's office carried Mrs. Maplethorpe out on a gurney. Her frozen body was still bent as it had been in the freezer, and the sight of a dark cover over her angled corpse was grotesque.

Jerry was in the living room, trying not to watch as his mother's body was taken away. His face was buried in his hands, and he was crying. I sat next to him, my arm around his shoulder. I said nothing; there was nothing to say. I stayed with him until Officer Mark Houghton called me over to get my statement.

Saturday, 3:30 pm

I was driven home in a squad car, which I'm sure impressed the hell out of my neighbours. An evidence technician followed behind us. Another cop said he'd drive my father's sedan home for me. They didn't ask how my dad's car had come to be there, and I didn't volunteer anything.

"This is the stuff that belonged to Mrs. Maplethorpe," I said to the alpha-male cop who'd taken the lead. "Her son confirmed it was hers. The clerk at the store should be able to confirm that it was Mary Carmen who sold it to him."

The technician bagged the brooch, rings, and pearl necklace.

"Here's my receipt from the pawnshop," I said. "Don't suppose I'll get reimbursed?"

"Not likely," the cop, whose name was Oxford, said. "Sorry."

"These are the things that belonged to Gaston, the pimp. Here's my receipt. I probably won't get reimbursed for this, either, will I?"

Again Officer Oxford shook his head as the evidence technician bagged and tagged the watch and the rings.

There were a few questions about chain of possession and continuity, but combined with everything else, the cops expected the case against Mary Carmen to be a slam dunk.

"You might also want to check the video surveillance tape of the ATM near St. Clair West subway station," I suggested.

Oxford looked up from his notepad. "Why's that?"

"I'm almost positive Mary Carmen doesn't have a bank account here, but I saw her using that bank machine the other day. I have a hunch there was at least one unauthorized withdrawal from Mrs. Maplethorpe's account."

"Interesting." He flipped open his cellphone.

Fifteen minutes later Officer Oxford and the evidence technician were both gone, and I was glad it was all over.

I never would have expected that a missing person case would lead to two murders, a shooting, and me running topless down a quiet neighbourhood street in a good part of town. Or that a crazy woman would want to kill me with a kitchen knife.

Damn, if I'd thought I'd needed a drink last night, then how might I rate today? Itching, yearning, hankering, pining, *ah*, yes, thirsting for a tall icy gin and tonic. A very strong one.

I poured my drink and went out to the backyard. The house was still hotter than hell, and I made a mental note to call the air-conditioning repairman again. Then, sitting on the deck, I took a sip of my drink and finally had a good cry.

Monday, July 27, 10:00 am

"Here you go." I handed my room key back to Agnes the Slum Lord, whose track pants today were egg-yolk yellow. The pale hue drew attention to her girth, and the pants fit snugly enough to emphasize every waddle and every jiggly bit of flab below her waist. How very unsexy. "I found a new place, something more permanent."

"Did ya move out all your things? Is the room clean?"

"Yes. It's in the exact same condition it was when I rented it last week." Exactly as dingy, scummy, and seedy as the day I'd "moved in." A lifetime ago. Literally.

"I gotta go up and check the room for damage," she said. "Wait here."

I hung around by the front door and waited. Fritz limped by and tried to growl at me. I growled back at him, and he skulked away. I wanted to run up to Mary Carmen's floor and nose around, but I knew better. Besides, the cops had already been through it, collecting whatever they needed to put together their case against her.

Poor girl. I would have felt sorry for Mary Carmen if she'd stopped after Gaston. His death was no great loss, but Vivian's was calculated and selfish. Unnecessary. I felt so sorry for Jerry.

"Hey, you've missed a lot of drama around here. Your friend Mary Carmen got busted." Carrie Jo was on her way out, but stopped to chat with me in the front hallway.

"Yeah," I said. "I've heard the whole story."

"Between Mary Carmen and Todd, things have been awful around here."

"I bet they have. I won't be around for any more of the drama, though. I'm leaving. Agnes is just checking my room."

"I don't blame you. I want to get the hell out of here, too. Maybe Todd and I can look for a place when he gets out of the hospital."

"How's he doing?"

"I'm actually on my way to see him. He's out of intensive care. Want to come with me?"

"Sure."

"Good." Then Carrie Jo shot me a strange look. "I hope you don't mind me saying this. My hairdresser's salon is on the way to St. Mike's. Maybe we can stop in and book you an appointment? Don't take offense, but you're having a really bad hair day."

This from a woman with dirty feet and toe jam?

Monday, 3:03 pm

"Dave, we need to talk," I said.

"What the hell are you doing calling me at work? How did you get this number?" Horndog Dave sounded less than thrilled at hearing from me.

"I have some computer files you might be interested in."

"I don't know what you're talking about."

"Computer files. You really don't want to get into this on the phone, do you? Meet me in the park beside St. James Cathedral. Fifteen minutes."

He grunted yes and clicked off without saying goodbye.

"Be careful," Mark Houghton said. "But don't be too worried."

"I doubt he'll be armed," I said. "He only used a gun on Candace because one was handy. It's not like he packs a concealed weapon as a matter of course, at least I hope not."

"We'll be keeping an eye on you. Try to sound natural. Just get him to talk. We have two guys on that bench." He indicated two men from the Geritol

Generation who were absent-mindedly feeding pigeons. "And the dumpster diver rooting through that trashcan over there is one of ours, as well."

"I'll be okay. Are you sure this thing's on?"

Mark and Toronto's finest had outfitted me with some pretty snazzy listening and recording devices. The Bic pen in my shirt pocket was actually an ultrasonic, low-vibration microphone capable of picking up any frequency between twenty and twenty thousand hertz.

"It's on. And the soccer moms parked in the green minivan on the corner will be recording everything. Sit right here so we can keep an eye on you." Mark indicated the shaded bench on the east side of the cathedral.

I sat down, carefully avoiding the dried-up plops of pigeon poop on the cast-iron bench. I was nervous. I closed my eyes and mentally rehearsed for about the thousandth time what I was going to say to dirtbag Dave Bowring. I was so focused on the pending sting that I didn't hear him approach, and almost jumped out of my skin when he spoke.

"I think you're taking the private-eye thing too far," Dave said. "I only agreed to see you in the hope that this will be our last encounter. I have nothing to say to you, nothing to hide."

"Bullshit."

"I admitted to seeing the Mexican girl once or twice a few months ago. There's nothing more to it than that. If I didn't know better, I'd think you were using this exaggerated and rather sordid story as a way to extort me."

"Candace had backup files in her office upstairs. You saw Mary Carmen eleven times between March, April, and May."

"Who cares if I did?"

"Your fiancée might care. So might the partners at Gopnik, Guralnick, Purdy, and Roth." I gave him a look of contempt that I hope made him feel like the bag of snot he'd shown himself to be.

"How did you find out where I work?" he asked.

"That's really not the point of this discussion, Dave. I know you shot Candace."

"I have no idea what you're talking about."

"I talked to Tonya."

"Who?"

"Give it up, Dave. You know perfectly well who I mean. I was onto her from the beginning. She was there when I gave Candace my contact info, and it was that night that she came and spray-painted threats on my house."

"I had nothing to do with that—"

"That little bitch was blackmailing a couple of clients, and she was going to extort you next, wasn't she?" I said.

"I have no idea what you're talking about. This is crazy. I'm out of here." His words had lost their bluster, and he didn't really make a move to leave yet, but I knew I'd have to wrap this up fast.

"I don't think so, asshole. The cops put a bit of pressure on Tonya. They threatened to charge her as an accessory, so she spilled her guts."

"I never…uh…no, wha—"

This is my favourite moment – when I know I have

the bad guy cornered. Like others in similar situations, Dirty Dog Dave began sputtering and stumbling over his words. He could recite the alphabet right now, and it still wouldn't be convincing.

"Maybe it would be easier if you turned yourself in," I said. "Perhaps you could avoid a trial and the publicity."

"You can't prove I shot her."

"Well, she's not dead, and when Candace comes to, she'll be able to identify you."

"You mean she didn't die?"

"Nope. The bright side is that you won't be charged with murder. The downside is they'll nail you for attempted. Tonya already told the cops you paid her to tell you when Candace would be alone in the house. That makes it premeditated, asshole."

"How much?"

"How much for what?"

"How much money do you want to keep your mouth shut?"

From bravado to whimpering in less than five minutes. "Don't waste your breath."

Neither of us said anything for a moment. I was on edge, worried that he'd try something. I glanced towards the undercover cops and hoped they'd give me a signal or something. I really wasn't sure what the endgame was.

Dave's voice cracked. "I just wanted to reason with her. I never meant to shoot her…"

That sounded good enough to me. Checkmate.

"See the two women in the green van over there?"

"Yes, why?"

"See the bum digging through the garbage over there?"

"Yeah… What do they have to do with anything?"

"They've been listening to our conversation and have recorded all of it."

His face blanched. "Oh, no, fuck, no…"

"The game's over, douchebag."

Friday, September 11, 11:30 am

"Just trust me," I said to Candace. "Be patient."

Candace and I were sitting at a picnic table in a park across the street from an elementary school in Don Mills, a completely uninspired residential area in northeast Toronto. Once upon a time, the neighbourhood might have been noteworthy as one of Canada's first postwar planned communities. Now it was as interesting as watching paint dry, a template for every cookie-cutter bedroom community marketed to middle-class commuters.

"I'm in your hands," Candace said.

I'd seen Candace a couple of times while she was in the hospital, but we hadn't connected since then. She'd recovered fairly well, and it was nice to finally catch up.

"Your hair looks good," she said. "The extensions blend in nicely."

"I wish it were my own hair, but it'll eventually grow back. Anyhow, what about you? You're a lot more scarred by this than I am."

"I'll be okay. I always somehow manage to land on

my feet."

"But you're definitely out of the business?"

"Yes, and I'm okay with it. One knows going into something like that that it's finite."

"So what will you do?"

"There's no rush. I have money." I was well aware of Candace's more than solvent status, a fact that was well-reflected in the generous bonus she'd given me. "Maybe I'll write a book. Perhaps I'll try to do the lecture circuit or talk shows."

"Hell," I said, "with what you've seen and done, you could probably host your own reality series."

We chatted for a while about her plans. The bordello side of things may well have died out, but she still had the lovely old house.

"I might try to turn it into an actual bed and breakfast," Candace said. "It's a gorgeous building. I could probably make that work."

"You'd probably get a lot of bookings from people who heard about what happened there. It's just the sort of twisted thing that could make the place really popular. Guests would whisper among themselves about the room where the shooting was, or they'd speculate about the hookers and the clients."

"I could exploit the whole saga and make it work for me. Another kind of prostitution, really. Speaking of which, what ever became of the drag queen? The one who was assaulted? How did he connect to everything?"

"Actually, he didn't. Other than the fact that Todd lived in the same rooming house as Mary Carmen, his attack was unrelated to you and the bordello and everything."

"Was it just a coincidence?"

"More like 'wrong place, wrong time.' He was trying to score some coke. He had cash on him from the *Divas in Drag* gig; he'd had a few drinks after the show; he was on a mission and he was feeling punchy."

"I can see what's coming..."

"Yup. He was just tipsy enough to flirt with danger. Thought he'd do a few lines and then pick up a john. Or do a few lines with whatever john he picked up. He approached the wrong guy, got mugged, and had the crap kicked out of him."

"So that's that," Candace said. "What about the car that tried to run you down? How did that fit into everything?"

"I really don't think it had anything to do with this case. I think it was a drunk driver. It could have been Tonya, but I'll never know."

"Perhaps it's best not to know. Anyway, now tell me, why are we here? I have a feeling I know..." She looked around the park and the schoolyard.

"Well, when the lunch bell sounds in a few minutes, I want you to keep your eyes on the door that leads out to the playground."

"This is about my son, isn't it?"

"Yes. I'll point him out to you. It's up to you where you take it from here."

Her eyes welled up at the same time as a smile spread from cheek to cheek. Neither of us said anything. What was there to say?

My cell bleeped at about the same moment as the school bell clanged.

"Hello," I said.

"Hey, gorgeous."

Ah, Derek Armstrong. I hadn't heard from him in a

couple days. He'd been busy with a trial, and I'd been busy with rehearsals for tomorrow night's reunion gig.

"So are we still on for dinner tonight?" he asked.

"You bet, but it'll have to be an early night. I'm doing a final run-through with the band tonight."

"I can't wait to see the show."

"I still think it's crazy that you're planning to come tomorrow night," I said. "You won't know anyone there."

"Doesn't matter. I wouldn't miss it for the world."

"I hope you like it. Oh, wait, sorry, hang on," I said, covering the mouthpiece of the phone. "Candace, look at the boy over there. The one in the light blue shirt. That's Adam."

Excerpt from

The Lies Have It

Sasha Jackson's next adventure.

Coming later this year.

Saturday, September 29th, 7:00 pm

"See a penny, pick it up, all day long you'll have good luck," my friend Jessica said, as she leaned over to grasp the shiny copper cent on the sidewalk. We were heading into the Stealth Lounge, the private party room on the second floor of The Pilot Tavern.

"See a penny, let it lie, then bad luck will pass you by," I replied. I've never let it cripple me, but I do happen to be kind of superstitious. Penny or not, I didn't have a great feeling about the evening ahead of us.

Bound for Glory, a sado-masochist fetish club was booked into the Stealth Lounge tonight. The same group had rented the place two weekends ago, and poor Jessica had been the only bartender on duty that night. Dear friend that she is, Jessica had suggested that I pinch hit on the bar with her this evening. I do have a real job as a private investigator, but all too frequently I find myself needing to supplement my income. Friends take pity on me, and occasionally offer me casual jobs that even welfare recipients would turn down, but I don't have that much pride. Besides, The Pilot's one of my favourite watering holes.

"Hand me the knife, will ya?" Jess asked as she dumped a bunch of citrus fruit on the bar.

She got busy slicing lemon and lime wedges while I stocked the beer fridge. We were in the midst of setting up the bar for the evening when Ian Dooley, the guy who spearheaded this dominance and submission social club, arrived.

"Hey, I'm Ian," he said, leaning against the bar. His voice was a little on the high-pitched nasal side, and had more than a hint of a Maritime accent.

I expected some wimpy little milquetoast with a sign on his forehead saying "beat me". Instead, when I looked up, I saw a hefty but solid guy in his late thirties. He was tall, easily six feet two inches. He was wearing a red plaid shirt and faded jeans, and had thick scruffy dark hair, and a firm jaw. He looked like Paul Bunyan's long lost cousin.

"Nice to meet you. I'm Sasha and this is Jessica." I wanted to be polite, but I didn't stick my hand out for him to shake. Something about a dude who hosts fetish parties gives me the heebie geebies.

"Ian and I met couple of weeks ago," Jess said.

"Oh yeah," I said.

"It should be a really good crowd tonight. I've promoted the party a lot more than last time," Ian said.

"Sounds good."

"I'm gonna start bringing stuff up, but can I leave this behind the bar for now?" He handed me his jean jacket and a Nike backpack. I tucked them onto the shelf where Jessica and I had stashed our purses.

"Could one of you unlock the back door for me?" Ian asked.

"I guess so. Jess, do you have the key?" I asked.

"Can you grab it?" she replied. "My hands are sticky. It's under the drawer of the cash register."

"Okay."

"Thanks," Ian said. "It's a lot easier to bring things up the back way; I can pull my truck right up to the back door." Ian headed out to collect the accoutrements for the S&M funfest.

Once we got everything set up behind the bar area, Jessica and I took a moment to freshen up.

"Do you think this colour is okay on me?" Jess puckered as she applied a shiny coat of Candy Apple lip gloss.

The bright red tone flattered her complexion and suited her chestnut hair, but I'm not one to toss off compliments freely.

"Yes my dear," I mumbled through the bobby pins I was holding between my teeth. "All the bondage boys are going to be begging for you." I was trying to get my hair to cooperate, but gave up, and just stuck it into a random pile at the back of my head. My hair these days is a lost cause. A good chunk of it was burned during a fire a few weeks ago, when I wrapped up one of my more unusual cases. It had started with a missing hooker and had ended with me dousing out flames on my head. All in a day's work. I had some hair extensions put in, but right now they seem like more bother than they're worth.

By nine o'clock, the Stealth Lounge had been transformed into a spank-me paradise. The stocks were in place, a St. Andrew's cross had been set up, the lights were dimmed. An upside down hangy thing that Jess had described to me after the previous event was set up. I looked it over, and could not figure out who was supposed to use it, or how. Ian reclaimed his knapsack and went into the men's room to change into his party clothes. He came back shirtless, wearing only a black leather "kilt" and black lace-up army boots. I couldn't tell if he was wearing socks.

He passed his knapsack back to me, and flexed his muscles and asked, "Whaddaya think?"

I checked him out from head to toe, and really didn't have any opinion, except for flinching when I noticed his pierced nipples. Ouch.

"So, is it true that men don't wear anything under their kilts?"

Shortly after nine o'clock, the first few partygoers began to straggle in.

"Coupla Stolies, neat," commanded a man in a leather hood as he dropped a fifty dollar bill on the bar. He groped and grabbed at his partner while I poured their drinks. The man looked like he wanted to devour the woman for breakfast, and she hung on his arm like the ditz I'm sure she is. After the guy paid and scooped up all his change, I gave my hands a quick rinse. Everything about this evening felt grimy. It suddenly seemed like my uncareer had been downgraded from unconventional to uninspired. I reminded myself that I had options. I could go back to school and train as a nurse or something.

The next twosome to belly up to the bar were in character, and they dashed the career choice I'd just made. She was Florence Nightingale in a micro-mini and see-through blouse. A cute little nurse's cap with a red cross on it was perched jauntily on her head. He was in green hospital pants and a white lab coat, and looked ready to give her a cervical exam.

The missing hooker case I had worked on this past summer had exposed me to the world of commercial sex. I had learned more than I wanted to know about what people do behind closed doors. However, my education in this field is all anecdotal, and I've never actually *seen* anyone acting out their fantasies like I was seeing here tonight. In fact, in another former job of mine, I'd talked people through their fantasies, but that had been on the telephone. I usually played Solitaire or surfed the Internet while horndogs got their rocks off, but I digress. Tonight was a real eye-opener.

Ian greeted guests as they arrived, high-fiving some of the guys. He pointed to the coat rack on the left where they could dump their jackets and bags and things, then he steered people towards the bar to order themselves a glass of liquid courage. Yet another couple walked in, and they too were dressed to play. They were all in leather, though she had on considerably less of it than he. The red-haired chick had a studded dog collar around her neck, and her partner had a leash attached to it. He didn't pull the leash taut, but the message was clear.

They came straight to the bar and I asked them something along the lines of "what's your poison" although I reworded it – some jackass in this crowd may have taken the cliché literally. Jess threw a smirk my way as she handed a Corona to a wrinkly old man wearing nothing but assless leather chaps and a pair of handcuffs dangling from his left wrist. I didn't watch to see where he kept his wallet. The Master and Slave duo in front of me looked at the array of bottles behind the bar.

"Johnnie Black and Coke. On the rocks," Master said. I was about to ask his pet what she'd like, when her master continued, "She'll just have water." I didn't ask if I should pour it into a bowl or serve it in a glass. The girl never even made eye contact with me.

I have to admit, the people – at least those who were permitted to speak – were generally rather nice and polite. With some customers, it was hard to hear their orders – the music was blaring, and leather facemasks aren't especially conducive to enunciation.

I flirted with a couple of the wussier looking guys, correctly guessing they'd respond well to a stern dominatrix, a role I'd learned to vocalize during a period of financial meltdown, when I'd briefly worked at an X-rated call centre. There's something to be said for transferable skills. You'd think that someone with my rather sullied curriculum vitae would be blasé about bartending at a fetish party. I wasn't necessarily offended by what was going on, but it was beyond my ken, although sort of interesting and rather surreal. Right now, I kind of wished I were a pothead. A joint might have helped make sense of this night. Alas, I'm not a toker.

I made the next customer beg me for his bottle of micro-brewed light beer.

"Are you sure you want it?" I purred as I uncapped a bottle of organic lager. "How badly do you want it?" I held the bottle just beyond his reach.

"Oh Mistress, you know I want it… bad… Please, please tell me you're going to give it to me," the guy replied.

A couple feet away, Ian, who'd been watching this whole transaction, gave me a thumb's up.

Jess rolled her eyes at me, and poured a Scotch on the rocks for a woman wearing nothing but Saran Wrap.

"Careful not to spill any on your lovely outfit," Jess deadpanned as she handed the Saran Siren her drink.

Although the night had started off rather slowly, by eleven o'clock, the party was in full swing. I suppose, if one were to choose, the Stealth Lounge is the ideal setting for a fetish party. The walls are painted one shade lighter than black. There are several over-sized ornately framed mirrors hung at odd angles behind the bar. I glimpsed myself in them, and thought for the hundredth time that it would have been funny to replace them with the convex and concave mirrors found at funhouses and carnivals. I checked my reflection and was satisfied with the appearance of the slender blond girl in a slim-cut, short black skirt and a scooped-neck, clingy white top who smiled back at me.

The furnishings of the Stealth Lounge run to glass and chrome, the upholstery is a velveteen zebra print. Pairs of loveseats at right angles to each other arc at the far end of the bar. Exposed ceiling beams, with their guts painted matte silver, give the room an industrial feeling. Blue tinted lighting completes the mood. The music, all techno-heavy instrumental, with throbbing, reverberating bass, comes over an audio system with crystal clear sound. Yeah, I guess if I were to host an S & M party, this would be the place to do so.

Couples and trios had started to pair off, and they were strapping, whipping and spanking each other with reckless abandon. Most of this pheromone themed hand-to-hand combat took place in the loveseats near the back. Those who hadn't yet met the bolt to go with their nut were milling about the bar area like dogs in heat. No doubt some of the sexual tension came from folks who had miscalculated the targets of their pick up lines – one dominant trying to pick up another dom was just not good for anyone.

"Hey Jess," I said, "maybe next time we should offer sticky name tags and pass them out at the entrance: S for submissive, D for dominant, B for bondage, and Y for why the hell don't I find another job?" Jess laughed.

Moose, a florist by day and the Stealth Lounge's doorman by night, was busy manning the entrance. I imagine it's rather difficult to be macho and intimidating when you smell like roses, but Moose seemed to be doing okay. A dark haired Latino behemoth, Moose checked IDs and names on the guest list, plus he had the dubious task of screening people for dress code infractions.

"Oh c'mon, lemme in! I wanna check it out!" slurred a skanky looking bit of trailer trash who looked like she'd be right at home in a bowling alley.

"Sorry, but, your name's not on the list." Moose's face was impassive.

"Wassa matter? I don't look sexy enough? Here, how's this?" she wailed as she unbuttoned her shirt and flashed her saggy boobs at poor Moose and the folks standing near the entrance.

"Let me in!" She cupped her breasts and continued to demonstrate her lack of both dignity and self-respect.

Her toothless Neanderthal of a date tried to finesse his way in with a bribe. He slipped $2 into Moose's palm and said, "That oughtta take care of things."

Moose scooped the Neanderthal into a headlock with his right arm, and firmly gripped Skanky's wrist with his left hand, and unceremoniously ushered them downstairs. A twenty might have worked, but not a deuce.

"That woman was unreal, wasn't she?" he asked me when he came back into the bar. I chuckled and slipped him a shot of vodka. He tossed the $2 onto the bar as a tip.

The bar area was quiet for a moment; everyone's drinks had been replenished. Jess and I leaned back against the beer fridge and simultaneously sighed, smirked, and surreptitiously stared at the group before us. A rather pudgy woman was prancing around wearing a nipple-less pink teddy on top and nothing, *nothing* on the bottom. She had a fluffy purple feather boa around her neck and was asking guys to slap her cottage cheese butt. Ian, ever the gracious host, happily obliged, while I averted my eyes and tried not to toss my cookies.

Jess had seen most of this crowd at the previous soiree and she filled me in on whatever catty gossip she had about them.

"See that guy?" she asked, indicating a well-preserved senior with giant nipple rings, "he's into golden showers, giving and receiving. I think he left alone last time. Can you imagine being into that?"

I cringed. "Never, no way, not in a million years." Right now, I kind of wished I were wearing a medieval chastity belt.

Jess continued, "See those two bottle blonds with black roots over there? Wearing fishnets? They're looking for a third chick who likes to talk dirty and wants to be paddled. Do you ever think of switching teams? I could introduce you."

"Ha ha. Piss off, Jess, or I'll give Assless Leather Chaps your cell number. Besides, Derek satisfies me more than anyone in this room ever could."

Derek Armstrong is the new man in my life. Our romance is still in its nascent days, but I swear that since we started seeing each other, the skies are bluer, the sun is brighter, and the birds sing more sweetly. Oh barf. I don't do well with mushy sentiments, but Derek really rocks my world. I couldn't imagine doing any of this kinky stuff with him, although handcuffing him might be fun. And maybe gagging him, but that's only because there are times when I'm not even remotely interested in him for conversation. *Sigh*. Derek had left on Tuesday to work on a trial out of town. I was really starting to miss him.

Beyond the bar area, in the dimly lit corners of the room, there was a lot of yelping and moaning going on. Ian and several people were clustered around the stocks, and another group was parked near the upside-down-hangy thing, so I still couldn't see how it was being used. Perhaps it was best not to know. A moment later an extremely sexy man, wearing nothing but a pair of skimpy red underwear, approached me. He set down his toys – a gaudy looking crown and sceptre – on the bar.

"How ya doing?" he said.

He was so handsome and cocky, standing there in his undies, without even a hint of self-consciousness. It unnerved me and I got all tongue-tied.

"Great! The fun sure seems party… I mean, it seems like everyone's having a good time."

He winked at me and said, "How about a Bombay Martini? Shaken. Really dry, with a twist."

I tried to look cool, holding the martini shaker in one hand, and shaking it in rhythm with the music. This guy's smile was electric, and he radiated sex appeal. Why do guys like him instantly make me feel self-conscious? I tried to think of Derek, but His Royal Hotness in front of me was just too yummy to ignore. Besides, there's nothing wrong with *looking*. I sucked in my tummy and tried to look cool. The charade came to an abrupt halt as my hand slipped, and the lid from the martini shaker flew off, splashing icy gin all over the front of my top.

"Guess I'm the top contender in the wet T-shirt contest." I discovered the hard way that my little white shirt is fairly transparent when it's wet. Oh dear.

I measured out another couple of ounces of gin and started again. "Interesting crowd. I guess you know most of the people here," I asked, holding the shaker a little more tightly this time.

"I've talked to most of them online, but this is only my third or fourth party. I come to whichever parties I can. It's a great community. Everyone's completely at ease."

I tried not to stare, but his undies left nothing to the imagination. Some lucky woman was in for a treat later tonight.

"Oh. That's interesting. I never really thought of it as a community," I said, effortlessly demonstrating my stellar conversation skills.

"Yeah, Ian hosts this group—"

"They're called *Bound for Glory*, right?" It was a safe bet that the fetish group hadn't named themselves after a Woody Guthrie song about a train.

"Yeah. And there're lots of other groups and chatrooms too, you know, like Second Life, Fet Life, and sites like that. I belong to those as well. I like this group because all their events are downtown."

"How convenient."

I passed the cocktail to His Royal Sexiness and was instantly repulsed. He reached into the front of his undies and whipped out a gold Amex to pay. Eeeeeewwww! The credit card was warm.

"It's on the house, handsome," I forced a smile and nudged his card back to him. I washed my hands again, this time with scalding water.

Around one-thirty, the party started to wind down. Some people paired off with others to go to hotels, and a few partiers invited their sex slaves home for a night of obedient lovemaking. Only three or four partiers left alone, including the Golden Shower Guy and King of the Red Undies. Other than them, the fetish crowd seemed to be batting just under a thousand. Ian was practically chained to Minerva, a raven-haired barracuda with never-ending cleavage who had shown up around eleven o'clock. Minerva looked like she had a long list of commands in store for Ian.

"I've packed up everything I can for tonight," he said. "I'll come back tomorrow for the rest of the gear."

"That's cool," Jessica said. "Everything will be locked up when we leave, but I won't be here tomorrow. I'm starting my vacation in about half an hour, as soon as this shift ends."

"Well then, bon voyage. Is there someone else I should speak to tomorrow?"

"Just ask whoever's on duty downstairs to open up the second floor for you."

"Thanks."

I passed Ian his things from behind the bar and bid him adieu.

By two-thirty, thanks to some help from Moose, we had cleaned up, cashed out, and were ready to go home.

"Just let me set the alarm, then we're outta here," Jessica said.

"Do either of you want a ride home?" offered Moose.

"Absolutely," we both answered.

"I'll get the lights," I said.

"Here, Sasha, don't forget your phone."

"Duh." I stuck it in my purse as Jess locked the door behind us.

Sunday, September 30th
8:47 am

"C'mon Winston, get the ball. Good boy."

The limping retiree with the brown Fedora could hardly keep up with the goofy Black Labrador, but that didn't make the morning dog walk any less fun. Winston ran for the ball and took his time dawdling back to his owner. The old man threw the ball again, not very far this time. He never threw it very far; his tired old arm didn't have the range or strength of his youth. The ball rolled along the flat sandy area and stopped just before the scrubby shore. Winston loped lazily after it.

"Bring it back, Winston. C'mon, boy, bring it back." Up ahead, the dog was circling, his nose to the ground. The old man hobbled towards the dirty Toronto waterfront where the Labrador was now barking with great import.

"Good lord. What the hell is this?"

A man was lying facedown at the edge of the shore. Dirty Lake Ontario water slopped up against his body. An empty Frito Lay chip bag splashed up onto the back of the man's upper legs, and landed between the man's thighs and the hem of his black leather kilt. The brightly coloured synthetic package fluttered slightly in the slow morning breeze. The man's torso was covered with welts and scratches, but neither of these seemed as lethal as the two bullet holes in his back. Another wave lapped the shoreline and lifted the hem of the kilt, exposing the man's welt-covered buttocks. The chip bag floated away, along with some watery streaks of pale red blood.